LISA MARIE RICE
A *Fine* SPECIMEN

Ellora's Cave
Romantica Publishing

An Ellora's Cave Romantica Publication

www.ellorascave.com

A Fine Specimen

ISBN 9781419960208
ALL RIGHTS RESERVED.
A Fine Specimen Copyright © 2009 Lisa Marie Rice
Edited by Kelli Collins.
Cover art by Syneca.

This book printed in the U.S.A. by Jasmine-Jade Enterprises, LLC.

Electronic book publication March 2009
Trade paperback publication December 2009

The terms Romantica® and Quickies® are registered trademarks of Ellora's Cave Publishing.

With the exception of quotes used in reviews, this book may not be reproduced or used in whole or in part by any means existing without written permission from the publisher, Ellora's Cave Publishing, Inc.® 1056 Home Avenue, Akron OH 44310-3502.

Warning: The unauthorized reproduction or distribution of this copyrighted work is illegal. Criminal copyright infringement, including infringement without monetary gain, is investigated by the FBI and is punishable by up to 5 years in federal prison and a fine of $250,000.
(http://www.fbi.gov/ipr/)

This book is a work of fiction and any resemblance to persons, living or dead, or places, events or locales is purely coincidental. The characters are productions of the author's imagination and used fictitiously.

A FINE SPECIMEN

Trademarks Acknowledgement

The author acknowledges the trademarked status and trademark owners of the following wordmarks mentioned in this work of fiction:

Armani: GA Modefine S.A. Corporation Switzerland
Brillo: Church & Dwight Company
Dick Tracy: Tribune Media Services, Inc.
Diet Coke: The Coca-Cola Company
Glock: Glock, Inc.
Hugo Boss: Hugo Boss A.G.
Identi-Kit: Smith & Wesson Corp.
Jacuzzi: Jacuzzi Inc. Corporation
Kevlar: E. I. du Pont de Nemours and Company
Lurex: Sildorex S.A. Corporation
Mercedes Benz: DaimlerChrysler AG Corporation
Montblanc: Montblanc-Simplo GmbH Corporation
Nasdaq: The Nasdaq OMX Group, Inc.
Nike: Nike, Inc.
Palm Pilot: Pirani, Amin
Ramen: Nissin Shokuhin Kabushiki Kaisha DBA Nissin Food Products Co., Ltd.
RoboCop: Orion Pictures Corporation
Sleeping Beauty: Disney Enterprises, Inc.
Starfleet Command: Paramount Pictures Corporation
Styrofoam: Dow Chemical Company
Versace: Gianni Versace S.p.A Corporation
Viagra: Pfizer Inc.

Chapter One

ಸಾ

"What the *fuck*!"

Lieutenant Alex Cruz's bellow could be heard clear across the station house. He fucking meant it to be heard. He was seriously annoyed and he didn't care who knew it.

"Yo, boss." Sergeant Ben Cade cautiously stuck his head around the door and looked at him out of half-moon glasses. He pulled a pencil out of a Brillo-pad head of graying red hair. "You barked?"

"What the hell does this mean?" Alex tapped the report in front of him. Just touching the ink on the paper disgusted him. Alex had definite ideas on the way things should be and what was in the report violated every single one of them.

Ben moved warily into the room, leaving the door open. Ben was a friend, except when he screwed up. Alex knew he was leaving the door open on purpose, in case Ben thought he needed a quick escape. Alex was also aware his temper was the stuff of urban myth and he did nothing to quell the rumors. He knew perfectly well that he was used as a boogeyman to scare new recruits.

The rumors that he ate newbies for breakfast were highly exaggerated.

He'd once overheard Ben telling a wide-eyed rookie that when Lieutenant Cruz was in a mood, his office was Never Never Land—you never, *never* wanted to go there. It wasn't true. Not much, anyway.

Except for right now.

Ben knew when Alex was pretending to be mad and when it was the real thing. Right now was definitely the real deal. Alex was furious.

"Ah..." Ben said, looking from the report to Alex's face — gauging blowup potential — back to the report, Alex's face, the report. The very molecules in the air crackled with tension. Whatever Ben was going to say was lost as he closed his mouth with an audible click.

"He gave you the slip." Alex's mouth tightened, his jaw muscles clenched. He found it hard to speak, he was so furious. "The fucking sonovabitch just fucking upped and...slipped away from you."

Ben didn't have to ask who "he" was. "He" was Martin "Ratso" Colby, the man they were all hoping would lead to the downfall of Angelo Lopez, a mobster who had been terrorizing Baylorville for years. PD had learned through a snitch that Ratso had been keeping the mobster's books. At this point, Ratso would know enough to put Lopez away for twenty years on tax evasion. The scumbag had murdered at least four people that Alex knew of, but nothing could be pinned on Lopez. Tax evasion was okay, if it could put him behind bars. A lot of evidence would come out once Lopez was safely put away. Cockroaches would come out from under rocks and start singing.

Tossing Lopez in the bucket had become Alex Cruz's personal crusade. Alex ate, slept and dreamed of Lopez — behind bars. Off the streets, the latest girlfriend of some Aryan Nation bruiser.

Alex loved the idea of that.

So far it was proving impossible, though everyone knew what Lopez was. Lopez was too savvy to leave hard evidence behind. He operated through layers of minions and was untouchable. But once Alex had found out that Ratso was keeping Lopez's books, that muscle in his chest that in other people was a heart simply warmed. Alex knew Ratso Colby. Everyone on the Baylorville PD knew Ratso Colby. They all

A Fine Specimen

knew he had two passions—money and staying out of jail. Ratso could be induced to spill the beans on Lopez with the threat of jail time.

If, that is, the police could ever get their hands on him. Ratso had disappeared. There'd been a Baylorville Police Department BOLO out on Ratso for a week, but up until now they had come up empty-handed.

Ratso was the Bill Gates of numbers, no one better, but other than that, he was no rocket scientist and had zero street smarts. Alex couldn't figure out what Baylorville PD was doing wrong. He could feel the tension rising as day after day went by with no Ratso.

And today they'd almost caught him.

Fuck! They'd almost caught him!

"How?" Alex's jaws clenched so hard he was surprised his back teeth didn't shoot out his ears. "How the *hell* did that runt get away from four of Baylorville's finest? Wrestle them to the ground?"

They were both silent for a moment, thinking of Ratso's miserably puny physique.

"No, um..." Alex had watched Ben interrogate hardened killers while munching on a sandwich, but now he was breaking into a sweat. "To tell the truth—"

"Yes, Sergeant? Please do tell me how it happened," Alex interrupted silkily, and Ben winced. Ben knew him well. When Alex used that tone, a smart man, a *prudent* man would turn tail and run. Alex watched Ben eye the open door with longing. The hell with that. He wasn't getting away that easily.

Alex placed his hands palm down on his desk and leaned forward. "So please tell me how a punk like Ratso could escape four armed and well-trained police officers. Did I waste Baylorville PD's budget buying every single one of my officers a brand-new 9 millimeter Glock 17? Well, Sergeant? Did I? *Shit!*" Alex slammed his fist on his desk, making papers flutter. He felt like his head was going to explode. "You guys *know*

Ratso has the goods on Lopez. You *know* we can get him to talk. All we have to do is apply a little bit of pressure and Ratso will crack like a nut. We were *this close*," Alex's index finger and thumb were half an inch apart and half an inch from Cade's nose, "*this close* to possibly nailing Angelo Lopez." He made a disgusted sound in the back of his throat, the growl a frustrated wolf would make. "I've got half a mind to have you all transferred to Hubcaps."

Assignment to the boring busywork of the Stolen Vehicles Department was every cop's worst nightmare. Cade took a deep breath. "Look here, boss —"

"I'm not the boss," Alex interrupted. "Ray Avery is. And will continue to be until he retires."

Cade shrugged his heavy shoulders. "In a coupla weeks. But okay, whatever you say — you're the boss." Everyone in the station house had long ago accepted the fact that when Avery retired, which was at the end of the month, Alex would be the new captain.

Alex didn't give a shit what other people thought. His own loyalty to Ray was absolute. As long as Ray Avery was formally captain, Alex was his. Ray was The Man. Always had been. Always would be.

"So tell me how you let him slip through your fingers." Alex sat back in his chair, fingers steepled under his chin. Calm, still, watching. Alex focused his attention like a laser beam. He didn't mean for Cade to be comfortable.

Cade shifted his shoulders, trying and failing to look away for a moment. "Well, we were down digging around the Trey."

Cruz nodded. The downtown block between 33rd and 3rd was a cesspool. The perfect swamp for a bottom feeder like Ratso.

"And we cornered Ratso at the Fat Lady. He gave up without a fight. Then he asked to go to the john." Cade lifted his shoulders and sighed. "I mean — what you gonna do? I'm not getting any younger. I'm starting to have those problems too. We let him go."

"Did any of you jokers actually check the john?" Alex asked softly.

"Hey." Cade puffed up in indignation. "Of course we did. What do you take us for?" Alex didn't even blink. "Okay…okay. Yeah. I went in with Ratso. It was a perfectly normal two-stall bathroom. No one else was there." Cade held up a large-palmed hand. "I checked. Honest."

"What you didn't check, apparently, were the windows," Alex growled.

"Window," Cade corrected. "*One* window, for the record, and it was fucking tiny. One miserable, filthy, tiny window. A foot by a foot. Who woulda thought—"

"*You* should have thought," Alex interrupted heatedly, leaning forward, hands clutching the edge of his desk with white knuckles. "Ratso's built like a boy. He just slithered through and was in the wind before you guys finished picking the lint out of your bellybuttons." He picked up a black pen and began tapping it on the desk, staring as Cade squirmed. Finally he sighed. "Well, that's that. Put out another BOLO—"

"Done," Cade said hastily.

"And fill out a warrant, just in case—"

"Ditto."

"Well." Alex sat thinking for a few minutes, running scenarios through his head, but it all came back to the same thing. His men had fucked up. He drummed his fingers once, hard, on the scarred oak desk. It sounded loud in the silence. He blew out a breath to relieve a little stress. "Okay. Okay. There's not much more that can be done until Ratso resurfaces. And when he does, we'll nail him and he'll flip. We can book him on a few minor counts that carry some jail time and he knows it, so he'll talk. Oh yeah, he'll talk." Alex pursed his lips and treated Cade to a long, level gaze. "I guess that's it for now."

Cade blew out a long sigh of relief himself, knowing it was all over. Alex's men knew that he might blow up, but it blew over quickly. And he didn't hold grudges.

Alex was already putting Ratso's escape from his mind when Cade cleared his throat. Clearing throats was not a good thing, particularly coming from someone who should have already disappeared, grateful that Alex hadn't handed him his ass on a stick.

Alex looked up to see Cade obviously trying to brace himself. He had something else to say and it wasn't going to be good. What was this? Alex's bad news quota today had already been exceeded. His mouth tightened. "What?"

"Here, boss." Cade handed over an envelope.

"I'm *not* the boss," Alex said between his teeth.

"Right, boss. Anything you say."

Alex rolled his eyes then glanced curiously at the white envelope. His name was neatly laser-printed in block letters. "Who's it from?"

"Um, Captain Avery. Sir. He said to say he was sorry he couldn't stay, but he had to go out of town." Cade was shifting his considerable weight uneasily from foot to foot, casting longing glances at the door. Alex narrowed his eyes. He could read body language. Cade knew what was in the letter and it wasn't good. "Captain said to be sure to give the letter to you in person," Ben added.

Alex had already slit the envelope and was quickly perusing the contents. Then he frowned and started over again. Even after he'd read it two times, it still didn't make sense. What the fuck was this?

Alex began from the top again, though the letter wasn't making any more sense the third time than it had the second or first. *Behavioral psychology major...dissertation...C. Summers...seven days...*

What the fuck kind of sick joke was Ray playing on him?

A Fine Specimen

"What's this crap?" Alex asked, his voice low and dangerous. He lifted his eyes from the letter. Sergeant Cade squirmed again, his stomach following a second behind his shoulders. It wasn't a pretty sight. "Did you know about this?"

"Nope. Not until, ah..."

"Do you know what the old man wants me to do?" Alex's voice rose as he leaned forward. He was feeling angry and aggrieved. This was *not* what he needed. Not today. Not tomorrow. Not ever. "There's some fucking *scholar* who wants to study..." Alex frowned at the paper he held in his hand then frowned at Cade, equally displeased with both. "'Dominance Displays in Law Enforcement'. Can you imagine that? I'm supposed to allow some fucking pencil-dick *geek to* follow me around! Starting today. *Fuck*! Right when we're in the fucking middle of this fucking mess. Right when I'm ready to nail that fucker Lopez. Now how the *fuck* am I supposed to do my job when—"

"Excuse me," a soft voice broke in.

Alex switched his glare from Cade to the woman standing in his doorway.

No, not woman—girl. Some high-schooler, to judge by the bag of books at her feet. Alex was too much of a cop not to notice everything about her and the more he looked, the more out of place she seemed in the cop shop.

Pretty, not too tall. Long, pale blonde hair tied back in a messy ponytail, tendrils of which had escaped and were curling around her face. Big, pale blue eyes behind round metal-rimmed glasses. Very pretty. Wispy, ankle-length light blue dress. Long Indian-print jacket. Sneakers. Very, *very* pretty.

What the hell was a high-schooler doing in a police station at eleven o'clock on a Friday morning? Why wasn't she in school?

Cade, the traitor, had slipped out while Cruz was focused on the girl.

"Lieutenant Cruz?" Her voice barely rose above the background noise of the squad room behind her. She angled back and looked at the name stenciled on his door, then back at him. "Lieutenant Alejandro Cruz?"

She wanted *him*? What the fuck was this? How did she have his first name? "Yeah, that's me, miss." Alex's hand hovered over the morning's reports. And yesterday's reports. He was behind in everything and he didn't need this. "You'll excuse me if—"

She cleared her throat. "May I speak with you a moment?"

Alex pinched the bridge of his nose. Hard. It was shaping up to be one of those days. First Ratso Colby slithering his skinny frame through the toilet window of a skanky dive, taking with him Cruz's best hope of nailing Angelo Lopez this year. Then Ray Avery siccing a geek on him. And not just any geek, no sirree. A geek who was supposed to spend a week glued to his side, getting in his way while he was working night and day to put Lopez away. What the fuck was that about? Ray knew better than that.

And now fucking *babies* wandering in off the street, asking for him.

Be polite now, Alex reminded himself. *Don't snap*. The kid was going to grow up and vote some day and every police circular stressed good relations with the community.

"Look, miss," Cruz said in his best talking-to-baby-civilians voice. "This is not where you want to be. Trust me on this. Now if you go back down to the ground floor you'll find a big desk, and behind that desk is the muster sergeant. He's the one you want to talk to."

"No, I don't want the muster sergeant." The girl widened her stance, picked up her book bag and held it in front of her like a shield. She took a deep breath. "I need to talk to Lieutenant Alejandro Cruz."

A Fine Specimen

"Well, that's me, all right." Alex tried to stretch his mouth into a reassuring smile and felt rarely used facial muscles balk. "And who the fu— Who are you?"

"Caitlin Summers," she said.

"Well, look, Miss Summers, I don't know what you want from—" Alex broke off, appalled. His brain spun. Caitlin Summers.

Jesus. C. *Summers.*

He rose slowly and his eyes widened in horror. "Dear sweet God, don't tell me you're—"

"The fucking pencil-dick geek," Caitlin Summers said softly. "Yes, I am."

Chapter Two

Lieutenant Alejandro Cruz was the most *alpha* alpha male Caitlin had ever seen. Wow, this guy was definitely the leader of the pack, top gun, the apex of the food chain.

A dominance hierarchy in a police station was just as necessary as in a wolf pack, and for the same reason—to maintain order and reduce conflict in a group of aggressive beings. Otherwise the group—or pack—would disintegrate into prolonged bouts of dangerous, possibly fatal fighting. So someone had to be the alpha male—and the lieutenant was definitely it.

On her way toward Lieutenant Cruz's lair—*office*—Caitlin had noticed how, the closer she got to it, the more the easy banter and noise the officers made seemed to gradually fade, until silence reigned outside his office. Now that she'd seen him, she could understand why.

Lieutenant Cruz was authority personified, alpha in every way there was. Totally a textbook case. His power didn't rest with a huge physique or with status symbol clothes. Standing, he was much taller than she was, but then she wasn't very tall. He had broad shoulders and was clearly very fit, but there were bigger men around. The man who'd been talking to Lieutenant Cruz, for example. He was a walking meat mountain. For all his size, however, that man could be overlooked in a room. Not Lieutenant Cruz. All eyes would immediately turn to the prime male.

Lieutenant Cruz's clothes were nondescript. White shirt, black tie, black trousers, black leather belt, which again was textbook. He didn't need Armani or Versace or Hugo Boss clothes to prevail. He didn't need to dress for power. He *was* power.

There was power in the dark eyes, in the chiseled jaw, in the corded neck. Strength, authority and responsibility were right there, in every feature of his face, in every line of his body.

He was watching her out of black eyes, his face without expression. The lines of his face were sharp, angular.

Not for the first time, Caitlin wondered at Ray Avery's advice. More than advice, really—insistence. Ray had been urging her for weeks to spend time in a station house to round out the information in her dissertation on Dominance Hierarchies in Law Enforcement.

You'll like Alex, Ray had said. *He's a nice man.*

Caitlin wasn't entirely sure *nice* was the right word to describe Alejandro Cruz. *Overwhelming,* maybe, oh yeah. *Intimidating,* certainly. But *nice?*

Caitlin stepped forward, feeling with each step as if she were moving into a force field. A power greater than her own. If she'd been convinced her studies had taught her how to deal with the male of her species, she had to think again. This was an entirely different order of magnitude from dealing with a fellow graduate student or an associate professor or even—God!—the dean.

This was raw, unadulterated male power, backed up by the weight of the entire U.S. government—not to mention a gun—and she couldn't possibly match it in any way.

But she'd promised Ray, so she walked forward slowly, as if through a sea of molasses. Caitlin stopped at Lieutenant Cruz's desk. Solid, uncompromising, enduring, a little scarred—just like the man behind it. She glanced at the chair in front of the desk and started to sit just as he said, "Please have a seat." His voice held faint tones of irony.

"Thank you." Caitlin hated the touch of breathlessness in her voice, but she couldn't help it. This was going to be much,

much harder than she'd imagined. She sat down, raised her eyes to his and tried to still her wild heartbeat.

"So." Lieutenant Cruz had a deep voice, slightly raspy, as if he didn't use it much. He probably didn't have to. One look from him and underlings would scurry to do his bidding. She felt like doing a little scurrying herself.

The lieutenant tapped Ray Avery's letter with a blunt fingertip. "It seems we have a problem here." His face was as cold as his voice.

Caitlin clasped her hands together. Not to stop them from trembling. Of course not. Just to have something to do with them. She didn't dare show shaking hands or allow her voice to tremble. She didn't dare allow herself any show of weakness at all.

Studies had shown that hyenas can smell blood ten miles away. This was a man who could smell weakness at a thousand paces. He held all the power and she was here asking for a favor. Conditions didn't get more lopsided than that. It was true that she had a secret weapon, maybe. But it might also be a weapon that would blow up in her hands.

Caitlin drew in a deep breath, wondering if the lieutenant noticed that it hitched slightly. She opened her mouth to speak, hoping she could keep her voice firm, then turned in gratitude as someone came in through the door of Lieutenant Cruz's office without knocking, bearing two steaming Styrofoam cups of coffee.

A woman in uniform. She had dark, curly hair and a round, lined face. Caitlin sent up thanks for the presence of a member of her gender in the room, to counteract the pure male pheromones Lt. Cruz was emitting by the ton.

"Hi," the woman said, slipping a cup in front of her with a friendly smile. "Sergeant Kathy Martello, hear you're a friend of Captain Avery's. Pleased to meet you." She put down the second cup in front of the lieutenant hard enough for some of the coffee to slosh over. "We like the captain a lot, so anyone he sends us is very welcome here. Isn't that right, Loot?" She gave the lieutenant A Look and walked out.

"Loot" took a long gulp of his coffee, though Caitlin could see steam coming off the cup. Maybe one developed a calloused gullet the farther one rose in law enforcement hierarchy? Her own cup was steaming too, and smelled awful—of dishrags dipped in turpentine.

Still, Sergeant Martello had made the effort, so Caitlin gingerly brought the cup to her mouth, hoping it hadn't been recycled. Budget cuts were everywhere. She sipped the hot, bitter brew and nearly gagged. It was one of the worst cups of coffee she'd ever tasted. Worse even than the Sociology Department cafeteria coffee. She remembered Ray commenting on that.

Whoa.

Maybe there could be a paper in this.

Bad coffee, Good Policing: A Causal Link. The journal of her professional society published several satirical articles a year and this would make a good one. Maybe she could get a lab to make analyses of the coffee in, say, all the police stations in the tri-county area, and correlate the organoleptic data with arrest figures—

Caitlin struggled to bring her mind back to the moment. Her mind wandered at the best of times, which often got her into trouble. Now, with Lieutenant Cruz watching her out of cold, dark, steely eyes was no time to be wool gathering.

"So," he said again. "I take it—"

"Hey, boss." The face that peeped into the door of the office was arrestingly ugly. Sparse red hair straggled back from a long, narrow freckled face with broad features. A wide, gap-toothed mouth smiled at her seraphically. He looked like an aging, goofy Howdy Doody on Quaaludes.

The man stared at her for a minute then shouted over his shoulder, "She's okay!"

"That's it!" Lieutenant Cruz slammed both hands down on his desk, got up and circled it. He stood framed in the doorway, a tall, broad-shouldered figure, and looked out at the squad room. Caitlin leaned a little to the right so she could see beyond him. Everyone in the squad room was frozen, as if caught in a game of "red light, green light".

"Okay, you jokers," Lieutenant Cruz growled. His voice wasn't loud but it carried. "If one more person comes through this door, there's going to be hell to pay. And you know I mean it." Caitlin watched the back of his head as he slowly quartered the room. Wherever he looked, people's eyes dropped. The only sounds were the rustling of papers and tapping of computer keyboards as the officers ostentatiously got back to work. "I trust I've made myself clear," he added icily.

She heard soft coughs and phones ringing in the distance. The lieutenant lingered in the doorway a moment longer then closed the door of his office just hard enough to make a point. Caitlin's heart jumped at the sound of the sharp *snick* of the door.

They were alone in the room.

Lieutenant Cruz made his way back to his desk, his tread as soft and dangerous as a panther's. He settled back smoothly into his chair and looked at her for a long, nerve-racking moment.

"Okay. Let's get down to business here." His deep voice was vibrant with frustration as he eyed her across his steepled fingers. "Precisely what is it that you want from me?"

"*I* don't want—" Caitlin began, then bit her lip. She'd argued with Ray Avery for three days running over this but he had finally convinced her that she should visit the station house, so now it was her decision to be here and she had to take responsibility for it. She looked into the lieutenant's eyes and immediately realized her mistake. They were dark, mesmerizing, hostile. She felt like a titmouse facing a cobra, paralyzed. What would the titmouse do?

Distract the cobra.

"Do you know, Lieutenant, I did some research on the history of the police force in Baylorville. This is a far cry from the very first police station," she said, looking around his neat, austere office. His office was utterly different from the cheerful clutter she'd observed on the other officers' desks. There was nothing in Lieutenant Cruz's office which even remotely hinted at anything personal. Besides his neat, uncluttered desk and the chair he was sitting on, the room had a computer workstation next to his desk and bookshelves filled with law textbooks and California police yearbooks, arranged in chronological order. No photographs, no bulletin board with notices tacked up, no wanted posters, nothing.

"The first station was built in 1858 where Willard's Department Store is now, at the Horace Street entrance. They called it the lockup. There were three police officers, only they were called constables then. Part of their duties was to ensure that every woman who attended a public dance was wearing a corset. It was written in the contract."

He blinked. "Oh yeah?"

She had distracted the lieutenant, she could see that. Maybe even thrown him off his stride. His annoyed look faded.

"Well, that's very int—" He caught himself and scowled again. "Look, Miss...ah, Ms. Summers. To come back to the matter at hand, I don't know what Ray told you, but we do *not* run training courses for students at this station."

Well, what a stupid notion.

"No, of course not," she said earnestly. "I certainly don't expect a full-blown *course*. That would be ridiculous and probably illegal. Good heavens, you have enough to do and I wouldn't think of taking staff away from their duties. And anyway, I don't need a course because I'm something of an expert on law enforcement myself."

He looked absolutely blank for a moment, his jaw hanging open slightly, before closing his mouth with a snap. His eyes narrowed until only the pupils showed, gleaming blackly under the harsh overhead neon like a sword in moonlight. "You're an expert on *what?*"

"Law enforcement." Caitlin watched, fascinated, as the muscles in his jaw worked and the cords in his neck stood out even more. It looked as if each muscle in his body—and he had a lot of them—tensed. She was so vividly aware of him that she hardly had a sense of herself. This was ridiculous. She had to get herself under control and stop allowing him to distract her so. She needed him to take her seriously, but he wouldn't if she simply sat there like a ninny, fascinated by his muscles.

Caitlin bent down to rummage in her book bag for the copy of her paper in *The Law Enforcement Review*. She was proud of that paper. It was a great paper. It held some original and truly groundbreaking research and had taken her two and a half years to write. Once the lieutenant read it, he would see that she knew what she was talking about. "Here," she said eagerly, thrusting the copy across his desk.

The lieutenant reached out with a frown. "What's this?"

His hand closed over hers, hard, warm, so incredibly, powerfully male. Caitlin jumped as if an electric prod had touched her. She jerked her hand away and knocked over his coffee cup—dumping the steaming contents straight into his lap.

There was a tense silence, broken only by the steady drip of coffee from the lieutenant's trousers onto her paper, which had fluttered to the floor in the terrible slow motion of disasters.

"*Oh. My. God!*" Caitlin breathed. There was a fierce internal battle inside her, as an intense desire to flee combated an equally intense desire to laugh. She clapped her hand over her mouth and stared at him, horrified.

He stood up, holding his sodden trousers away from his skin. Caitlin realized that the boiling coffee must have burnt him.

"Oh!" She completely forgot her intimidation as she rushed to his side, kneeling, pulling her book bag behind her. She'd once burnt herself with boiling water and could still remember the stinging pain. She had a small hand towel in her bag and as she pulled it hastily out to sponge away the worst of the mess, her 2008 hardback edition of *Theories of Policing in Western Societies*—all one thousand, forty-seven heavy, glossy pages of it—spilled out and landed squarely, heavily on the lieutenant's shiny black lace-up shoe.

"*Ow!*" This time he cried out and instantly his office door opened. Sergeant Martello stuck her head in and frowned at the sight of the two of them, the lieutenant slapping his thighs and Caitlin kneeling at his feet, doing…something to him.

"What's going on here?" A sharp indrawn breath of outrage. "Lieutenant Cruz, you should be ashamed of yourself! Why, that poor child—"

"This poor child," he said between clenched teeth, "is doing her best to kill me, and she's doing a very good job of it. Now if you'll just leave, Sergeant, we can let Ms. Summers finish me off in peace."

Caitlin looked up at the lieutenant in surprise.

He has a sense of humor? Apparently, he did. Heavy-handed humor, it was true, but it was a minor miracle he had it at all—she'd been expecting a burst of rage. Instead, though his face was drawn into long lines of pain, his eyes, those dark, fascinating eyes, had something in them which in a lesser man might be called a twinkle.

It was probably an effect of the light.

"I'm really, really sorry, Lieutenant," Caitlin said humbly, sitting back on her heels. She wrung out her little hand towel over the wastepaper basket and watched the brown sludge drip down. Maybe the coffee would taste better now that it had been filtered through Lieutenant Alejandro Cruz's pants and her towel.

"Yes, I can see that you are." His voice was unexpectedly gentle as he put a hard hand under her elbow and lifted her effortlessly to her feet. "Nonetheless, I'd be really grateful if you would just sit down over there while we finish our conversation and *don't move.*"

Caitlin sat down and folded her hands in her lap, totally unnerved at the thought of what she'd done. She got very clumsy when she was nervous, so she tightened her hands in her lap and resolved to remain calm and focused. And to breathe from the diaphragm the way her yoga instructor had taught her.

"So." As if unconsciously echoing her, he put his own clasped hands on the desk in front of him. Caitlin stared at his hands. Large, long-fingered, powerful, graceful. Short black hairs on the backs. Nails trimmed, unbuffed. There was a small white scar on the back of his right hand, like a lightning bolt in the flesh. Was that a *tattoo* on his wrist? She jerked her head up.

"I beg your pardon, Lieutenant?" He had said something and she had been lost in contemplation of his hands.

"I said," he repeated patiently, "would you please explain to me exactly what it is that you want?"

To study you, Caitlin wanted to say, but couldn't, much as she'd like to. Lieutenant Cruz was a walking, talking display of dominance. She'd give her eyeteeth to be able to film him for a year. They'd give her the Nobel. Certainly she'd make her name in academia. She'd get tenure immediately. Probably at Harvard.

"I'm a graduate student at St. Mary's over in Grant Falls and I'm writing my dissertation on...certain aspects of law enforcement," she said finally.

"Dominance displays," the lieutenant said dryly.

"Well...yes." Caitlin coughed discreetly. Best to simply glide over that aspect. Couldn't have the lieutenant thinking she would be studying *him* specifically, though now that she'd seen him, she couldn't even imagine studying anyone else. "I've done most of the preliminary research, but Ray—Captain Avery—convinced me that my dissertation would profit from time spent actually observing firsthand the workings of a police force."

"You said you were an expert but I don't get it. How on earth can you be an expert on law enforcement if you aren't a police officer?" he asked. He sounded genuinely puzzled.

Caitlin tried not to smile. How many times had academics in the social sciences came across this prejudice? You could explain to practitioners until you were blue in the face that professions needed a theoretical underpinning, but it never sank in. And yet, what academics did was important. They created a framework within which experience could be fitted. Without that framework, experience was lost, energy dissipated. "Easy. Most research on the subject is done by academics, not practitioners. It's the same in most fields, you know. However, most academics research secondary sources. That's why Captain Avery's classes were so priceless," she said earnestly, leaning forward in her eagerness. "They were incredibly popular. He gave us so many precious insights into the practice of policing. Just absolutely fascinating."

Lieutenant Cruz straightened in his chair. "Captain Avery's classes?"

"Why yes." Caitlin stared at him. "Captain Avery taught a seminar at St. Mary's, The History of Law Enforcement, during the spring semester. Didn't you know?"

Alex froze and stared. So *that* was where Ray had gone off to? Off to teach nerds at some school? What was with that? What the fuck was he doing teaching instead of doing?

And yet, it explained a lot.

Ray'd been disappearing for weeks at a time over the past six months, leaving Alex in charge. Ray had had tons of accumulated leave to use up. Everyone knew he was retiring soon and no one had asked questions, least of all Alex. Ray had the right to do what he wanted, when he wanted, but still, Alex missed him something fierce.

He'd always bounced ideas off Ray, vented his frustrations with him. The day hadn't been complete without a cold beer with Ray at The Shamrock, an Irish pub run by a Singaporean-Irishman named Li O'Shannesy.

Everyone assumed Alex wanted to take Ray's place as captain, but Alex didn't. He'd rather have Ray remain as captain, and friend, than rise in rank.

"No," he said slowly. "I didn't know."

Alex focused on the young woman in front of him. Messy ponytail. Pale, perfect, poreless skin. Straight little nose with delicately flared nostrils. Full, unpainted lips. Perfect oval face. Clothes ancient and shapeless. Take away the untidy externals and she was extraordinarily beautiful—and she looked about sixteen.

This was not good. When she'd been ineffectually patting his trousers with her small, pale hands to sop up the sludge known here as coffee, he'd felt the first stirrings of his cock in, fuck...way, *way* too long. He tried to think back to the last time he'd had sex and came up blank.

Jesus, maybe the last time he'd gotten laid had been with that gorgeous barracuda of a real estate agent he'd hooked up with...what? Around Christmas? Fuck, that long ago?

She'd been smart, beautiful and scary as hell. For just a moment, as he put his cock in her, he wondered if he'd ever get it back.

Had he had sex since? Nope, he decided, after a quick consult with his dick. And after that brief, unsatisfactory liaison, the hunt for Lopez had heated up and he'd been putting in sixteen-hour days at the cop shop.

He needed to get laid again, fast, if a student could turn him on. At work, no less. Alex believed strongly is keeping work separate from the rest of his life, and that included sex. Of course, lately, his entire life *was* work, with no time for anything else. There really wasn't any rest of his life.

Only that would explain a semi-hard-on because Caitlin Summers' hands had come perilously near his groin. She wasn't his type at all. He liked women who knew the score. And though she said she was a graduate student, she looked so impossibly young...

"How old are you?" he asked abruptly.

Caitlin Summers blinked. "Twenty-eight. Why?"

Alex let out a breath he didn't know he'd been holding. The reaction he'd had to her patting his groin would have been inappropriate—*illegal*, actually—had she been as old as she looked. The last thing he needed was to turn into a dirty old man at the age of thirty-eight. Since when did he get turned on by school kids? Okay, so it had been a long time since he'd gotten his rocks off with anything other than his fist—so sue him, he'd been busy—but being turned on by jailbait would have been over the top.

However, his reactions were perfectly normal, not to mention legal—though still inappropriate at work—if she was twenty-eight.

"Never mind," Alex muttered. "So I guess you took some courses from Ray?"

"Yes," she said enthusiastically, head bobbing, wisps of platinum hair flying around her face. "Oh yes. He gave some incredibly interesting lectures. We were all so enthralled. The stories he told... He gave us such fascinating viewpoints from...the field, I guess you'd call it."

"I guess I would," Alex said dryly. He'd always thought of policing as strictly a hands-on business. As practical as it was possible to be, like being a plumber or a vermin exterminator or a proctologist. People broke the law and he and his men tried their best to check them into the Gray Bar Hotel. Nothing theoretical about it.

She leaned forward earnestly. "Anyway, Captain Avery insisted that I gain information firsthand. He said that even if I couldn't put it in the footnotes, it was important to know what law enforcement *feels* like."

"Like crap," Alex muttered, thinking about Ratso's escape. Thinking that Angelo Lopez was going to spend another day as a free man, free to wreck lives. That sucked, big time.

"I beg your pardon?"

"Never mind," Alex said. "Listen, Ms. Summers. It's been very interesting talking to you, and I'm glad to hear that Ray has been using his time profitably teaching you police theory while we've been running around foolishly wasting ours chasing crooks, but I'm afraid that there's no question of you hanging around for a week. Or even ten minutes, for that matter. This is a working police station, not a lab for out-of-work academics." He placed his hands palm down on his desktop. "Now if you'll excuse me—"

"Lieutenant Cruz," she said softly, looking up at him. "I have something else to say to you." She was gripping her hands tightly together. Her hands were pretty, slender and delicate, with a little ink stain on the middle finger of her right hand. A scholar who actually wrote with a pen? He thought people didn't know how to write with pens anymore.

Alex had four snitches, a sergeant and a district attorney waiting for him, so he was sorely tempted to stand, stride to the door and open it in a not-so-subtle invitation for her to leave. He didn't, but sat impatiently to hear what else she had to say. Ray had sent this girl—woman—so if she had one more thing to say to him, he was honor-bound to listen to her. Then he'd say "no way" as gently as he could and escort the girl—the woman—to the door. Ray would expect him to be polite.

A Fine Specimen

He resisted looking at his watch, but it didn't make any difference. He knew how to gauge time. Caitlin Summers had another three minutes with him, tops. Then he was going to tell her to fuck off.

Politely, of course. She was a civilian.

And after all, Ray had sent her.

Caitlin realized that so far the interview had gone more or less precisely as Ray had said it would—except that Ray could never have guessed that she would manage to burn the lieutenant's thigh and mangle his foot. Ray had insisted that she say what she was going to say next, but her instinct told her that the lieutenant was not going to like it.

"Okay. Say what you have to say," he growled. The lieutenant didn't even bother to put hostility in his voice. He didn't have to—the boredom and indifference were enough.

He wasn't fidgeting and he wasn't rolling his eyes, or drumming his fingers on the desktop or tapping his foot. He was perfectly composed. But he hummed with frustrated energy as he sat there, clearly hating to waste even another minute with her.

Caitlin could feel the force field of his impatience from across the desk and it was almost frightening how powerful it was. It wasn't even a power ploy like some executives pull—*I am so important I cannot waste even a second more of my precious time with you.* She recognized those subliminal messages from her research into corporate culture, where half the time the executives had absolutely nothing on their schedules besides two-hour lunches and were otherwise busy trying to make themselves look important with pretend work.

No, this was the real thing—a powerful man with important work to do, impatiently biding his time, his spirit already somewhere else.

Caitlin drew in a deep breath, unobtrusively—dominant males of any species recognized distressed breathing patterns instinctively.

She didn't want to say what was coming next, but Ray had insisted. She'd better just get it out and get it over with.

The lieutenant was already rising.

Caitlin bit her lip and forced the words past the tightness in her throat. There was no polite way to say it, so she just blurted it out. "Ray—um, Captain Avery—said to tell you that you owe him. And that he's collecting."

To her astonishment, he dropped back heavily into his chair as if he'd been suddenly weighted down with lead. Or knocked in the head.

He looked sucker-punched.

"I owe Ray," he repeated slowly, "and he's collecting."

He hadn't betrayed his feelings other than by narrowing his eyes, but he'd had the wind knocked clean out of him, that was clear. Whatever hold Ray thought he had over Alejandro Cruz, it was real, at least in the lieutenant's eyes. She couldn't imagine anything else stopping the lieutenant, other than a bullet to the head.

They stared at each in silence. Caitlin didn't dare look away—a sure sign of weakness. She didn't even dare so much as blink. Though her chest felt constricted, she tried to breathe normally.

She couldn't read his face at all. Though years of study in the behavioral sciences had taught her how to read more or less every human expression in a number of different cultures, she was stymied here, for the first time.

Faces are extraordinary tools of human communication. She'd studied under Professor Hamilton Barstow, an expert on facial expressions in cultures throughout the world. So she could decipher even deadpan expressions by slight corrugations of the brow, by the muscles around the mouth, by the tilt of the head. Neurolinguistics was a big help too, studying the direction the eyes traveled.

And if the face didn't work, there was always body language, another field of expertise for her.

However, none of her training, experience or book learning helped right now. There was simply no way to decipher what Alejandro Cruz was thinking by any physical means. He'd learned impassivity at a tougher school than the Department of Social Sciences at St. Mary's.

This was a master.

Caitlin did the only thing she could do—she simply sat back and waited.

There was nothing she could do or say to sway him in any way. She'd said her piece—repeating Ray Avery's words—and now whether Alejandro Cruz acknowledged his mysterious debt to Avery or not was entirely up to him.

"Okay." He slapped the desk with flat hands and surged out of his seat as she gaped up at him. "Come with me, Ms. Law Enforcement. We're going out on a Code Seven."

A Code Seven! Wow! Ray was *right*! This was going to work after all! She was going to get some field experience. And a Code Seven at that!

Caitlin stood up too. "All right," she said, trying to still her hammering heart. "A Code Seven! Oh my gosh, that's so exciting! Thank you!" She was hastily gathering her things, including the book that nearly lamed him. A pen fell out of her bag and she stuffed it back in. "What's a Code Seven? An emergency? No, that's in hospitals, I remember that from *ER* and *Scrubs*. Is a Code Seven a robbery? Arson? A kidnapping?"

"No." The lieutenant strode out of his office and she rushed to catch up with him.

Caitlin tried to thread her way quickly through the desks and past the officers loitering and laughing in the large squad room. As she hurried past a desk, her book bag caught a pile of CDs. They spilled to the floor with a clatter. "Sorry," she mumbled as she bent down. The lieutenant had stopped at the door on the far side of the room, waiting while she scrambled to pick them up, red-faced.

"That's okay, honey." Kathy Martello bent to help her. "It's much too crowded in here. I'm always bumping into things."

Caitlin looked around furtively, hoping the lieutenant wasn't watching her too closely. Those dark eyes were far too observant. Her hands scrabbled to pick the CDs up.

"Quick," she whispered to Sergeant Martello behind her hand. God forbid he hear her. Ray had described the lieutenant as having preternaturally acute hearing.

Actually, his exact words had been, "Alex can hear a fly fart in the next room."

Sergeant Martello looked at her kindly, brows raised, as Caitlin asked, "What's a Code Seven? I'm going out on one with Lieutenant Cruz."

Kathy Martello straightened suddenly, eyes wide, hands full of CDs. "You're going out...on a *Code Seven*? With the Loot?" she repeated, looking stunned.

"Yes," Caitlin hissed, fairly dancing with impatience. God! This was so exciting! "What is it? What's a Code Seven?"

"Whoa, I am sooo not going there." Kathy looked over to the lieutenant, standing with his arms crossed, then looked back at Caitlin. She shook her head with a grin, miming zipping her mouth. "You'll have to ask the Loot himself what a Code Seven is, honey."

Caitlin Summers approached him gingerly after picking up the mess she'd made. Alex watched her as she made her way toward him, weaving gracefully among the desks. The usually noisy squad room grew quiet as she walked by, heads swiveling, phones on shoulders, fingers lifting from keyboards. When she finally reached him, she stopped, clutching her book bag with white knuckles.

Fuck, but she'd thrown him. *Ray said to tell you that you owed him.*

Oh yeah. He owed Ray. And how.

Well, looked like Ray had finally called in his chips.

Ray was absolutely right, no question. Alex owed the man, big time. Twenty years ago Alex had been a worthless punk, a piece of shit running with a gang like a rat in a pack, with maybe a year or two left to live, if he was lucky, before he got wasted in a shootout or in a revenge killing by a rival gang.

For some reason known only to himself and God, Ray Avery had seen something in him. Something Alex himself had taken years to see.

Certainly neither his alcoholic mother nor his drug-addled father had ever taken the time or the energy to look beyond Alex's size and strength and toughness to see whether there was anything else there.

Ray had. Ray had singled him out, roughed him up and generally knocked some sense into him. And then Ray had hounded him until he had joined the Police Academy. Where Alex had surprised himself and his instructors — but not Ray — by being a natural.

Alex would have given anything he possessed to Ray, anything at all — certainly his life. That was nothing. His life was Ray's for the asking. But Ray had refused everything he wanted to offer him, even thanks. All he said was that one day he would collect.

Well, looked as if that day was finally here, in the form of a very, very pretty woman who was going to fuck with his schedule and his head and his dick for the next week. A crucial week, during which he was expecting to have to all but camp out at the station house as they ran Ratso to ground.

Alex ran a hand down his face, stalling, but there was no question in his mind what he had to do. If Ray wanted a pint of blood and a pound of flesh, Alex would gladly, unquestioningly give it.

But Jesus, not this. Somehow, this was worse.

He looked again at the girl—no, dammit, *woman*—standing in front of him. She was looking at him anxiously out of enormous blue eyes, the same color as her dress. The same color as the sea at dawn. The same color as the spring sky...

Alex drew in a sharp breath, willing his dick to stay down. It had taken enthusiastic note of how incredibly pretty she was underneath her studenty getup. It didn't care at all that she wasn't Alex's type, all it wanted was to get into her pants...

Oh fuck. How was he going to get any work done with this...this *distraction* next to him?

"Um, Lieutenant Cruz?"

"Alex." If she was going to fuck with his head and his week, at least they should be on first-name terms.

She nodded. "Okay, Lieu— Alex. Um, Alex?"

Damn but she was pretty. Even her voice was pretty, soft and light. Was that a touch of the South he heard in her voice?

She was watching him, pale blue eyes unblinking.

Alex sighed. "Yeah?"

"Um, what's a Code Seven?"

Alex didn't answer immediately but instead stared out, jaws clenched, over her head at his men, sending out the silent signal—*showtime's over.*

His men snapped to.

In Alex's mind, even the women were his men. One look from him and it was like the scene in *Sleeping Beauty* where the castle comes to life. Inside of a minute, there was the usual hustle-bustle. Even the phones starting ringing again.

Alex gave one long last look at the squad room. He longed to stay here, with his men. This was where he belonged.

Today's fuckup with Ratso made him even more anxious to get moving on a report of Lopez's finances that had come in from the forensic economists at the FBI. He had a four o'clock meeting with the shrink who'd carried out the compulsory psych evaluation on one of his men who'd shot a scumbag last week. The SWAT guys were begging for new ceramic plates to add to the Kevlar body armor and he was moving heaven and earth to find the money for them. Today was not a day he wanted to be babysitting, not even for pretty girls sent to him by Ray. Not even if the pretty girl in question was waking up his dormant libido.

"What's a Code Seven?" he repeated, taking her arm and moving to the stairs. "Lunch."

Chapter Three

They were walking down the big marble staircase Caitlin knew had been built in 1934, at the height of the Depression, as part of the WPA. She knew everything about the building, about its history and the role it had played in Baylorville. She'd been looking forward to working here for the next week.

Now she had the distinct feeling that if Lieutenant Cruz—Alex—had any say in the matter, she'd never walk back up this staircase ever again.

The meeting had gone more or less precisely as Ray had said it would. Caitlin had been dead set against telling the lieutenant she was here to collect on a debt. Didn't make any difference what she thought though, because Ray insisted. Ray was another super-alpha male.

Caitlin had hated saying what she'd said. It sounded horribly like blackmail, but Ray had insisted and he could be very...forceful. Though Ray was short and stout, with bright blue eyes and a bushy white mane of hair—the physical opposite of the lieutenant...Alex—they both shared the kind of personality it was hard to say no to.

Ray had simply straightened his shoulders, deepened his voice, sharpened his gaze and had gotten his way.

That was probably part of the psychological profile of a police officer, she mused. A certain...persuasiveness. It was an interesting point and there was a lot of literature to back it up, starting from Anderson Carter, who had noted that in his groundbreaking study in the '50s...

Caitlin emerged blinking into the bright light of a Southern California June afternoon.

She needed to pay attention here. Alex was very cool and very smooth. She'd just been herded out of the police station without anything to show for it. He very definitely had not said that she could spend time in the station for her research. All he'd committed himself to was lunch.

Man, he was good. A real player.

He put a large hand to her elbow to turn her right and she instinctively followed his lead, behaving humiliatingly like a little lamb in the presence of a wolf. This wasn't good. She knew better than this. She had to take back the initiative.

Over lunch, he was probably going to start listing the reasons why she'd be in the way, why she'd impede important police work, why there was no question of her interrupting his officers. He would be extremely persuasive and he had a very dominant personality. There was a real risk here of coming away empty-handed.

Pulling Ray out of a hat like a rabbit would only work once. The Loot, as Kathy called him, was perfectly capable of somehow twisting things around so that she spent time in the Archives instead of the station house. Then, technically, he'd be off the hook with Ray.

"You don't need to feed me, Lieutenant," Caitlin said. "I don't want to take you away from your work. All I need is a few moments of your time and your permission to talk with your officers."

"I told you to call me Alex." He wasn't even listening. "Here, let me carry that." Before she could even think of protesting, he'd shouldered her heavy book bag.

Caitlin thought she would have to scramble to keep up with him, but he adjusted the stride of his long legs to hers and she was able to walk at a comfortable pace by his side.

She tried not to watch him as he walked along beside her, but it was hard to keep her eyes off him. The man moved with a strong, easy grace, an alpha male animal in its prime, head high, shoulders back, gaze direct. His jacket covered the shoulder holster with its weapon, but he didn't need it. He had the classic dominant male posture. As he walked, he signaled he was master of all he surveyed.

This was his street, his turf, and here he was the king. Everyone on the street acknowledged him in classic submissive or acceptance behavior. Passersby on the sidewalk dropped their eyes to the ground. A news vendor across the street waved, a woman behind the counter of a bakery shop smiled at him. A taxi cab driver gave a tiny hoot of his horn as he drove by. Alex nodded to everyone.

It was all very pleasant, all very civilized.

Caitlin had no doubt that the street they were on had suddenly become the safest one in the Western hemisphere. No crook in his right mind would attempt a mugging or a holdup in the area with Lieutenant Alejandro Cruz walking around with his Glock 19, the new weapon of choice of most police officers in the county—she'd checked—snugly fitted into his shoulder holster. He probably had a backup weapon in an ankle holster and his hands looked large and sinewy and strong enough to be considered weapons themselves. He exuded mastery and danger as he walked silently alongside her.

Were cops natural predators, Caitlin mused? Or did the job turn them into predators?

There was a lot of literature on the fact that cops and crooks were the obverse side of each other, operating on different sides of the law, but similarly equipped by nature to prevail. She could even see Alejandro Cruz as a crook. A super-crook, the kind who could coolly steal a billion then fade into the night.

It would be really interesting to see him a bit farther afield, not so close to his home territory, so to speak, and observe his body language.

Law enforcement communities are closely packed entities working toward the same goal, like a wolf pack on the hunt.

Most police officers spent more time at work—all of it intense—than with their families. There were ties in a station house fortified by adrenaline and sweat and shared danger. The strict hierarchy allowed it all to work. So how did the alpha male—used to instant obedience and deference in the workplace—function in the outside world? Was he able to impose the ironclad rules of a small nondemocratic fiefdom to the broader world outside?

How would one set up a field study? Caitlin's heartbeat sped up as she began drawing up a plan in her head for collecting data correlated to a map, to ascertain whether signs of deference and submission decreased proportionately to the increase of the distance from the station house. Surely there would be a mathematical correlation—

A flash of blue, a current of wind whipping at her skirt, a loud car horn honking angrily...

Caitlin found herself hauled back violently and held tightly against a hard, broad chest. In self-defense, her arms had gone up to shield herself instinctively and now they were splayed on his chest, hands over his pectorals. He was in instinctive male protection mode—one hand to the back of her head, one hand around her waist, protecting her vital organs and bringing her flush up against the front of his body.

They stood there for long moments while the sound of the car horn faded into the distance. Caitlin could feel the lieutenant's steady, strong heartbeat—nothing like her own trip-hammering heart. She could feel crisp chest hairs through the stiff cotton of his shirt and she could feel...

Oh God. His penis, stirring against her.

That often happened to her on dates. A too-tight embrace for a goodnight kiss and her date's cock surged. Men were programmed that way. A little contact and wham! Off they went. Or rather, *up*.

However, this time there was something different. For each surge of his penis, there was an answering surge of heat and blood in her womb. It was uncontrollable, unstoppable, pure instinct, wildly delicious.

The lieutenant shook her, hard.

Her mind jerked back to reality, heart pounding. She'd almost been run over by a car and only Alejandro Cruz's fast reflexes had saved her. His partial erection was a known male reaction to the adrenaline released by danger. Hers, on the other hand...

What was she thinking of?

Finally, reaction set in and she started trembling. The lieutenant's arms tightened for a moment, then he held her away from him with both hands. There was no expression on his face except for anger. If she hadn't felt it with her own senses, she'd never have believed that he'd had a partial erection. With her...*for* her.

"Damn it, woman, what's the matter with you!" he blazed, jaw muscles tensely bunching. "Do you have some kind of death wish? If you want to kill yourself, do it on your own time! Not while you're walking with me!"

"I'm sorry," she whispered, eyes wide, seeing the anger on his face. He looked furious, the skin taut across his cheekbones, eyes narrowed until only a black glitter showed.

"Damn it, on this planet a red light means stop!" He gripped her shoulder to turn her slightly, waving at the traffic light with his other hand. He shook her lightly. "What the fu— What on *earth* were you thinking of?"

You, Caitlin wanted to say, but couldn't. *I was thinking of you, your power and how to measure it.*

She was *still* thinking of him. It was hard not to think of him as she was still *feeling* him.

All over.

She could feel the steely imprint of his fingers on her shoulders, his hold only now relenting a little. His arms had banded about her as he had pulled her to him, to safety. She could still feel the hard muscles of his arms, the solid strength of his chest, his cock surging against her.

But now the lieutenant was holding her away from himself and she looked up into the furious face, all harsh angles, an angry red flush under the olive-toned skin.

Distract the cobra.

"I'm sorry," she improvised. "I get so carried away by my thoughts sometimes that I get myself into these messes. I was mulling over a point made by a colleague about the relationship between armies and the police."

He dropped his arms. She watched, fascinated, as his jaw muscles bunched angrily. If he continued biting his teeth so hard, he'd grind them down to stubs and need massive dental reconstruction.

The department would pay for it. She'd reviewed the PD's employment contract and health plan before coming. She knew exactly what was refundable under the health plan. Viagra yes, birth control no.

He opened his mouth then shut it with a snap. Lieutenant Cruz was biting back harsh words with all his strength. "Well, I hope it was a thought worth dying for," he ground out finally.

"No," Caitlin replied, pushing her glasses back up to the bridge of her nose. "No, it wasn't. Not at all. Just a minor footnote in a paper." She stepped back to get a better look at him, gauging his interest. He was listening. "My colleague was speculating that throughout history, when the military divided up into army and police, it signaled the beginning of civilization. Like when the Normans set up the traveling judges for the shires. A police force, separate from an army, means a society can begin the move toward democracy."

"Well, that's a dumb thing to be so wrapped up in that you nearly become roadkill—" he began heatedly, then stopped.

Caitlin watched him mull this over. It wasn't really such a dumb thing, after all. Most police officers never really thought deeply about the history of what they did. They were so busy becoming cops and then *being* cops that they never gave much thought to the *idea* of cops. Mostly they assumed that the police had always just...been there. But they hadn't.

She'd often seen the wheels whirring in their practical, reality-focused heads when she mentioned this point, as they wrestled with the idea of when policing actually sprung up. Policing started after the dinosaurs and before TV, obviously, but when?

He was standing there on the corner, lost in thought. She tapped him on the shoulder and he looked down, blinking. "What?"

Caitlin grinned and pointed at the traffic light across the street. "On this planet, the green light means walk."

The diner was called the Garden of Eatin', and Lieutenant Cruz was clearly a treasured customer.

Caitlin was amused by the fact that though a number of attractive women diners and two of the younger waitresses stared at Alejandro Cruz with open appreciation, he didn't seem to notice them. Instead, he honed in on a bony, middle-aged waitress and swooped down to give her a swift hug.

"Alex," the waitress said, pleased. A nametag with "Martha" written in pen was pinned to her flat chest. She hung onto the lieutenant's arms and smiled up at him. "Hey big guy, haven't seen you around lately. What is it—crime rate suddenly go up? You're so busy you can't stop by to see your friends?"

"You know how it is, Martha," Lieutenant Cruz said solemnly, releasing her and stepping back. "Been working hard putting the bad guys away. Keeping you guys safe."

"Yeah, well, you weren't doing a good job of it the other night. Our cook was mugged by a coupla guys on his way home."

His gaze sharpened. "Hank?" he frowned. "What happened? Was he hurt?"

Martha shrugged. "They beat him up some. Cracked a rib and would have cracked his head if it wasn't so hard. Took two hundred bucks off him."

Alex had whipped out a notebook and was taking notes. "Did Hank get a good look at them?"

Martha shrugged again. "Dunno. Hafta ask him."

"Well, tell Hank to stop by the station house and we'll run a lineup for him. Round up the usual suspects and let him see if he recognizes anyone."

"What's the use?" Martha gave the weary sigh of someone who was used to the cruel ways of the world, with the odds tilted against the powerless. "You're never gonna catch 'em anyway."

"We can try." Alex's deep voice was quiet, firm. Caitlin knew full well that the statistical chances of finding muggers almost twenty-four hours after the fact were practically nil, but Alex sounded so reassuring, she almost believed he actually could somehow magically produce the two muggers, with Hank's two hundred still unspent.

Alex released Martha and put a hand to Caitlin's back, ushering her into a booth with cracked red vinyl seating. Once she'd been seated, he took his place across from her, sliding over the menu Martha had placed on the table. "The cheeseburger's good here. So are the burritos."

Caitlin didn't open the menu. "I'll have the cheeseburger then."

Alex signaled and Martha came up, placing two glasses of ice water in front of them. "Here's two on the city. So—what'll it be?" She pulled a pencil from behind her ear. "The usual for you, Alex," she said without looking at him, "and what'll it be for you, miss?"

"Cheeseburger," Caitlin replied.

"C.B. and a burrito," Martha said, writing. "And to drink..." She looked at Caitlin, her brow wrinkling heavily. "And don't even bother asking for anything alcoholic, because we don't serve liquor to minors."

Alex's hard mouth curved slightly. Lord, was that a *smile*? "Relax, Martha, she's of age." He raised an eyebrow at Caitlin. "So, what's your poison?"

"Iced tea," she said.

"And black coffee for me."

He brought his attention back to Caitlin as Martha bustled off, crossing his arms on the faded linoleum tabletop and leaning forward. He eyed Caitlin for a long moment. His gaze was so intent she felt as if he were seeking the secrets to her soul. Good thing she wasn't a criminal and had nothing to confess, because she would have. In a heartbeat. Who on earth could withstand that intense black gaze?

"Okay." His jaw muscles bunched as she watched him try to line up his arguments against her staying at the station house for ten days.

However, something had happened in the past hour since she'd been with him. It wasn't so much that she'd acquired a backbone—she already had one. Living off peanuts while working on a PhD dissertation took guts, thank you very much—but rather that she'd become a convert to Ray's thesis. There wasn't anything that could stop her now. Alex could rant and rave or—since that probably wasn't his style—talk himself blue in the face, but she wouldn't be swayed. Oh no. Not when she'd seen with her own eyes how fascinating he was. Just an hour in his presence and she'd written a whole chapter of her dissertation in her head. Not only that, but now she knew she had a powerful weapon in Ray.

A Fine Specimen

Still, it was going to be fun watching him try to dissuade her.

His jaw muscles bunched again. "Okay, Ray wants you to spend a week in the station house. That I get. But I don't get what it is that you want from us. Or what Ray thought you would get by spending time with us."

Caitlin took a sip of the ice water. Not stalling for time, really. Just marshalling her thoughts. You didn't let your mind wander around Alejandro Cruz. He was watching her with piercing dark eyes, his normally full, surprisingly sensuous mouth pursed tight...

Caitlin shook herself slightly and took a deep breath. She had to convince him she was serious. She knew now that she was going to be spending the next week in the Baylorville Police HQ, but it would make a huge difference whether Alex Cruz was going to be quietly obstructive or helpful. So she had to watch her step and she had to find the right words.

"Look. I've got a double masters in behavioral psychology and sociology." She leaned forward as he had done, looking straight into his black eyes and trying to make him understand. "I've always been interested in law enforcement theory and I'm writing my dissertation on it. I have basically all the material I need but, as I told you, Ray insisted that I spend time at a police station and I think he's right, because fieldwork in testing theories is always so important.

"I won't be a bother, I promise. I have a slightly modified Thematic Apperception Test which I'll be asking your officers to take, but they can do that whenever they have a spare moment. I would like to interview them as well, but I can easily arrange to do that when they have some down time, if they're willing. I won't interrupt anyone's routine and I promise not to get in the way. When I go back to my hotel in the evening, you won't even know I had been around."

It was as if she hadn't spoken about her work at all. He honed in on something else entirely. "You're staying in a hotel? Where? Which one?"

"The Carlton," Caitlin said, wrinkling her nose. She'd been a student all her adult life and was used to ratty student conditions, but the Carlton was, hands down, the worst place she'd ever slept in her life.

He reared his head back. "The Carlton. That's in Riverhead."

She blinked at the flat, disapproving tone of his voice.

He shook his head, a sharp blur. "You're crazy. Riverhead is the worst section of Baylorville, worse than the Trey. Someone who looks like you, someone who gets lost in her thoughts, is ripe prey for the scumbags in Riverhead." He rapped his knuckles on the tabletop once, hard, and blew out a quick breath. "I knew it. You *do* have a death wish."

"No, I don't." Caitlin sighed. "I didn't know the area would be like that. My travel agent probably didn't either. I told her I wanted a budget hotel. I'm sure she didn't realize how...how unsavory the area is." She shrugged. "It's only for a few days, anyway."

"A few days are enough for you to get tossed, maybe killed," he said bluntly, and nodded as she flinched involuntarily at his harsh words. "Good. The more scared you are, the more wary you'll be."

He was trying to scare her away, but he didn't know her. Caitlin didn't scare easily. "Like I said, it's only for a few days. I'm expecting—hoping—to be awarded a year's grant by the Frederiksson Foundation. Once I get the grant, I'll be looking for an apartment."

Caitlin tried not to squirm under Alex's dark, intense, disapproving gaze. She simply met it with her own, keeping her face neutral. But she could feel his strong will beating against her from across the table. To her relief, Martha arrived, neatly sliding his burrito and Caitlin's cheeseburger in front of them.

As if she didn't have a care in the world, Caitlin bit into her burger and munched. "Wow. This *is* really good."

He was barely listening, simply glowering at her. Caitlin refrained from rolling her eyes or showing impatience in any way as she ate the delicious cheeseburger. She didn't want to do anything to tip the balance, because they were at a stalemate. His power against her stubbornness. The first person to blink lost.

They stared at each other, Alex doing a very good imitation of a smokestack with steam coming out of it.

After a while, it got ridiculous. Caitlin tried a little conversational distraction. She finished chewing and smiled. "Ray told me the cheeseburgers in Baylorville were special."

Alex just stared. He didn't want her at the station house, but just as clearly, he was compelled, for reasons she didn't understand, to accede to Ray's wishes. As long as Caitlin didn't do or say anything that could put ammunition in his hands, she'd won.

They were at a tipping point. Caitlin suddenly realized that she needed for him to obey her on something, to establish a precedent.

She nodded at his burrito. "*Eat,*" she said, trying to inject stern command into her voice.

He looked down, startled, at the food in front of him, as if he'd forgotten all about it. At her command, he picked up his fork.

Though she kept her face impassive, Caitlin rejoiced inwardly.

Yessss!

If he obeyed her once, he would obey her again.

She was going to win this battle. And after the battle, the war.

The aromas of Hank's food wafted straight into Alex's system, reminding him that he was running on empty. Or on station house coffee, which was worse.

Alex picked up his fork to dig into his burrito then stopped, running through what Caitlin had said in his mind. He lifted his head, surprised.

"The Frederiksson Foundation?"

The Frederiksson Foundation was the pride of the city — one of the best-known think tanks in the country, run by two Nobel Prize winners.

Alex looked again at Caitlin Summers, this time looking past the incredible prettiness, the absentmindedness, the grad student messiness.

Now he saw the intelligence.

He hadn't noticed it before because she was so fucking pretty and looked so damn innocent. He didn't know any pretty, intelligent, innocent women. Most of the intelligent women he knew were cops. A cop didn't stay innocent after Day One on the job.

She swallowed and smiled at him. "You've heard of it? I suppose you would have, being from Baylorville. I'm really looking forward to being a fellow there, if they offer it to me." Caitlin pursed her lips. "Even though it *is* full of pencil-dick geeks." Flashing an amused grin at him, she bit into her cheeseburger again. A drop of Hank's homemade ketchup dripped from the bun. She licked it off her lip with a small pink tongue.

Alex opened his mouth to reply but was sidetracked by the sight of that little pink tongue. This was another aspect of Caitlin Summers that he'd been trying to ignore, but that quick, mischievous grin, that tongue sneaking out to lick her luscious lips — making him think of her licking *him* — blindsided him.

Alex kept sex and work strictly separate. Not that there had been that much sex lately to keep separate. He'd been busy. But still. If he met an attractive woman with any connection to the job, Alex just flipped that switch in his head that kept his dick down between his legs.

That switch just broke.

He'd already noticed how attractive she was but it hadn't really affected him beyond a knee-jerk male reaction when she'd nearly become roadkill. He'd just filed it away as a distinguishing characteristic, as if compiling an Identi-Kit. *Large, luminous eyes the color of a summer sky, beautiful pale blonde hair so thick it frothed out of its ponytail, high, sculpted cheekbones, long graceful neck. Five-four, slender build. Utterly gorgeous.*

But now all that feminine attraction seemed to reach out and grab him by the dick, forcing him to notice, to look at her as a woman. She wasn't wearing any perfume, she didn't have any makeup on, her clothes were cheap and wrinkled. His cock didn't give a shit. It just reared straight up, the fucker.

Damn Ray Avery! This woman was going to be a *huge* distraction. And now was the wrong time for him to be thinking with his little head. Just when he was zeroing in on Angelo Lopez...

Maybe all this was happening because he hadn't had sex in a while, sort of like punishment. Like going too long without giving your car a lube job. He had to see about getting laid, double quick, only not with Caitlin Summers.

Not only was she definitely not his type, she'd been sent by *Ray*. It'd...it'd be like fucking Ray's daughter. Ray didn't have a daughter, he'd never married, but still.

"Lieutenant?" He looked at her. Shit, even her voice was attractive. Soft, a faint hint of honeysuckle, though without that coyness he hated in Southern women. He shifted uneasily in his seat. The boner was *not* going down.

Caitlin put down her cheeseburger and leaned forward earnestly, light blue eyes searching his. "Look, I've interviewed literally thousands of people at the workplace. What I said before is true. I can promise you that I won't cause any trouble or distract anyone from their duties. I'll be so discreet you'll hardly notice I'm there. All I want to do is talk with the officers, get to know them well enough to evaluate the questionnaire. Find out how they feel about their jobs. Find out what their concerns are."

"Well hell," Alex said, disgusted. "I can tell you that right now, without having to interview them. They want to put away the bad guys and stay in one piece while doing it."

"Of course they do." She nudged her little round scholar's glasses back up to the bridge of her nose. "But in order to do that, they need a strategy. A survival strategy. Cops are both predator and prey, so like any animal in the wild they need to hunt while convincing their enemies that they won't make an easy meal."

Laughter rumbled in Alex's chest but he refused to give in to it. This was *not* a laughing matter, damn it. He absolutely refused to be charmed by Caitlin Summers, no matter how pretty, no matter how smart she was. She was going to be a burden and a distraction.

He was going to open the doors of his station house to her under duress and only because Ray Avery had asked him to. And Ray was the only human being alive he'd do this for.

"Academic theory always has a positive rebound effect on the object of its study, sooner or later," Caitlin said softly. "So you really won't have been wasting your time or the time of your officers."

"Rebound effect?" Alex heroically refrained from rolling his eyes. "You mean you think *you're* going to help *us*?"

Alex knew he was in intimidation mode, but to his surprise, she didn't back down. She clearly felt she was on safe ground here.

Caitlin nodded. "Sure. A large part of behavioral psychology is based on the fact that we're animals and we

A Fine Specimen

follow the rules any animal species does. You eat or be eaten. You mate and defend your young. You keep the troop or the flock or the pride together and orderly by following the rules of hierarchy. Aggression must be used under controlled circumstances or the group suffers. In this one aspect, the human species differs from all other animal species. No other species has as many rogue elements as humans. No other species requires that a percentage of the energies of the group go into keeping order. It's also very unusual in primitive human tribes. That's what makes modern law enforcement so fascinating."

Alex grunted and looked down at his plate, astonished to see that he hadn't started eating yet. He'd been starving and she'd made him forget his food. Ms. Caitlin Summers was proving to be an even bigger distraction than he had originally thought. Not much could get between him and one of Hank's burritos when he was hungry. Deliberately, he sank his fork into the now lukewarm burrito.

Caitlin tilted her head and studied him. "Go ahead, Lieutenant. Why don't you tell me about a case you're working on and I'll tell you what academic theory can do."

Alex stopped with his fork halfway to his mouth, turning her words over in his head.

No. No fucking way. Police business stayed in the force. He wasn't about to go blabbing about their problems to the first pretty face who asked.

And yet...and yet. Alex was a good cop because he used everything he could, because he never spurned help, because he thought outside the box. And this was a woman who'd spent years studying law enforcement. Surely that counted for something...

Shit.

He was thinking about it. What was the matter with him? Had he suddenly gone loco?

"You don't have to give me names or details, Alex. Just give me the general outline of the problem." Caitlin smiled at him, lips curving gently upward. It occurred to him that some women were smart not to use lipstick. Her lips were a very pretty color all their own—a smooth, glistening pale pink. He could kiss her without getting glop on his face. His cock pulsed at the thought of kissing her, diving into that pretty mouth, licking into it...

He jerked himself back to reality. *Think about something else*, he ordered himself.

Ratso escaping and Lopez laughing all the way to the bank came to mind, and his cock subsided.

"We're looking for someone," he found himself saying.

"Someone?"

"Yeah." Philosophically, Alex finally put the fork in his mouth and started chewing. With an inner sigh, he realized that he was going to tell her about Ratso Colby. He didn't want to, but he was going to anyway. "He's the bookkeeper for the man we really want, a major bad guy. We found out that the bookkeeper had been keeping the bad guy's accounts—and I'm not talking about filing for the IRS here. If we can get this guy we're looking for to talk, we can put the mobster away for a long, long time. Unfortunately, word is out on the street that we're looking for the bookkeeper, so he's on the run. From us and now from the mobster, who probably knows by now what we're up to."

"What incentives are you offering this bookkeeper to flip?"

She knew the lingo, that was for sure. Not only that. With a stab of surprise, Alex realized she'd cut straight to the heart of the matter. "Well, our bookkeeper has also been a bad boy in the past—he knows it and *we* know it. There are two or three counts we can nail him on. Minor things, but he's been caught twice before and this would be the third time."

A Fine Specimen

"Three strikes and you're out," Caitlin said softly, her eyes never leaving his.

"That's right," Alex said with rich satisfaction. "And our friend spent some quality time in stir and hated it, and would do anything not to go back in. So we think he'll give us names and dates about how and where our bad guy washes his money whiter than white. And so bang! We nail the bad guy."

"And what happens to the...bookkeeper?"

"Witness Protection Program, probably," Alex said, watching her as she winced. "What?"

"I imagine that's as unacceptable as prison for your bookkeeper. He'd be relocated somewhere at the discretion of the Marshall's office, given an identity they choose for him, doing a faceless, nameless job the office chooses, always looking over his shoulder...he's in a tight spot."

"Yeah, yeah. That's just tough," Alex said unsympathetically. "He should have thought of that before going to work for Lo— For the bad guy. So, are you going to look into your crystal ball and tell us where he is or not?"

Caitlin looked up sharply but Alex wasn't making fun of her. He wasn't really sure if anything she might say could be helpful, but he waited politely for her response just the same.

"There are basically two types of anti-predator behavior," Caitlin said. "Escape behavior and crypsis, hiding to make prey detection more difficult. Do you think he's escaped?"

"No, he was spotted this morning, as a matter of fact."

"So there's probably a reason why he hasn't fled and you might want to look into that. Maybe he's waiting for something or someone."

Waiting. Alex thought it over. He'd been astonished to hear that Ratso was still around when it would have made sense for him to get out of Dodge fast, what with both the cops and Lopez looking for him. The cops to make him talk. Lopez to shut him up permanently. So why hadn't he skipped town? Something or...*someone*, she'd said.

Alex thought it over and rejected the notion that Ratso had a love interest. The two things Ratso loved most in the world were himself and money. Now money... Maybe he'd stashed away some money and was trying to get his hands on it before leaving for good. It was a line to pursue.

"Well," he said, signaling Martha, "this particular predator has to get back to work." He frowned as he watched her fumble with her purse. "What are you doing?"

Caitlin froze, blinking. "Er...getting my wallet?"

His frown deepened. "What for?"

Caitlin looked around the four walls of the café as if they could help her. "Um..." She bit her bottom lip. "To pay my share of the bill?"

Martha slipped the check near Alex's right elbow and Caitlin reached for it. Alex clasped her wrist, feeling her skin warm and soft under his hand.

"No, really," Caitlin protested, "you must let me—" She pulled her wrist out of his grasp and knocked Alex's glass of ice water straight into his lap.

Alex closed his eyes for a second against the icy wet sensation in his groin. As opposed to the burning wet sensation of the coffee an hour before. He opened them to see Caitlin Summers' mortified expression.

Well, at least being doused with ice water had made his dick go permanently down. Count your blessings where you can find them, Ray used to say.

"Tell me the truth, Ms. Summers," Alex said dryly as he threw two tens on the table and stood up. "Did my dry cleaner send you?"

Chapter Four

"What are you doing here at this hour?"

Caitlin jumped at the harsh, deep voice behind her. She had no doubt who it belonged to. Lieutenant Alejandro Cruz's voice was unmistakable. It wasn't just the deep timbre of his voice, but the firm tone of command. Yes, it was definitely Alex Cruz.

She stretched and then turned around slowly, blinking and trying to clear her head to deal with the man. He always seemed to catch her at her worst moments.

They'd walked back to the station house in silence after lunch, Caitlin's cheeks red with embarrassment. Alex had disappeared into his office and Caitlin had wandered around, getting a feel for the layout, chatting with the officers.

After a couple of hours observing the workings of the station, she'd asked Sergeant Martello if there were somewhere private where she could do some paperwork. Sergeant Martello had led her to a big corner room just off the squad room with INTERROGATION etched on the frosted upper panel of the door, and Caitlin had simply dived into the questionnaires.

She knew that interrogation rooms were supposed to be windowless and featureless, stripped of any decoration that could distract a suspect's attention during the interrogation so that the questioning could be focused. Almost a form of sensory deprivation. Unfortunately, since there were so few distractions, the room was also guaranteed to put her into a study trance, where she promptly forgot about the outside world and about time passing.

The lieutenant brought her back to earth with a thump. Reflexively, she glanced at her watch and was horrified to see that it was almost quarter to eight.

"Oh my God!" she gasped, rising and quickly shoving her papers together. In the windowless room, she hadn't been able to see day fading to night. "Thanks for reminding me how late it is. I have to hurry. The last bus to Riverhead leaves at eight o'clock."

He stuffed two big, heavy books into her book bag and hefted a third in his hand. "I'm glad *these* aren't landing on my foot," he said wryly, then glanced sharply at her. "You don't have a car?"

"No." Caitlin tussled briefly with him over who was going to carry her heavy book bag, then let him do it. She didn't have time to waste arguing. It was a twenty-minute bus ride and it would be almost completely dark by the time she got to Riverhead. And it was at least a fifteen-minute walk from the bus stop to the Carlton. Ten if she hurried. She would definitely hurry. The thought of walking through Riverhead after dark was terrifying.

Caitlin ran down the two flights of stairs to the ground floor, barely noticing that the lieutenant was right behind her. She had to battle her way down through laughing, joking officers walking up. The night shift was coming on. She was about to push her way through the heavy oak front doors when her elbow was caught in a hard grip.

"Lieutenant," she said hurriedly, trying to tug her arm free while reaching for her books. His grip didn't hurt, but it was firm. "Thank you for carrying my book bag, but now I have to run—"

He was glaring at her grimly. "You're not running anywhere, Ms. Summers, you're coming with me."

Caitlin stopped, all semblance of thought flown from her head. In gripping her elbow, he had swung her close to him. So close she had to look up to see his face. So close she could

A Fine Specimen

see the beginnings of a dark beard—he was the kind of man who probably had to shave twice a day if he went out in the evenings. So close she thought she could smell him—a faint tang of soap and leather and gun oil—over the station-house smells of must and sweat and disinfectant. Even though he was glaring down at her, Caitlin had an insane desire to move even closer, to see if he felt as wonderful as she remembered.

Temptations were there to yield to—and she shuffled half a step closer to him.

Oh God, yes, he felt so delicious. So very unlike anyone she'd ever touched before. Most of the men she touched were students, with soft, thin limbs. Touching them had never been a turn-on.

Last fall, she'd dated a biology major who was hooked on weightlifting and could bench press her late, unlamented car. He had muscles coming out his ears. He'd felt lumpy and hard, like rocks in a sock. He had been so involved in his own body that kissing him had been like kissing her arm. That hadn't been a turn-on, either.

This was a turn-on, feeling that strong, lean, fit body against hers. The temptation to reach up and cup her hand to that dark face, just to see if she could soften it up, was almost overwhelming.

Clearly the man played havoc with her thought processes and that was dangerous as hell. This was not a man you played around with. Not only was he tough and emotionally remote, she needed his cooperation for the next week. Touching him was out of the question.

She curled her fingers into the palm of her hand and stepped back immediately.

"I have to go now, Lieutenant," she said, trying to tug her arm free. "The bus—"

"I told you to call me Alex. And you're not catching that bus."

Caitlin blinked. "I beg your pardon?"

He released her elbow and put a large hand to the small of her back. "You have to call me Alex if I'm going to be your babysitter."

Intimidating or not, Caitlin felt her indignation rise at his words. She'd lost her father at a young age and she'd held down a job of one kind or another since she was twelve. She'd put herself through college and graduate school by dint of sheer hard work and was used to taking care of herself. In fact, she prided herself on her independence.

Caitlin stopped dead in her tracks, glaring up at him. "I don't *need* a babysitter, thank you very much. I'm perfectly capable of taking care of myself. Which right now means making that eight o'clock bus, otherwise I'm stuck without a ride and I don't have cash for a cab." Caitlin was trying to be forceful and make him understand that she had to get out of the station house fast, but he was almost pushing her to a side door.

"You have a ride," he said. "Me."

"Lieutenant Cruz—"

"Alex."

"Alex," she said between clenched teeth, and dug in her heels. This was terrible and counterproductive. The last thing she needed was for him to feel that she was going to be a burden on him. That would be giving him ammunition to get rid of her as soon as possible. "There is no reason whatsoever for you to feel that you have to babysit me, or feed me, or drive me around. Now, I would stay and argue the point with you, but I really, really have to *catch my bus.*" She looked down pointedly at her arm, where he still held her by the elbow. He dropped his hand.

"Ray sent you." The lieutenant's deep voice made the statement as if it were the clincher in an argument. He shrugged.

Caitlin glanced at her ancient cheapo faux Swatch and the panic rose. *7:55.* Another minute more and she'd be too late to catch the bus. "I realize you feel you should drive me back to the hotel, Lieutenant, but there's no reason—"

"Alex."

"*Alex*," she repeated, feeling hunted. *7:56.* "There's no reason at all for you to feel that way. Captain Avery didn't expect you to look out for me. All he asked was for you and your officers to give me some of your time."

"Ray sent you. Frankly, he would have my head if I let you wander around Riverhead all on your own at night."

Caitlin gritted her teeth and swallowed her words. She knew perfectly well she looked younger than her years. Part of it was that she dressed so badly. She simply didn't have the money to dress as an adult out in the working world. But the combination of her looks and her clothes had people constantly underestimating her and it rankled. She wasn't a dummy and she wasn't without street smarts. "I won't be *wandering around*, Lieu— Alex. I have every intention of being careful, believe me. I know how to behave in dangerous areas. You really don't need to worry at all."

Caitlin might as well have been talking to the wind. He'd taken hold of her elbow again in a grip that was just shy of painful and totally unbreakable. She was being walked toward a side door and there was absolutely nothing she could do about it, unless she wanted to create a scene or leave her elbow behind. A big clock in the lobby showed the time. *8:00.*

Hell, she though. *The bus has gone.*

They exited through the side door into a parking lot. The lieutenant—Alex—pressed something in his jacket pocket and a sleek black car in a slot with "Lt. Cruz" stenciled on the brick wall in front of it unlocked its doors for him with an expensive-sounding *whump*. It wasn't enough that he had police officers and herself obeying him, Caitlin thought resentfully. Even his *car* sprang to attention, damn his hide.

Caitlin sighed and thought of her ancient car, Marvin, named after a particularly limp boyfriend who, like his namesake, often left her flat when she needed him most. Marvin—the car—had died a geriatric death last month and she simply had no money to replace it. It hadn't had a remote-control opening or power steering or air conditioning. She was lucky it had had four tires, though all of them were bald.

Alex opened the passenger door for her, releasing her arm only when she was settled in the passenger seat. "Seat belt," he said as he slid behind the wheel, cop to the end.

"Yes *sir*."

He glanced over, not visibly disturbed by her slightly acerbic tone. "It's the law, you know."

Caitlin probably knew the law better than he did. The law wasn't the problem, *he* was. "Well, the law certainly doesn't say anything about feeling responsible for me or having to accompany me to my hotel."

He backed quickly, skillfully out of the slot. "The law might not be clear on that point, Ms. Summers, but there are rules."

"Caitlin," she said on a sigh. "If you're going to babysit me, we might as well be on first-name terms."

Traffic was heavy. The ride took almost forty minutes. Twilight was edging into night by the time Alex pulled up in front of the decayed old hotel which had never seen better days.

Across the street from the Carlton was a burned-out apartment building. To the right was a rubble-strewn empty lot and to the left was a boarded-up building which, according to the poster on the splintered door, had been condemned by the city authorities, though no one had cared enough to actually demolish it.

The instant they'd entered Riverhead at the Madison Street turnoff, the change was startling, like day into night. The few people on the streets were badly dressed, some stumbling, some simply standing, eyes blank, high on the drug or drink of

A Fine Specimen

their choice. The buildings were old, built when people had stoops to beat the summer heat. Many of the stoops had people sitting listlessly on the steps, a bottle between their legs, staring indifferently at the few cars that drove by.

Riverhead had twice the number of reported crimes as the rest of Baylorville, but the real figure was much higher. Most of the crimes went unreported, for the simple reason that most of the victims were criminals themselves. There was, on average, a murder every three days, two rapes a week, four muggings a day and countless episodes of domestic violence. About four million dollars in drugs changed hands every day.

Then again, drug dealing was just about the only viable economic activity in the neighborhood.

The life expectancy of Riverhead residents was thirty years less than that of the residents of the rest of the city, and for a good reason. If you lived here, you were poor and either a drug addict or an alcoholic, maybe even both. Either that or you were married to one or your parents were in the life. There was almost no hope of escape from here except feet first in a coffin, which happened to a statistically significant portion of the teenagers in Riverhead.

Alex had grown up here — six blocks down and an alley over from the Carlton, actually. Even what had passed for his family — a drunk of a mother and a drug-addict father — had grown up here. Riverhead was in his genes. He'd been destined from birth to live here and to die here. His fate was to end up like the other lost souls in Riverhead — to live fast, die young and leave a big stain.

Thank God for Ray.

Alex remembered the Carlton from his misspent youth. The Carlton was where businessmen from the downtown area used to take the young, easy women of Riverhead for an hour on their lunch break for a quick fuck.

No mistresses down here in Riverhead, no fancy ladies set up in luxury flats, no expensive call girls. The women here were lucky to get ten bucks for a blowjob in a car, maybe twenty for a longer session in the Carlton, which helpfully rented by the hour.

A few years ago, there had been a fleeting interest in cleaning up Riverhead. The Carlton had been painted and the roof repaired, just enough of an effort to make it look like a semi-respectable hotel. But now the paint was peeling again and Alex suspected that it was being used for things more dangerous than a little illicit love.

He parked directly in front of the entrance, figuring that the dim glow cast by the entrance porch light might be enough to keep the scumbags from boosting his hubcaps for, oh, maybe fifteen minutes. Twenty, tops.

Alex killed the engine. "Welcome to the Ritz," he said dryly, looking over at Caitlin. She'd been very quiet on the trip out, watching out the window as the scenery grew danker and grimmer.

Shit, she was so fucking out of place here. Right now, in the uncertain light of the flickering lamp over the Carlton's entrance, she looked twelve and helpless. In some parts of the world that was a guarantee of safety, but not here. Not in Riverhead. Here, what she signaled was—*come and get me.*

"It isn't much, is it?" Caitlin said quietly.

Fuck no, it wasn't.

Alex came around to the passenger door and opened it. She stepped out onto the cracked pavement.

A bell echoed distantly as Alex pushed down on the heavy brass handle of the hotel's front door and shouldered it open. He let Caitlin pass then followed her in. His disapproving gaze took in the peeling wallpaper and cracked flooring.

His disapproval turned to fury when he saw that the front desk was unattended, the keys hanging on a plywood board.

"What's your room number?" he murmured to Caitlin.

"Four forty-six," she replied. "Why?"

Alex reached across the front desk and lifted her key from its hook. He pocketed it just as a dark-skinned man with a stained turban came in from a side door, still chewing something. The smell of curry wafted in from behind the door. The man's polite smile turned genuinely welcoming when he saw Caitlin. "Ah, Ms. Summers. Good evening."

"Good evening, Hassan."

"You want key? Number four forty-six. Is right?" He searched the board. "That is strange..." Hassan turned back to them and froze when he saw Alex's hand holding a BPD shield two inches from his nose, Alex's face right behind it. "S-s-sir?"

"Baylorville Police Department," Alex growled, trying to contain his anger. This dirtbag could get Caitlin raped or killed. "You are very lucky today, Hassan, because I am not going to haul your sorry ass downtown on a charge of reckless endangerment. Nor am I going to inquire about your status with Immigration."

Hassan turned pasty white under his dusky complexion.

Alex dangled Caitlin's key in front of him. "Listen up, Hassan, because I'm only going to say this once. Never, *ever* leave this key unattended. If you absolutely have to leave the front desk, you take Ms. Summers' key with you. If you don't, and if someone gets into Ms. Summers' room and she gets hurt, I will personally make it my business to see that you are put away for the rest of your natural life." Alex's gaze was fierce. He meant Every. Fucking. Word. "*Is that clear?*"

Hassan jumped. "Yessir, yes! Yes indeed." He placed his hands together and bowed his head. "Most clear."

Alex stared at him for another long moment then put a hand to Caitlin's back and walked her to the battered steel doors of the elevator.

Caitlin was silent until the doors closed and the elevator started creaking slowly upward. She rounded on him. "How *dare* you speak to poor Hassan like that! There was no need whatsoever to terrify him like you did."

"Are you joking? There was every need!" The elevator jerked to a stop and Alex stepped warily out into the corridor. The lighting in the hallway was dim and there were pockets of darkness down its length. Room 446 was at the end of the corridor. "Anyone could just walk in off the street and grab your key." The thought of it had him in a sweat. It would take nothing to notice her, follow her back to the hotel and find out what room she was in. Then steal the key while ol' Hassan was in the back office scarfing curry rice.

Caitlin wasn't listening. "Hassan only arrived in this country from Pakistan a year ago. He's working to save money so he can study agronomy, and here you are, frightening the poor man to death. Threatening to call Immigration, for heaven's sake! I'm sure he's got his green card, but still— Alex? What are you doing?"

Alex used the key to open the door to room 446, though the lock was so flimsy he could have picked it in two seconds. He stood to the side of the door, opened it, scanned the room then stepped inside. A few more large steps took him to the opposite wall. The Carlton didn't exactly splurge on space. He quickly checked the small closet and the even smaller bathroom.

Caitlin was standing in the doorway, her arms crossed. "Well?" she asked sweetly. "No dope fiends hiding under the bed? No serial killers in the shower stall?"

"Nope." Alex walked back to her. Caitlin's skin seemed to glow in the faint light from the corridor. Her pale blue eyes widened slowly as he approached, his eyes never leaving hers.

Alex picked up her hand and pressed the key into it, his fist closing over hers. Her hand was slender and soft, and to his surprise, he couldn't let go. His brain seemed to stop functioning, though the cop in him noticed Caitlin's irregular breathing, the way her eyes were fixed on his mouth then rose to meet his eyes, the way her soft, pale pink lips parted...

Without thinking about it, without planning it, without even *wanting* it, he found himself bending down to her. Her

A Fine Specimen

wide blue eyes watched him then drifted shut as his mouth closed over hers.

He could feel her breath sighing out as her mouth opened under his. He moved closer, one hand behind her head to hold her still for his kiss, the other around her narrow waist.

Alex had a number of very, *very* good reasons not to do this.

A. Though Caitlin Summers was twenty-eight, she looked like a teenager. And though Alex was technically only thirty-eight in human years, he was about one hundred ninety-seven in cop years. This was not a good match.

B. He liked his women savvy and experienced and unbreakable. He was a love-'em-and-leave-'em kind of guy, always had been, always would be. He wasn't looking for a relationship.

C. This girl—*woman*—had relationship written all over that gorgeous face.

D. Ray had sent her. She was Ray's student, sort of like his daughter. Ray was the closest thing to a father he'd ever had. Sex with this woman would be like...like incest. Wouldn't it?

E. She was going to be in the cop shop for a whole week, messing with his head. Sex would make it worse, make him fumble, make him lose his mojo—because knowing she was around would make him think with his cock instead of his head...

He never got to F because the heat in his dick fried his logic circuits. Her mouth tasted as luscious as it looked, without the syrupy sensation of lipstick he now realized he hated. She was so delicious he didn't even do what he usually did—make it a delicate, tentative kiss until he got signs from the woman that his advance was welcome.

No, sir. He dove in, licking, sucking, biting, as if she were a cream puff and he were a starving man.

It was like plunging into a sea of warm, fragrant flowers that caressed him back.

She moved her arms to cling to his neck and dropped her heavy book bag right onto his foot, probably breaking a few small bones. He didn't give a shit. That same heavy heat that took out his brain cells had zapped down to his feet to remove his pain receptor cells too. He felt no pain whatsoever and impatiently shoved the bag out of his way with his foot because it created maybe half an inch of distance between them and that was totally intolerable. He had to be as close to her as it was physically possible to be. Closer. His grip tightened as he angled his head for a deeper taste of her, so incredibly delicious he would have laughed if his mouth had been free.

His cock was having a good time too, way up, hard as steel and happily rubbing against the lips of her sex. The flimsy material of her dress and panties couldn't hide the shape of her. He could feel it all, every little ripple through the cloth. If this was so great that it felt like the top of his head would come off, wouldn't feeling her naked flesh be better?

Oh yeah.

Alex's right hand moved from her waist. It took only a second to bunch that lightweight skirt over his wrist as his hand slowly rode up that long, soft thigh, arrowing straight toward…

Ahh!

That was it. He cupped her in the palm of his hand, tightly. They gasped at the same time, out of excitement and to get some oxygen, their lips never parting, then Alex kissed her again, harder, deeper. It was so great he almost forgot what his right hand was doing. Almost. There was something hugely annoying under his hand, keeping him out. Impatient, he tugged viciously, barely noticing the ripping sound because his fingers were there, sliding through the soft, wet heart of her. Softer than the finest silk. He outlined her with the tip of his finger.

A Fine Specimen

She moaned when he entered her with one finger, then two. The sound of her moan echoed in his mouth.

She was so wet and so impossibly tight. His entire world had narrowed to his mouth, his cock and his fingers. There was no way he could get his cock in her without stretching her first. He separated his fingers and she jolted wildly, shaking. With every breath came a little moan, as if she couldn't help herself.

And then he felt his fingers pulsing and with the few brain cells left, he wondered if his hand was coming.

No, it wasn't his hand — it was Caitlin Summers. Coming.

He'd never felt anything like it. Her little cunt contracted against his fingers in rhythmic waves, her entire body welling up against him, bursting with joy. She came against his mouth, against his chest, against his hand, in long swells rippling through her body.

Alex had unzipped himself — God! The release felt so good! — and was holding his cock, ready to plunge inside her, when he pulled out of the kiss for a fraction of a second. He needed air.

Looking down, he froze.

Caitlin looked pale, shocked, lost. Wide blue eyes alarmed, soft mouth open, wet from his own.

Jesus. She was panting and shaking, completely out of her depth. This wasn't some easy lay, happy to have a quickie against a hotel doorframe. With the door still *open*. What the *fuck* was he thinking?

Alex stepped back for a second and winced as he looked down at his inflamed cock, huge and red. He withdrew his hand, sliding it out of her. Her skirt dropped back down over her legs and Caitlin was restored to a semblance of dignity. He, on the other hand, was standing there with his cock jutting from his unzipped pants, hard as a rock, weeping drops of come. He looked like an ass.

Alex hadn't lost control of himself like this since…since when? Not even in high school. Hell, especially not in high school. He'd had so much sex in high school there was no way it would have thrown him like this. He was so incredibly excited simply because it had been a long, long time since he'd gotten laid. *Now* wasn't when he should be making up for lost time. The world was full of women to fuck, now that his hormones had been kick-started.

He took another step back as he tried to stuff himself back into his pants, wincing with pain. It fucking hurt.

He bent to pick up a ripped piece of material from the floor. Her panties. Oh Jesus. He'd fucking ripped her panties off. Alex was smooth, he didn't do ripped panties. What the hell was wrong with him?

"Here." His voice came out a croak. He cleared his throat. "Here," he repeated. "I'm sorry I, um, tore them."

She was standing there, staring at him, soft mouth slightly open. He picked up her hand and placed the torn panties in her palm. "Sorry," he said again.

"That's okay." Her voice was breathless. She looked down at her hand, holding a now-useless piece of material that used to be underwear, looking like a ten-year-old whose doll had been smashed by a bully.

Her hair was even more disheveled than usual from his fingers. Strands which had escaped the ponytail curled around her face, lying in gleaming coils along her slender shoulders.

He had to get out of there or he'd push her onto that rickety bed with the stained bedspread and climb right on top of her. Slide right into that warm little cunt, soft and welcoming. Start fucking, hard. Because he wanted that so badly he was shaking. He stepped back.

"Lock the door after me and put a chair under the handle." His voice came out harsh and guttural.

She nodded. It wasn't enough.

"Tell me what you're going to do."

A Fine Specimen

"Lock," she said breathlessly. "Chair under the handle."

"Lock the windows too. I don't care how hot it gets."

She nodded. "Okay."

"You don't open for anyone but me. Ever. Is that clear?"

"Yes." Her breathing had slowed a little. Caitlin was watching him steadily out of those clear, pale blue eyes.

"You should be okay taking the bus in the mornings. I'll be driving you home in the evenings."

"I— Okay."

"You don't talk to anyone here." Nail it down. "Understood?"

She nodded, eyes huge.

Christ, he had to get out of there. She was unspeakably beautiful with the flush of the orgasm pinking her cheeks. Alex knew that if he didn't go now, he wouldn't be going at all.

"I'll see you tomorrow."

She nodded again.

"Lock that door." He stepped out and waited as she closed the door, locked it, and didn't leave until he heard the scrape of the chair on the floor and the bump as it was leaned against the door.

Okay, he thought. *I can go* now. But he didn't. He stayed right where he was as if his feet had been nailed to the stained carpet and stared at the door. For five minutes, ten, until he finally told himself to stop being such a dickhead and get out of there. His heart thundered as he walked down the dim corridor.

Why the fuck had he done it? It was going to make for complications and he didn't need that.

He didn't need complications, he didn't need *her*.

He didn't need anything or anyone, except maybe Angelo Lopez. Behind bars.

Chapter Five

The next day, Caitlin did her best to stay out of Alex's way. Luckily he was ignoring her too, which was good because, after all, what could she say? *Sorry I behaved so unprofessionally. It's just that you smelled so good and felt so good and tasted so good I simply lost my head.*

How could she say that?

She couldn't even begin to imagine what had gotten into her, except that she had been taken utterly and completely by surprise. Lieutenant Alejandro Cruz had seemed so...so incredibly un-kissable — right up until the moment he'd kissed her.

And kissed her and kissed her and touched her and made her come.

Wow, that was another surprise. Caitlin had had what she considered the requisite number of lovers for her age and socioeconomic status. Not too many, not too few. None particularly memorable and not one — not *one!* — capable of making her climax within a few moments with only what her grandmother would have called heavy petting.

If anything, she was slow to climax, as a couple of former lovers had complained.

Not with Lieutenant Alejandro Cruz, oh no. A kiss and a touch and it was like holding a match to a fuse. She'd simply blown apart.

It was all immensely embarrassing.

Even more embarrassing was the fact that she hadn't slept all night, and not just because the bed was hard and lumpy and smelly. She'd tossed and turned until the sky outside her window turned gray. The whole night she'd relived every second, from the moment his mouth had touched hers. She'd squirmed with embarrassment, it was true, but also with heat.

Even the memory of the few moments with him had been way more exciting than actual sex with her last two boyfriends.

Caitlin felt irrevocably changed. Instead of being a rather uptight scholar who was better with books than men, she'd morphed into a siren, a woman who could tempt a man as luscious as Lieutenant Alejandro Cruz—even if only for a few moments—and who could climax almost on demand.

Wow, that put her up into sex goddess country.

Pity her sex goddess phase was so short-lived. The instant Alex had lifted his mouth from hers, *he'd* morphed right back into Mr. Hard-Ass. You'd have thought that a man who had taken a woman to climax in four minutes, tops, with only his mouth and his hand would have had a self-satisfied look on him, happy to have strutted his stuff so successfully. Maybe looking forward to Stage Two on the bed, naked.

Instead, Alex had looked appalled, as if he wanted to arrest himself. Then he'd gone into protective overdrive as he backed away, pretending his only concern was keeping her safe.

His backing away was the cue for her head to start working again instead of other body parts. And as soon as the blood returned to her head, she was stricken with remorse. What had she been thinking? Of nothing at all, apparently.

God, she'd made a terrible, terrible mistake.

Caitlin prided herself on her professionalism. Melting in the arms of a man she'd just met and who was crucial to her work was as nonprofessional as it got. Caitlin would never get anywhere, all her sacrifices would be in vain, if she became the kind of woman who hopped into bed with the first authority figure who crossed her path.

So now that she was clear on the fact that Alejandro Cruz messed with her mind in a major way, she had to avoid him as much as possible and keep her cool when she couldn't.

Caitlin had precious few resources in this life. She had little money, no status, no job, with only the possibility of the fellowship. The only real things she could count on were her mind and her reputation. If she wasn't careful, Alex Cruz would destroy both.

When she'd walked into the station house at 8 a.m., together with the incoming morning shift, Caitlin had resolved to stay well out of Alex Cruz's way. It wasn't hard to do. She hadn't even caught a glimpse of him during the entire morning, which she happily spent interviewing officers.

She didn't see him, but she did, however, get an earful *about* him.

Every single interview eventually veered, sooner rather than later, to the subject of the Loot. They'd start out with a discussion of, say, cycles of criminal activity, work schedules or local crime patterns, and within five minutes the officers were discussing the man everyone knew was slated to become the new captain. That was the only thing the officers really wanted to talk about — Alejandro Cruz.

They loved him. They hated him. They respected him. And they all deeply, deeply wanted him to get a life so he would get off their backs.

Kathy Martello told Caitlin about Cruz's background. "Alex was a punk himself once. Long time ago," Kathy told her over a cup of the bitter station-house brew. "It's how come he's so good at catching criminals. He knows how they think. He knows exactly what makes them tick. Alex's got one of the highest arrest and conviction rates in the state, did you know that?" Kathy had shaken her head in admiration before sipping her coffee. "Guy's a genius at anticipating a criminal's next move, it's like he's got a sixth sense for it. And with all that, for all his smarts, he doesn't have a clue about emotions or feelings. Not his or anyone else's. Not a clue."

A Fine Specimen

Ben Cade, the meat mountain, was even more direct. Caitlin interviewed him in the interrogation room. He was huge, jovial, dressed in vibrant, clashing colors.

Caitlin found out that Ben had been an insurance adjuster before becoming a cop, that he had another ten years until retirement and that he was dating a pretty Frenchwoman who had just moved to Baylorville to open a French pastry shop. He was studying French to impress her.

"Alex's a great guy, a great cop, the best, but I guess he gets a little...single-minded, some might say obsessed, when he's on someone's trail. Hasn't had a Sunday off in years, hasn't gotten laid in—"

He broke off, eyed Caitlin and sighed. "Anyway, right now he's got Angelo Lopez in his sights and I tell you he eats, sleeps, *breathes* the fuck— Er, Lopez. He's always got Lopez's file in hand. But Alex's gotta let off steam somehow or he's gonna blow. Years ago, when he joined the force, he was a real okay guy. We'd go out drinking and carousing." Ben smiled reminiscently and shrugged a broad plaid shoulder. "Which is prob'ly why my second wife divorced me. Anyway, Alex had a string of women panting after him then. But he just got so wrapped around the axle on this job, it's all he can see anymore. He's been a mean-tempered sonovabitch lately, I can tell you that. There are a lot of officers who'd be really happy if he...you know...got hisself a life. Lightened up a little. Met some nice girl, settled down some, got laid on a regular basis, know what I mean?" Ben's eyes bored directly into hers. "Toot sweet."

* * * * *

In the early afternoon, while Caitlin was finishing her second interview with Kathy Martello, Alex showed up.

Caitlin was startled. She'd already told him she was planning on leaving early and taking Saturday and Sunday off. Her plan was to take the 2:30 bus back to the hotel, go over her notes and write them up. Over the weekend, she'd take the bus into town for her meals. There certainly wasn't anyplace in Riverhead she'd trust enough to eat in.

She wouldn't be traveling back to Riverhead in the evening again until the beginning of next week. She hadn't expected to see Alex Cruz until Monday evening.

Alex stood in the doorframe, filling it, glowering. He turned to Kathy Martello. "Sergeant, there you are. I want that report on the Branson shooting on my desk by Monday morning."

"Yes sir," Kathy said. She looked up at him. When he gave no sign of moving, she added, "Was there something else, sir?"

Alex turned his scowl on Caitlin and she straightened in her chair. Was something wrong? Why was he looking at her like that? "Tomorrow evening," Alex said, pointing a finger at her. "I'll pick you up at 7:30 at your hotel."

"Tomorrow...evening?" Caitlin repeated, bewildered. Her brow furrowed. She couldn't make sense of what he was saying. "You'll pick me up—" She blinked. "Why?"

"Dinner," Alex said, jaw muscles bunching, and turned away.

Caitlin could hear his footsteps echoing down the corridor. Confused, she turned to Kathy Martello. "Dinner?"

"Dinner." Sgt. Martello kept her expression bland. She pursed her lips. "You know—that meal you eat in the evenings?"

"I know what dinner is, I just..." Caitlin made an exasperated sound and rolled her eyes. "Why does Lieutenant Cruz think he has to feed me?"

"I think—now don't quote me on this—but I think that Alex was looking at it more like a...a date. You know? You've just been asked out on a Saturday night date, hon. That's my reading of it, anyway. Though I'll agree the invitation left a lot to be desired."

A Fine Specimen

"A *date?*" Caitlin asked, turning the incident around in her mind. *That* was an invitation to a dinner date? Not where she came from. Even the geekiest scholar with the most abysmal social skills could do better than that. "I don't know...it didn't feel like he was asking for a date. It felt more like a...a summons."

"Alex is a little, um, authoritarian at times," Kathy said kindly, hitching her gun belt.

Caitlin sat still for a moment, thinking it over before starting to gather her papers. She wrinkled her nose. "Maybe he's taking his feelings of responsibility too seriously. He feels like he has to take care of me, not just ferry me back to my hotel. For Ray's sake."

"Nope, honey," Kathy Martello said as she walked out. "Take it from me. You've just been asked out on a guy-girl kind of date by the Prince of Darkness." She waggled her fingers and grinned wickedly. "Have fun."

* * * * *

There was a message waiting for Caitlin at the Carlton when she got back to the hotel at three. Hassan stepped warily out from behind the curtain that separated his office from the front desk area, saw that she was unaccompanied and visibly relaxed. "Miss Summers," he said gratefully. "You're alone."

"That's right, Hassan." Caitlin smiled at him. "May I have my key?"

He handed her the key, which he kept in his pocket, and an envelope. "This came for you about an hour ago, miss. A young lady left it."

"Thank you, Hassan." Caitlin checked the back of the envelope. It was from Samantha Dane, her former college roommate. Sam had found a good job in Baylorville as executive assistant to a major industrialist, one of the backers of the Frederiksson Foundation. She was one of the reasons Caitlin was hoping for the job at the Frederiksson.

If Samantha was writing, then there was news about the fellowship.

In her room, Caitlin dumped her bag on the bed and opened the envelope. She hastily read the contents, hissed "Yesss!" and pumped her fist in the air. She did a little victory dance around the tiny room, trying not to bounce off the walls, then sat down on the only chair and read the note again, more carefully this time.

Hi Caitlin, your mom told me where to find you. You weren't in, I don't have your cell number, so I decided to drop by and leave you a note. I just had to give you the good news right away! The Frederiksson Foundation Board meeting was this morning and you've just been approved for a one-year fellowship, renewable for two years! The fellowship grant is $45,000 a year. The Board will be making the public announcement on Thursday the 14th, so you should be getting official word by Wednesday, at the latest. You start on Monday the 18th. Congratulations! I'll be out of town for ten days, but let's go out to dinner to celebrate when I come back. Love, Sam.

Caitlin sat back in the chair, her mind swirling. Sam's words floated in her head, bright and golden, lighter than air.

One-year fellowship...$45,000.

In a daze, Caitlin called her mother with the news and received her congratulations. She sat down on the bed, took a deep breath and finally let her feelings rip. There were a lot of them and she let them all out in a whoosh.

Elation. Excitement. Relief.

It had begun.

After so many years of hard work and study, her life had finally begun. She'd been stuck in studenthood for so long, it felt as if she'd been living in a cloister. She loved academic life and she was happy with her chosen course but she was also soooo ready to go out into the world and *live*.

A Fine Specimen

God, there was so much to do! Close down the furnished rental in Grants Falls, find something suitable here in Baylorville, find some cheap furniture... Well, not *too* cheap.

Finally, some *money*. Real money, not a few miserly dollars hoarded from waitressing tips. God, she'd been living off student loans and what she'd managed to save from odd summer jobs for so long, it felt strange to think of actually having money, like an adult.

Well, dammit, she *was* an adult, though she'd been a student since she was four years old.

Caitlin looked down at herself and winced. Okay, she was an adult with an honest-to-god job—or the next best thing, a fellowship—but she sure didn't *look* like an adult. The clothes were pure Early Student. Worn sneakers, ancient, faded jeans and an old cotton sweater which bagged nearly to her knees and reached to her fingertips. Every item of clothing she had on, including her underwear, was at least five years old.

She had some money in her checking account that she'd been hoarding. Now she didn't have to hoard so much because money would be coming in.

Adult money, not student money.

She could buy some clothes. New clothes, new shoes, makeup. Go to the hairdresser. Tomorrow would be Caitlin Day. Celebrate the start of the next part of her life in *style*.

Maybe give the inscrutable Alex Cruz a surprise tomorrow night.

Hoo-ah!

* * * * *

Alex nearly swallowed his tongue whole when Caitlin emerged from the Carlton's elevator at 7:30 on Saturday evening.

Holy fuck!

She was right on time, as he'd expected she would be. She might look like a teenager, but she had shown herself to be serious, reliable and committed to her work.

Except Caitlin Summers didn't look like a teenager now. She looked like a woman. A drop-dead gorgeous woman. A woman he had a date with.

Jesus, not a date, Alex backtracked immediately inside his head. No, no way. He was just looking after her, like Ray would have wanted. And if he found himself wearing his new lightweight wool jacket and new loafers, well...you had to break in something new sometime, didn't you?

Thoughts of pants and loafers flew straight out of his head when Caitlin walked out the open doors of the rusty elevator. His head wasn't thinking straight but, Jesus Christ, his body was. It sent up as immense clamor. *That one*! it shouted. *I want that one!*

He'd been looking for another woman entirely when all of a sudden this...this siren stepped out. Alex had actually been looking at the wrong height for her head and found himself staring at her very beautiful neck. A quick glance down showed that she had on a pair of fuck-me shoes that on some women looked ridiculous and yet, on her, God! They made her legs look a mile long.

Caitlin was dressed in a sexy, clinging turquoise sheath which lovingly caressed curves that had only been hinted at before in her old, baggy clothes. She wore makeup that made her eyes enormous, her mouth look like something that would raise a man from the dead and accentuated high, slanting cheekbones. Her pale blonde hair had been caught up in some sophisticated hairdo, exposing a slim, graceful neck. Those high heels changed everything, lifting her mouth that much closer to kissing range...

Alex shook his head, as if to rid it of wayward thoughts. No kissing tonight, no, no, no. No kissing, no touching, no fondling. Nothing. Nada.

But she was like a human bag of potato chips. One taste and you couldn't stop.

Caitlin was standing right in front of him, looking up, while he was giving himself strict orders to behave. "Hi." Her voice was low, almost shy.

"Uh...hi." Nothing else would come out. Great. He'd managed to avoid swallowing his tongue, only to have it stick to the roof of his mouth. *Talk, you idiot!*

"You look, uh..." Alex waved his hand awkwardly. There weren't words to describe how she looked. "Nice."

They stared at each other in silence for a full ten seconds.

"You look, um, nice too," Caitlin finally said, and continued looking at him.

"Miss?"

Caitlin turned her head and gazed blankly at Hassan.

"The key...miss?"

"Key? I, ah—oh!" Caitlin handed Hassan the key and turned back to Alex. "Where are we going?" she asked and smiled at him.

It was her first real, full-fledged smile. It was a very good thing she hadn't really smiled before. Alex watched as two perfect dimples formed around her perfect mouth. Lushly pink mouth. Deliciously gorgeous mouth. Eminently kissable mouth. He remembered its taste perfectly.

She shouldn't smile. It wasn't fair, her having this perfect mouth that made him think of diving straight in.

Think about something else. Like...like her clothes. That was good.

Not good.

Caitlin's dress was held up by little straps over the shoulders—her round, smooth, creamy-shade-of-pale shoulders. She couldn't be wearing a bra. The bra straps would show under the spaghetti straps of the dress. And yet her breasts were full but high. How could that be if she wasn't wearing a bra? Did she have on one of those strapless thingies? Because who had breasts like that? And how come he hadn't noticed them before? Alex was a breast man, always had been, always would be. And these were spectacular on any scale.

In Alex's experience, any woman with breasts like that liked to show them off. Caitlin's had been lost in layers of clothing, which in his opinion was a real sin. It was like draping the Mona Lisa with sackcloth.

Alex pulled his mind back from contemplation of her breasts and realized she'd spoken. She'd said something about "going"? He seemed to have lost his place in the program.

"Out?" Caitlin looked up at him doubtfully. "Aren't we going out to dinner?"

Dinner. He'd asked her out to dinner.

Get a grip, Alex told himself. *Now*.

It had been way too long since he'd taken a woman out to dinner. That was it. His moves, once bright and shiny from frequent and successful use, had turned rusty while he wasn't looking. Eyeing a woman's breasts, trying to figure out if she was wearing a bra right at the beginning of the evening was *not* a smooth move. He knew better than that. He knew what he had to do—make eye contact to reassure her and start acting like an adult, not a horny teenager.

Alex raised his eyes to hers—and was lost. They were so fucking beautiful. Huge behind the adorable, scholarly glasses, with lashes so long he wondered how she could keep her eyes open, and this incredible sky-blue color you could lose yourself in...

Alex gritted his teeth and vowed that he was going to get his rocks off just as soon as he could. Maybe he should beat off every night before going to sleep—because the no-sex zone he'd been living in was messing with his head, big time. Determined to keep his eyes off her breasts—and her legs and her mouth and her eyes—and to be a good dinner companion,

A Fine Specimen

Alex cupped her elbow, forgetting completely that this was going to be a no-touching dinner.

He'd cupped her elbow a couple of times, but she'd had a sweater or a jacket on. This time he was touching flesh. Delectable flesh...soft, smooth flesh... Alex shook his head again, trying to concentrate.

He'd planned on taking her to the Garden of Eatin', or to a family style Tex-Mex cantina he knew. He'd planned on feeding her every night, though he'd had to skip last night because of a meeting. Good Samaritan Alex, that was him.

The thing was, anyone staying at the Carlton was seriously low on funds and the thought of her skimping on meals...well. Alex knew deep down in his bones what it was like to go without, to go hungry. A friend of Ray's wouldn't go hungry, not while he could do anything about it.

So there was this virtuous plan all set in his head...

First, take her to a fast-food family style place full of noisy families and no possibility whatsoever of an intimate conversation, where they'd have a quick bite.

Second, drive her back to the Carlton.

Third, make sure the room was secure.

And then fourth—leave, double-quick.

That and letting her interview his men went a long, long way toward paying his debt to Ray. And he'd let Ray know that too.

But then this poised, elegant beauty had stepped out of the elevator and he'd had to go immediately to Plan B.

The Garden and the cantina might be fine for Caitlin Summers, poor grad student, probably used to an evening meal of Ramen noodles or yogurt, but they would not do at all for this luscious, elegant young woman.

"Do you like Italian food?" Alex asked as they neared the car and he opened the passenger door for her, heroically not watching as her skirt rose inches above her knees as she got in.

"Italian, mmmm," she said softly, looking him full in the face once he was behind the wheel, giving him another one of those double-whammy smiles. Her eyes were luminous in the glow of the dashboard. Some womanly scent chock full of pheromones wafted over from the passenger seat. He clutched the steering wheel hard. "Spaghetti à la marinara, veal piccata, spumoni...I love Italian."

"I know a nice place downtown," Alex said as he started the engine. "Let's see if we can keep the marinara sauce off my trousers."

"That's not funny," she said primly as he drove off.

* * * * *

It's a nice place, Caitlin thought later, with nouvelle Mediterranean décor and a friendly, casual atmosphere. A collection of olive oil bottles, filled with what looked like top-quality extra virgin olive oil with a faint green tint, was ranged across one wall, a tile mural of a lemon grove on the other. Plants in enormous majolica vases were scattered around, providing privacy for the diners. Neapolitan rock came from discreet speakers hidden in the corners. A tiled counter separated the eating area from the kitchen, the source of mouthwatering smells wafting into the room.

It was warm, welcoming and unobtrusively, discreetly expensive. Not that in-your-face kind of expensive, with sober tuxedoed waiters standing around stiffly just waiting for you to use the wrong fork. Not at all. It was a place to have fun, eat well and spend a relaxing evening.

The waitstaff was young, friendly and numerous. The serving plates and stemware were beautiful. The food was creatively presented. Judging by the satisfied smiles of diners, everyone's food was as good as it looked.

The whole place was intimate and romantic, pleasing to every sense. Caitlin's heart thrummed to the luscious beat of the music.

A Fine Specimen

Alex chose a banquette and sat next to her, instead of across from her, though she noticed with amusement that he chose seats facing the entrance, with their backs to the wall—just like a true cop.

Caitlin's feeling that the restaurant was expensive was proved correct when she opened the oversized menu and saw that most of the entrées cost more than she spent on food in a week.

All her dates had been as broke as she was. Eating out with a date meant choosing the cheapest possible restaurant and scrutinizing the menu for the least expensive items.

She smiled to herself. Well, that part of her life was over. Maybe. With a little bit of luck.

Alex pinned her with his dark gaze. "You haven't even eaten yet and you're already smiling."

Caitlin thought briefly of telling him that she'd been awarded the Frederiksson fellowship. But she hadn't yet, actually. She only had Sam's word on it. No, she would tell him if and when the announcement was made. But in the meantime, she could hug the prospect of good news to herself and feel uplifted.

"Everything looks so good," she said.

"Everything *is* good." Alex looked up at the server slipping a tray of warm bruschetta in front of them and nodded his thanks. The server, a pretty, tall, well-built brunette, grinned. She held the grin for just a second longer than was necessary, stood just inside his personal space and took a deep breath, showcasing an amazing set of assets. Her body language was very clear.

Ditch the wishy-washy blonde, buddy, and I'm yours. Let's go out back and get it on.

Alex was much too astute not to catch that, but he handled it well, breaking off eye contact at exactly the right moment, leaning forward to push Caitlin's plate closer, eyes connecting with hers.

The message to the waitress was clear. *Sorry, not tonight.*

The smoothness with which he did it showed it was an automatic reflex. It was something he'd probably practiced every day of his life. He was a very handsome man, and she could tell he'd been a good-looking boy. He'd probably had to fend off dozens—hundreds!—of advances from women. Some subtle, some not-so-subtle. He'd perfected the art of the brush-off, and it had probably become so innate he hardly noticed it anymore.

Being sexually reticent herself, an observer by nature and training and not a doer, Caitlin had observed some amazing scenes from sexually adventurous women over the years. Just last week, she'd been in a bar with another TA drinking a beer when she'd seen a man walk up to a woman, introduce himself, then offer to buy her a drink. Within five minutes, the woman was fondling his crotch. Within six, they were gone.

Alex probably dealt with those kinds of situations daily, though not at work. She'd observed, and heard, that work for him was a very strict no-sex zone. Not that much was happening right now in his life outside work. Thanks to his colleagues at the station house, she got the impression that he didn't *have* a private life, and considering his looks, his charisma, his overpowering *maleness*, that was entirely voluntary.

If she were a company, she'd send a memo to herself. *Note—no way.*

She had to remember all of this, even though he seemed to have some kind of magical sex key where she was concerned and had managed to give her an explosive orgasm she could almost still feel on her skin, in her bones. And he'd done it with his mouth and hand. She shuddered to think of other body parts coming into play. She'd fall into a billion pieces.

In every way there was, an affair with Alex Cruz was a no-no.

Wanting Alex Cruz was perfectly pointless. Like wanting a Mercedes Benz or wanting to be taller. Not going to happen.

She had to enjoy the evening for what it was and keep her eye on the main goal, her dissertation.

Alex poured her a glass of wine from the bottle of Merlot the server had uncorked. He hadn't asked for either the wine or the bruschetta, so Caitlin could only assume that he came here often enough for his tastes to be known to the staff.

"I can recommend the tuna steak on a bed of pappardelle," he said, confirming her thoughts.

It was the most expensive item on the menu, she was amused to note. *Go for it*, Caitlin told herself. "Sounds good."

Alex gave their order and sipped the wine, an expression of pleasure crossing his face. He seemed utterly at ease, which somehow surprised her. She wouldn't have thought of an elegant, high-end restaurant as Alex's habitat.

Well, okay. He was at the top of the food chain and he carried that impression wherever he went. He would probably be equally at ease and dominant in a low-life dive or a royal palace. Nature had equipped him with the tools to prevail no matter what. She tried to think of him at a loss—and failed. Alex was the kind of man who knew what to do and how to do it in any kind of situation.

In bed, he probably—

Whoa! Don't even go there.

Too late. She'd already gone. Whoosh—in an instant, straight into forbidden territory.

Totally unbidden, completely unwelcome images arose in her mind, full-blown, complete, like watching a movie. Alex's dark face above her, eyes narrowed, intent gaze on hers, broad shoulders blocking out the light. Heavy body on hers, that amazingly large and thick penis she'd felt through his clothes, inside her, thrusting heavily...

Oh God.

She was exciting herself just thinking about it. One part of her was going haywire and the other part—the part that remained a scholar, a student of human nature—observed herself, partly amused, partly appalled.

She remembered every second of his kisses, how his five o'clock shadow had scraped deliciously across her cheeks as he angled his head this way and that to deepen the kisses. Kiss, actually. One. One kiss that never ended, that melted her bones, that lit up every cell in her body with heat and desire.

Amazing. Though her neurons had sputtered, she'd been aware every second that it had been entirely new territory for her, that her body had never had those sensations before and quite possibly never would again.

Immense heat prickling through her system, pooling in her breasts and between her legs. Skin so sensitive she could feel the air like a weight, his hands leaving electric sparks of pleasure wherever he touched. The world simply falling away, completely gone, as she concentrated on his mouth and hands on her.

The world falling away was not good. The world was big and bad and bit women who forgot the rules and lost their heads.

Caitlin squirmed for a second in her seat. The images of Alex's kiss had come with sensory input and she could actually feel the swelling of the lips of her sex. It was like a small sun blossoming between her legs, so brightly she was surprised it didn't generate light.

But just as her head could tell her body to forget about tiredness and hunger and lack of sleep, her head now told her body to wipe out those delicious sensations and allowed her to morph back into her serious, professional persona.

It took more effort than she liked.

The food arrived. The waitress had received the message loud and clear that Alex wasn't on the market, and placed the plates in front of them with an impersonal smile, angling now for a generous tip rather than Alex's body.

The smells coming off the plates were delicious, perfect. A million miles away from her usual crap fare. Lately, lack of time had been added to her chronic lack of money and she'd subsisted on yogurt and sandwiches these past few weeks.

Ah, her life was changing in so many ways, all of them good. She resolved to enjoy this evening and keep a tight rein on her reactions to the extremely powerful and extremely sexy man sitting next to her.

"Eat," he said, "and I'll tell you how the mayor got his nickname, The Lizard."

She looked at him, amused. How wonderful to get inside gossip. "Not because he has that leathery salon tan?"

"No, it involves a truck, a mistress and a hundred thousand dollars."

"One of those things you can't make up?"

"Absolutely."

It was a shaggy dog story, long, convoluted, funny. It saw her through the tuna and pappardelle, the pear and arugula salad with balsamic vinegar, and several bites of Alex's twelve-ounce *bistecca fiorentina* that he insisted she try.

It was delicious. *He* was delicious, perfect.

Oh *God*.

Caitlin had simply assumed that Alex Cruz was a job-obsessed monomaniac and that the police station was his natural habitat. He'd looked so at home there, with basically the whole station house at his beck and call. King of all he surveyed.

A one-dimensional man, even one as preternaturally sexy and attractive as Alex, was easy to resist in the long run. Monomaniacs are notoriously humor-challenged, devoid of all irony. Bad conversationalists, self-obsessed.

She'd dated her share of them, though to be honest, her type of monomaniac was usually an academic with an unholy interest in Tibetan literature or Italian *opera buffa* or Dutch voting patterns.

Though in theory she liked men, she did have to admit that they could be monumentally boring, and she'd expected Alex to be no different from the rest of his gender, only sexier than most. Happy only in one place, doing one thing.

And yet here he was, perfectly at home in this trendy, upscale eatery. Making light, fascinating conversation. Suave and urbane. So attractive it should be illegal.

This was *so* not good. Caitlin had never felt such a powerful, magnetic attraction to a man before. She hadn't even known she was capable of it. Last night's kiss and explosive climax was way off her radar. It was hard enough to keep her cool around him and not melt into a puddle at his feet when she thought he was just a tough, hard-assed cop. Good-looking, okay, that was a given—but horrifically lousy relationship material. A man who, out of bed, would bore her to death in the long run. That man was no temptation at all, other than sexual, though God knew that was bad enough.

Who knew sex was high on her list of priorities? It was news to her. If Caitlin had to list things that gave her pleasure, sex would probably be embarrassingly low on the list. Well, considering what her sex life had been up until now, finding a new library archive *was* infinitely more exciting than going to bed with William Trudloe or Marvin the Unreliable. But there it was, a statistical outlier—her treacherous body had lit up like a Christmas tree the instant Alex had touched her.

A worldly, sophisticated, entertaining Alex was truly frightening because he made her yearn. A worldly, sophisticated, entertaining sex god was guaranteed to ruin her for other men forever.

Caitlin made it a point not to yearn after what she couldn't have. She was really good at it because she'd had a lot of practice. Over the past few years, she'd watched high school and college friends get jobs and start rising through the ranks of life. Most of her nonacademic friends owned their own homes, bought designer clothes, drove fancy cars, ate at restaurants reviewed in newspapers and went on vacations to exotic places. Caitlin had known when she opted for the academic life that these things would be hers only later in life, if ever.

They'd also gotten engaged and then married. Or at least settled into steady relationships. She rarely admitted to herself how much it hurt to watch friends pairing up, while she seemed so relentlessly...*alone* all the time.

So it was a very good thing she'd decided early on in her career that she wasn't going to pine after the unobtainable.

Wanting a real relationship with Alex Cruz would break her heart. After last night, she'd factored in that they might have an affair if her willpower suddenly decided to take a hike. It wasn't very professional, but then she'd only have to deal with him professionally for another week or so. It wasn't as if he were a colleague or someone she'd have to work with on a steady basis, which would be a real no-no.

So, yes, if she had to be honest with herself, hot sex for the first time in her life sounded really, really good. They'd have fantastic sex and then part ways without any complications. That was the plan that had been brewing deep in her subconscious and was now beginning to percolate upward.

Caitlin always thought she'd end up late in life with some nice, low-key scholar. A sweater-and-suspenders kind of guy. They'd study together, have really good conversations and make polite love in the dark, under the covers.

She knew that beta males make great companions even though they don't, alas, heat the blood. Just this once, Caitlin wanted her blood heated. The memory of having had a hot time between the sheets with a true, unadulterated alpha male would warm her nights with her nice, tame future husband.

Hot, unforgettable sex with a man you knew you wouldn't want for the long-term was one thing. Hot, unforgettable sex with a fascinating man who made her want more...

Well. That was heartbreak waiting to happen.

"So, you getting what you need at the cop shop?" The question was asked out of nowhere in an idle tone, but his eyes were sharp as they watched hers.

Caitlin sipped the wine. God, even the wine was perfect. "Oh yes, thank you. Kathy Martello and Ben Cade have been particularly helpful. I've got a lot of useful data." *Including an extensive bio of one Alejandro Cruz.*

"You're doing it again," Alex observed mildly as he topped her glass.

They were on their second bottle and that, combined with the truly excellent food, filled Caitlin with a mellow glow. If you were going to get your heart broken, it might as well be in style.

"What?" She twisted the stem of her glass, watching the candle's reflection in the crystal blur and grow into a teardrop.

"Smiling."

"Tell me, Lieutenant, is smiling suddenly against the law?"

"Maybe it is. Or at least it should be, since here I was, telling you how the state should be run and you start smiling." They'd been talking about a recent state senate scandal and had found themselves in total agreement regarding who were the scumbags and who were the good guys. "You should be — at the very least — pursing your lips and nodding solemnly at the wisdom I was imparting."

Caitlin let out her breath on a long sigh. "Sorry. I was thinking of something else."

"Such as?"

She shrugged, happy that he wasn't telepathic.

"Are you going to tell me or am I going to have to call the maitre d' over and have him break out the rubber hoses to make you talk?" He leaned toward her and assumed a Peter Lorre accent. "Theeessss restaurant's dooongeon isss famous in four cown-treeeessss."

How the candlelight loved the planes of his face, hard and clean and sharply handsome. The black eyes gleamed with humor and intelligence, his skin dark against the pristine white shirt. His mouth looked hard but she remembered—oh-so clearly—how soft it had felt against hers, how, with a twist of his mouth, he'd opened her own. She also remembered how, when his tongue had touched hers, she'd felt it deep in her womb. Everything in her had fluttered when he'd kissed her, including her heart.

Caitlin put her hands on her lap and clenched them, otherwise she'd reach out and touch his mouth, his skin, run her fingers through his hair. He was sitting way too close to her, so close she could feel his body heat.

And she could smell him. He smelled simply fabulous. It wasn't cologne. It didn't have the undertone of alcohol all commercial colognes had. No, what she was smelling was clean clothes, his soap and shampoo and...his skin. A clean male smell designed by hundreds of thousands of years of evolution to entrap unwary females like herself. Over the centuries, how many women had been tripped up over a smell like that, coupled with dark, knowing eyes and a subtle, sexy smile?

Millions. And they'd been left heartbroken, every single one.

Their server slipped an earthenware bowl full of a frothy chocolate concoction in front of them and Caitlin sighed, glad of the distraction. Chocolate and cream were perhaps the only things on this earth that could drag her attention away for even a second from Alex Cruz. "Wow. Tiramisù."

"Nothing but the best." Alex picked up his dessert spoon.

Caitlin admired the serving bowl, decorated in bright, swirling colors. The heady chocolate smell of the dessert filled her nostrils. She glanced up, smiling, at Alex—and froze.

Fire. Fire in his eyes. His skin was drawn tightly over his high cheekbones and his full mouth was drawn in a hard, thin line. He looked as if he wanted to gobble *her* up instead of the tiramisu...

And the images that look conjured unnerved her so much that her hand jerked, tipping her dessert bowl straight onto Alex's lap.

Chapter Six

"I'm really, really sorry, Alex," Caitlin said contritely for the bazillionth time. She could feel her blush reaching down to her breasts. Hopefully she still wasn't the stoplight color she'd been at the restaurant. Alex opened the door to his house and put a hand to her back to usher her in.

What a nightmare trip across town, with the remains of tiramisù drying on Alex's thighs while her cheeks burned in the dark and her hands trembled in her lap, totally unable to speak a single sentence without "sorry" in it somewhere. Finally, she had just shut up.

"Tiramisù," he said philosophically, looking down at the chocolate-and-cream-covered disaster that was his pants. "At least it's partly dark. The cream sauce in the pappardelle would have clashed terribly."

Caitlin winced and looked away. His pants were dark, made of some expensive, superfine wool and covered in half-dried cream and chocolate. That mess on his thighs was all her fault. "Oh God. What can I say? I'm so sorry." Caitlin was horrified to hear the shakiness in her voice.

She wished he'd driven her back to the hotel instead of first detouring to his house to change. She could be huddled miserably on the dirty, lumpy bed with no one to see her humiliation instead of here, red-faced, gulping for air, blinking back tears.

"Hey." Alex's big hand caught her chin and turned her face up to his. His thumb stroked her cheek then touched a tear that was forming at the corner of her eye. "What's this?" His deep voice was gentle.

Caitlin jolted when he touched her. God, this was so scary. Even his casual touch felt electric.

He raised his eyebrows. "You're not afraid of me, are you?"

"N-no." Caitlin took a deep breath. It wasn't fear, but he definitely made her quake. "But sometimes you make me a little...nervous."

"I don't want to do that," he said, his deep voice sober. His beautifully shaped black eyebrows drew together in a puzzled frown and he shook his head slowly. "I'd have to go out and buy myself a whole new wardrobe and I really hate to shop."

"That was a joke, wasn't it?" she asked shakily. "Tell me it's a joke."

He wasn't listening. His hand had slipped into her hair to cup her head. His eyes were fixed on her mouth. She could feel his breath wash over her face. His eyes met hers for a second and the heat in them gave her heart a jolt.

She could feel herself swaying toward him, an irresistible movement, like iron filings to a lodestone. "Alex?"

He looked down at his pants then stepped away and it was exactly as if a force field around her had been switched off. She rocked back on her heels, the tension in her shoulders easing. She drew in a deep breath and realized she'd been holding it.

Alex turned. "I'm going to run upstairs and change. And then we can go back out if you want. There's a good little jazz club that fixes mean margaritas not too far from here. Or we could take in a movie. Or watch one here." He took the stairs two at a time and stopped on the landing, looking down at her. The light in the living room didn't extend far and all she could make out on the landing was the white of his shirt, as if he were a powerful ghost with a deep voice. "Put on some music in the meantime if you want."

"Okay."

A Fine Specimen

She was grateful for the reprieve. She needed time to get her emotions back under control.

Trying to distract herself, Caitlin looked around Alex's house. She hadn't the vaguest idea where they were except that they weren't in the downtown area. Caitlin had a little hobby of matching people to their habitats and she was seldom wrong. She'd imagined Alex Cruz living in an apartment in the city, close to the action. A low-maintenance kind of bachelor pad that served as a staging ground for his life, nothing more.

That's why she was so surprised when he had pulled into the driveway of a small, neat, two-story house in an upscale residential district about ten miles from the city.

Who would have pegged him for a suburbanite? He kept surprising her.

She wandered around the living room, curious to find out more about this man. It wasn't easy getting a read on him because there were very few personal effects. His house was like a machine for living. There were no knickknacks, no photos, no plants, no souvenirs scattered about like most people had—there was nothing in the living room that in any way betrayed the personality of the owner. The few pieces of furniture were of good quality, the whitewashed walls were bare of paintings or photographs, there was no hint of possible sports he might play or hobbies he might have.

There was absolutely no sign of a woman's presence, anywhere.

The house was neat. *That* she would have imagined. He was always very neatly dressed. His shirts—white—were clean and freshly pressed. His pants—black—had knife-edge creases. His shoes—black—were well polished.

So the neatness didn't surprise her. What did surprise her were the books—the walls were lined with shelves filled two and sometimes three deep with books. Alex was a reader. A voracious one.

He seemed so no-nonsense. So Mr. Macho Cop, the kind of man who'd spend his free time on the firing range or playing pickup basketball.

Curious, she bent to peruse some of the titles. He read history and popular science, biographies and travel books. Some science fiction. He read mysteries, which didn't surprise her, and westerns, which did.

Westerns? Who knew he'd have that in him? Surely a taste for westerns showed a hidden romantic streak? Or was she kidding herself?

God. Westerns.

Caitlin had a flash of Alex as he would have been in the old West. Dressed in black, an implacable force for justice, fast with a gun and his fists, eyes shaded by the brim of a black ten-gallon hat with a silver circlet around the brim, silver and mother of pearl handles on the pistols, dark eyes burning... She shivered and moved on.

On a high-tech metal stand was the largest home entertainment center she'd ever seen, with a ginormous flat-screen TV and a top-of-the-line Swedish stereo set.

She ran her finger along the rows of DVDs, all of them purchased. No pirated editions for Alex the Lawman. Classic movies, mostly, many she'd heard of but hadn't seen. The CDs, too, were all purchased—four shelves of them, alphabetized and orderly. She couldn't remember the last time she'd bought music, but then, she lived in a university environment. Students at college hadn't bought CDs since 2002. Curious, she ran her finger along the names of the composers and artists. Alex's taste in music was eclectic, running more to instrumentals than to vocals.

"The remote for the CD player is in the wooden bowl on the coffee table." Alex's deep voice came floating down from upstairs.

Caitlin found the remote and chose a quiet, bluesy album. The notes from a mournful sax filled the air, melancholy and moving. Caitlin swayed gently to the music, eyes closed, then sat down on the dark green leather couch and leaned her head against the back. The music washed over her, gentle, sad, seductive. Caitlin closed her eyes and let herself go, the tenor sax soothing her nerves.

"Here." Caitlin opened her eyes enough to see Alex holding out a crystal glass with a finger of amber liquid and a couple of ice cubes. "Ol' Coltrane knew what he was doing. He's good for the nerves, isn't he? So's this." He nudged the glass into her hand.

"Thanks." She gulped the whisky as Alex sat next to her. The couch dipped and it seemed as if the entire universe were conspiring to have her dip toward him too. She could feel his body heat, feel the force of his eyes on her. Nervous, she took another long swallow.

"Hey, go easy there." Alex's hard mouth lifted in a half smile. "I want to get you mellow, not soused." He leaned back into the couch with a sigh, one broad shoulder brushing hers. He lifted his left arm and hooked it over the back of the sofa, brushing her shoulders. The hairs on Caitlin's nape rose.

She turned her head slightly to look at him. He'd changed into a black tee shirt and pressed black jeans. Dressed informally, he looked younger than he did in his RoboCop incarnation—*just making the world safe for civilians, ma'am, now step aside*—though not softer or more approachable.

She thought of the men she'd dated, though at this particular moment she couldn't remember the face of even one. They'd been boys, she realized now, not men. That was what had been wrong with them. Soft, weak and, at times, petulant boys. Puppies. There was absolutely nothing boyish or soft about Alex Cruz. He was a powerful man in his prime, a big, magnificent animal, one of nature's aristocrats, like a tiger or a wolf. Powerful in every way.

He turned that handsome head to look at her, not even pretending to look at anything else.

Right now all that formidable power was focused laser-sharp on her. Totally. It was as if the very molecules in the air were charged and focused on her. Caitlin had to remember to breathe and she had to consciously expand her lungs to do it.

Sex was in the air, heavy, musky, pulsing to the rhythms of a tenor sax playing the blues. Caitlin could practically see pheromones dancing in the dim light. Everything in her body felt heavy—eyelids, limbs, the hot blood coursing slowly through her veins like sweet liquid honey. Everything, that is, but her head. That felt so light it was in danger of floating away.

The music stopped as the CD player changed discs. For a moment, the silence enveloped them like a blanket, a living thing in the dark room. The music had been keeping them company, like a third person in the room, but it had departed. Now there was only the two of them.

The music started up again, another tune, another tone—coolly slick and sexy. A clarinet and piano, a low, throbbing undertone overlaid with a sensuous melody. Pure sex set to music.

Every sense Caitlin had was heightened. She could hear her breathing and his, the soft whisper of a car passing down the residential street outside, her heavy heartbeats. Her skin had become one huge sensitive pad, feeling every inch of her clothes—dress, panties and shoes, all she had on. And the rest of her bare skin felt the touch of his gaze as clearly as if he'd reached out his big hand to caress her.

His face was all hard lines and shadows in the dim light. Something was waiting in the shadows. The very air was pulsing with something immense, something that was about to happen.

Caitlin felt like a diver hesitating at the top of the highest diving board, toes hanging in space, looking down, heart thumping with fear and excitement. The next few seconds would change her life, she knew that. She was afraid to move, to breathe.

A Fine Specimen

She jumped when a hard hand closed on the nape of her neck. Her hand shook and the ice tinkled in her glass.

Alex reached over and took the glass from her hand. "Careful," he murmured. "I'm running out of pants."

The whisky had obviously wiped out her indignation lobe. All she could manage was a weak, "That's not funny."

His fingers burrowed in her hair. "Not funny at all," he agreed. "I told you I hate to shop." Alex's thumb traced her jawbone. "So...do you want to go out?"

Out? Did she want to go *out*? What could she possibly want out there when everything desirable was in here, watching her with heated, dark, half-closed eyes? She shook her head. "No."

His expression didn't change, but it intensified. Everything about his face became clearer, sharper, more tightly focused.

He slowly removed her glasses and placed them carefully on the coffee table. She was nearsighted, so it didn't matter. Everything she wanted to see was only inches away.

Caitlin watched as his face came closer to hers. She could see a faint dusting of silver in the black wings of hair over his ears, she could see the floor lamp reflected in his dark eyes, the beard shadowing his face—and then she couldn't see anything at all because she closed her eyes as his mouth closed over hers.

A last lingering source of rationality told her to keep her cool, keep a sense of herself, not lose herself in the moment, not lose herself to *him*.

Too late.

At the first touch of his lips to hers, she was gone.

Alex knew it would happen. Oh yeah.

He'd been talking a good line to himself—*you keep your hands off her, she's too young for you, she's a colleague—sort of—*

and anyway, she's Ray's protégé. All in his best Stern Voice of God that worked wonders down at the station house. Yada yada, yeah yeah. He might as well have been whistling at the moon for all the attention his cock was paying to his noble intentions.

It was one thing to convince himself in the abstract that Caitlin Summers was off limits while they were having dinner. Not too much of a chance of ripping her clothes off and jumping her bones in a room full of diners.

But he was alone with her now, just the two of them, in his house, and every cell in his body was screaming for sex. They'd been screaming all through dinner and with massive self-control, he'd managed to shut them up. But now there was no more pretending, not with his mouth on hers. He gave up without even a struggle. Just touching her was explosive. Just his hand on her neck, feeling how silky the skin under her ear was, made his heart pound.

The skin under her ear was soft, tender. As were her eyes, her lips...

He drew back a moment to breathe, to catch himself. Caitlin's eyes were closed, the long lashes casting shadows over her delicate cheekbones. Her eyelids fluttered open and her gaze circled his face. In the dim light, her eyes looked silver, rimmed by a slightly darker blue. When she moved her eyes they flashed like lightning. It was fascinating to watch. He could barely take his eyes off her.

"Alex?"

God, even her voice was soft, with just that slight hint of honeysuckle that drove him crazy.

"Yeah?" If she wanted to have a conversation—well hell, knowing her, it would have to be an *intelligent* conversation— he was in deepest shit, because he could barely remember his name.

"Are we going to have sex?"

"Oh yeah," he breathed.

Ping.

That was the sound of all his restraints popping.

"Good."

With a groan, he bent down to her again at a sharper angle, his mouth claiming hers, his tongue licking hers. She had a wonderful taste—the bourbon, the faint overtones of the good Merlot at dinner and something else that was pure sex. Could surrender have a taste? If it did, this was it. Her mouth was completely open to his as her head fell back against his hand. Her arms snaked around his neck and he pulled her closer as neurons sputtered and died in his head from overload.

There was a protocol to kissing. You start out slow and build up—then you can stop kissing and get to have sex. But before then, still in the kissing stage, there's a moment when you understand whether the woman is signaling with her mouth that, yes, they'd be getting it on soon. Once he got to the kissing stage, Alex was rarely refused. So locking lips was a way station to fucking.

Not now, not with Caitlin. It wasn't a way station to something else, it was something hot and bewitching in its own right. This wasn't a lead-in kiss, soft little nibbles, delicate probing with his tongue.

He was way too excited for that.

He just plunged straight into her mouth. He placed his open mouth on hers and, to his delight, found her already open for him, soft tongue meeting his immediately. He stroked her mouth with his tongue and felt her sighs against his lips. Each stroke of her tongue sent blood straight to his cock until it was practically dancing in his jeans. His thumb was right against the artery in her neck and he swore he could feel her pulse picking up its rhythm each time his tongue touched hers.

Alex lost track of time, totally lost in the moment, his world reduced to her slim arms around his neck, her breasts against his chest and her open mouth against his. He held her head with both hands, angling it slightly to get a deeper, tighter fit, the smell and the taste of her going straight to his head, hotter and better than the bourbon.

He was hard as a rock, and had been since he'd touched her. Just his finger against the soft skin of her neck had made him swell and, with each stroke of his tongue against hers, he could feel his cock lengthening in hard surges.

Alex cupped her shoulders, feeling the small straps holding up her dress and the slim, strong muscles of her upper arms. His hands glided down to her waist then slowly worked their way back up to the top of the dress.

Ah, there it was. The gateway to paradise. The little zipper doohickey that you pulled to unzip.

He slid the zipper of her dress halfway down and separated the fabric. His hands encountered warm, silky woman and nothing else. He lifted his mouth from hers for just a second.

"All this time," he gasped, dick so hard it hurt. "All during dinner, I've been wondering what you were wearing under this dress." He smoothed his palms over her soft, warm, bare back. "And now I know."

"Now you know," she murmured as he ran his lips over her temple, down to her jaw. She jumped when he nipped her lightly.

He knew a lot of things now. How her breathing sped up when he kissed her, how her back arched when he clasped her small waist, how her breath shuddered when his tongue met hers.

He kept his hands slow, touching her carefully, but what he wanted to do was devour her. Crush her to him with all his strength, then strip her and take her, hard and fast. His head was filled with images of them together, him buried deep inside her, slamming into her, fucking her hard, harder than he'd ever had another woman. The desire that shook him was violent and it took more effort than he liked to keep his hands gentle.

He held his hands open by sheer force of will. What he wanted to do was clutch her, grab at her, sink his fingers into her soft flesh. He wanted to turn his hands into grappling hooks that would bind her to him so strongly she could never get away.

The images in his head frightened him. His hands were strong. If he gripped her as hard as he wanted to, he'd leave bruises all over that pale, creamy skin.

Sliding his open palms upward along the satiny planes of her back, he lightly cupped her head in both hands once more and delved deeply into her mouth. He picked the pins one by one out of her hair and shuddered as the shiny, heavy mass spilled over his hands, her shoulders. The sweet smell of shampoo rose from her hair, like a flower whose petals had been crushed. It was a heady scent, almost overpoweringly sexy.

"God!" he gasped, burying his face in her neck, feeling the soft curls like tendrils against his skin. Hesitantly, he licked her neck, feeling the vein pulsing there, wanting to bite her. He gave into temptation and nipped her. Not hard enough to hurt but sure as hell hard enough to mark possession. She jumped slightly, shuddered. Her breath caught and she let it out in a little moan.

Oh fuck, this was just so delicious. Absolutely everything about it. The feel of her, the smell of her, the taste of her.

He opened the edges of the dress farther and smoothed them forward over her shoulders. The lightest shift, a soft shimmy and slight lift of her hips and it was off. So easy, like something preordained. He hated taking layers off women, but this was like something out of a dream. A whoosh and the dress was gone.

He pulled away and held her at arm's length, staring hungrily. She was so perfect, small and delicate, with firm, smooth muscles. She blushed under his gaze, the color rosy, the color of arousal, so different from the stoplight-red she'd been before when she dumped a ton of chocolate into his lap.

That tiramisù in his lap was what had brought them to this moment. Bless it. He was going to have it bronzed.

Looking at her was good, touching her was better. He pulled her forward until he was nuzzling her neck, kissing the soft skin behind her ears, raking his teeth down a tendon. It excited her. She shuddered, gave a soft moan. He pulled back a breath and looked down. Oh yeah, her nipples had hardened.

"I don't know what to do first," he whispered. A finger reached out, circled her nipple. She shuddered again. His eyes rose, met hers. "Help me out here, Caitlin. What do I do now?"

Her mouth opened then closed. She huffed out a small breath in a laugh. "I have no idea. Surely the great Lieutenant Cruz isn't looking for *instructions* from me?"

The great Lieutenant Cruz hadn't had something this delectable under his hands in a long, long time.

"Well...I want to do things that please you. That's the general idea, and that's why I asked."

She was quiet a moment, light blue eyes wide. The color was amazing in the penumbra of the room. It was like she had twin searchlights in her head.

"Everything you do to me is pleasing," she said simply.

Alex lost it. Simply lost it.

Surging up from the couch with Caitlin in his arms, he made for the staircase, his mouth on hers. She was light as a feather, but even if she hadn't been, he was so blasted by lust he had superhuman strength. He would have carried her up if she'd been a solid bronze statue, because upstairs was where his bed was and he wanted her on it—and him on her—more than he wanted his next breath.

He stubbed his toe on the first step and muttered "*shit!*" into her mouth. Her lips curved under his.

A Fine Specimen

"Are you sure you want to do this?" she breathed against his mouth as he raced up the stairs. "You might throw your back out."

Fuck yeah he wanted to do this! "It's my night for living dangerously," he growled.

Alex didn't turn on the light in his bedroom. The curtains were open and a full moon shone in, bathing Caitlin in luminescence. He set her on her feet, this slim, pale column of woman, and spent about a second enjoying the view. He wanted to enjoy this view for hours, but he wanted his hands on her more.

She was wearing brief, white stretchy panties and high heels.

Jesus.

"Wow, I'm glad I didn't know what was under that dress. Or what *wasn't* under that dress." He buried his face in her hair. "I'd never have made it through dinner."

He ran his index finger around the elastic of her panties. When she clutched his shoulders and gasped, he caught her mouth beneath his and slipped his hand down over her flat little belly, past the elastic, and cupped her.

The heat was incredible. He waggled his hand gently from side to side and she obeyed the silent signal, shifting her legs to open them. Ah yes. That was better. He circled his finger around her opening, feeling the moisture welling. Perfect.

Her pubic hair was soft, almost as soft as the skin of her cunt, slick and warm and welcoming. He could feel her welcome as he slid his middle finger around her. Some women had steel traps for cunts but not Caitlin. The soft, plump folds were inviting him in and he took the invitation. He slid his middle finger into her, deeply, feeling her catch her breath against his mouth. She was aroused, there was no doubt about that, her cream coated his hand—but she was small and tight.

They were going to need as much cream as he could coax out of her.

Alex probed her pussy with his finger in exactly the same cadence and rhythm as his tongue exploring her mouth. She was caught by him, one hand clutching the back of her head tightly, holding her closely against his mouth, and the other cupping her between her legs, one finger embedded deeply inside her. She couldn't escape him even if she wanted to.

She didn't want to, that was clear. Her arms were tight around his neck, fingers in his hair. He could feel her skin warming up through his tee shirt, those lovely naked breasts rubbing against his chest. When he slanted his mouth to kiss her more deeply, she opened even more to him. When their tongues met, her little cunt contracted against his finger and he felt an answering throb in his dick. He moved his finger experimentally, in and out, and she gave a little cry as her cunt clenched tightly. She was seconds from coming, and so was he.

Not here. Not like this.

When it happened, he wanted them to be on the bed and he wanted to be on top of her, cock in cunt, riding her.

Alex didn't much care what positions he took with his sex partners. He often left it up to the woman and if she wanted to be on top, that was fine with him. More than fine. Less work for him.

But not this time, not with Caitlin. Not the first time. He wanted her spread out under him, that glorious hair a pale cloud around her head. He wanted to be on top, holding her down with the weight of his body, thrusting heavily into her. The missionary position, they called it, but he didn't feel like a missionary. He felt raw and primitive and he wanted to take her in the most basic way there was, male taking female, hard and fast and dominant.

It was a night for slow seduction. A plaintive sax throbbed in the distance. He held a beautiful woman in his arms. There was even a full moon shining right outside his window, the way it was supposed to. The music, the night, the moon, a beautiful woman...he should be slowly arousing her, plying her with kisses and caresses, murmuring words of praise.

He *should* be murmuring words of praise because she was, hands down, the most beautiful woman he'd ever held in his arms. He had no trouble sweet-talking other women, why was it he couldn't find the words right now? The heat in his head blasted all the words right out.

Alex knew how to do this. He had all the moves and God knows, he'd practiced them often enough. He knew how to juice a little romanticism into the moment. But all those savvy, practiced moves, all that knowledge about what women liked simply drained from his head, together with all the blood in it.

Make an effort. He pulled back from her lips, something so hard he should get a goddamn medal for it. "You're so beautiful," he croaked.

She blinked then pulled him down to her by his ears. "Kiss me," she said.

Okay. She didn't need words. Neither did he.

Hunger seethed in his veins. Instead of stripping her gently, he all but tore off her panties until they pooled around her ankles then lifted her up and away from them before lifting her onto the bed. He wasn't gentle about it, either. He dropped her so hard she bounced.

He placed a knee on the bed and bent down to take her shoes off. Very pretty shoes. Classic fuck-me shoes. He slipped them off her very pretty feet and tossed them over his shoulder, where they landed with twin thuds.

Her pale skin glowed in the moonlight. When she smiled at him and murmured, "Alex," he broke his own personal stripping speed record, flinging his clothes behind him in a blur instead of neatly folding them onto the wooden butler next to the chest of drawers, as he did every night.

Alex was about ready to jump on her when the two neurons left in his head sputtered to life.

There was something wrong with this picture. But what?

She was naked. Check. Wonderful.

He was naked. Check. Great— No, *wait*! He wasn't supposed to be completely naked, he was supposed to have something on...

Condom!

With shaking hands, Alex reached into his bedside table, where he used to keep his condoms, back when he used to have a sex life. Tearing a packet open, he pulled the latex ring out and handed it to Caitlin. His hands were sweating. He'd never get it done. "You put it on."

She looked startled as she sat up. "Oh! Okay. I haven't actually done this before, but..."

He nearly groaned when she put her small, soft hand around his cock and gently pulled it forward so she could work the condom over it. He was so stiff, he worried for a second that his dick was going to break as she tugged it away from his belly. Just crack off at the base from the pressure.

Sweetly awkward, Caitlin fumbled the latex ring over him. The wrong way around. "No, no," he said.

"What?" Her hands stilled as she looked up at him, eyes flashing silver in the moonlight. "What do you mean, 'no'?"

"No, not that way," Alex urged, "turn it around."

Caitlin said, "What?" again and pushed down, hard.

The condom bounced off his cock—which was as hard as a steel club—and flew across the room.

Alex followed it with his eyes in disbelief until it disappeared into the gloom. His heart beat hard and heavy in his chest as he contemplated utter and total disaster.

Oh God, this was terrible! He was feeling her, smelling her, touching her. Every sense he had was on overload. Visions of her on her back, legs open, soft, warm little cunt glistening with desire—all filling his head. All he could think about was tumbling her onto her back and entering her—a second later!

Jesus, putting on another condom meant...meant leaning over, pulling one out of the drawers, ripping it open... Whole seconds! Maybe a *minute*! He didn't have a minute, he was just about ready to blow.

With shaking hands, Alex was reaching for the bedside table again, hoping he could hold out long enough to get another rubber on, when her soft voice sounded in the darkness.

"I'm on the Pill," she offered. "I was having a few health problems, and the doc—"

Whatever she was going to say was drowned out by his mouth. And anyway, she probably wouldn't have had the breath to continue because he landed on her in a rush, kneeing her legs apart, holding her open—and slamming into her.

He was coming even as he entered her, in hot, uncontrollable spurts, shaking and spilling liquid from every part of his body—vast amounts of come from his cock, sweat out of every pore, even his eyes were leaking with the intensity of the experience.

He had absolutely no control over his body, over what was happening. It was like being on a freight train with no brakes. Every muscle he had was tense, strained, hard. He was digging his toes into the mattress in an attempt to drive even more deeply into her, though he could feel her clamped tightly around the root of his cock. He couldn't possibly go deeper, though he was trying like hell.

If he could, he'd have punched a hole right through her to get in more deeply.

Smooth, smooth Alex, who knew all the moves, who prided himself on being good in bed—was totally out of control.

He couldn't even move inside her, because that would mean pulling out a little and his cock refused. It wanted to stay where it was, deeply embedded, pouring out come in hot, hard jets while he shuddered with excitement.

It was so intense, it couldn't last. Finally, finally, he calmed down a little and his heart stopped trip-hammering with excitement...and just settled down to the normal rhythm it would have after a five-mile run.

It was like floating in space. For a long moment, Alex even forgot who he was, all consciousness wiped out, the frontal lobe of his brain turned to cream of wheat while he reveled in his senses, which were more alive than they'd ever been in his life, shooting wild messages of utter joy back to him.

His face was buried in the soft cloud of pale hair that smelled like apple shampoo, his lips just brushing the incredibly soft skin of her temple. She smelled so amazingly delicious—like fruit and candy and flowers—the smell of a desirable woman. Some unique scent that went straight to the most primitive part of his brain.

His breathing hadn't settled yet. He was still breathing in short spurts that moved a curl of hair lying across his lips. Each breath brought his chest into closer contact with those luscious, round breasts, the aroused little nipples stabbing into him. Even his fucking *toes* rejoiced, curled up against the bottom of her small, delicate feet.

His cock—ah, his cock was the happiest of all, deeply embedded into the sweetest, wettest little cunt it had ever been in.

Ah yes, he was one happy camper.

Until the blood returned to his head and he was able to put two thoughts together. Once that was a physical possibility, once his brain started working again, the joy and sensual delight fled. Time to take stock—and it wasn't pretty.

A Fine Specimen

Alex prided himself on treating his women well. He wasn't long-term mate material and he made sure his dates knew it, but that didn't mean he didn't treat them like ladies — even the ones who weren't — while they were with him.

Caitlin was a lady from the top of her head to the bottom of her pretty little feet — and he'd treated her like a two-bit whore.

Treating a woman right did *not* include jumping her like a rabid wolverine in rut. No foreplay, no easing in gently, no sirree. He'd just slammed into her with all the force of his hips. She was small too. She'd been aroused, no mistaking that, but he'd entered her so hard and so fast he might even have hurt her. *Jesus!* The thought made him slightly sick.

He was clutching her ass tightly, so tightly he was probably leaving marks on her delicate skin. He'd grabbed her ass in an attempt to get inside her as deeply as possible. Well, stopping his fingers from digging into her soft flesh might be a good first step toward reparation for the damage done.

With a wince, Alex opened his hands, braced them on the mattress and lifted his head, ready for anything.

Whatever she wanted to say to him, he deserved. Caitlin had every right in the world to be mad at him and he wouldn't blink at whatever name she wanted to call him. If she wanted to slap him, he wouldn't even try to duck the blow. He'd do anything she wanted, give her anything she needed, except for one thing.

He wouldn't — couldn't — pull out of her. His cock wanted to stay right where it was, forever. He hadn't even begun to get her out of his blood.

Trying to convince her to let him have another chance was going to be hard though, after slamming into her and coming one second after that. He was marshalling words and trying out possible angles and excuses in his head when he looked down at her.

His heart nearly stopped at the sight. Jesus, what a beauty. He'd looked down at countless women beneath him in his life, but never one as lovely as this one. The light from the full moon outside the window lit her face with a pale, unearthly glow, as if she were a pearl under water, silvering her pale blue eyes. She looked more like a mermaid than a flesh and blood woman.

She was silent, simply looking up at him, his face a mere inch above hers. It was impossible to tell what she was thinking. She wasn't smiling and she wasn't frowning as she stared up into his eyes.

"Caitlin," he whispered, hoping that she'd let him tell her how sorry he was for treating her like this before she started screaming and biting him. He had to let her know that—

"Oh God," Caitlin moaned and then said his name on a low whisper that raised the hairs on the nape of his neck. "Alex. *Alex*." Her back arched and her hips tilted upward, grinding against him, eyes half-closing. Then he felt her clenching around his cock in short, rhythmic bursts, like a little velvet vise, and his heart nearly stopped.

She was coming.

She was *coming*! Her legs and arms tightened around him in a silken embrace, the hot perfume of her skin filling his nostrils, soft, warm skin everywhere he touched her. Fuck, it was unbearably intense, feeling her little pussy contracting around him, milking him of the last spurts of come. He lowered his head until their foreheads met, feeling the sharp contractions of her cunt all over his body. It seemed even his heart pulsed to the same beat.

Caitlin sighed his name again, her breath sweet on his face, and closed her eyes.

Most women, in Alex's experience, looked tense while coming, as if coming somehow hurt. Their faces scrunched up and the veins in their necks stood out and their mouths turned down. Not Caitlin. Her face softened into a dreamy expression, as if she were reading poetry by the lake instead of lying under him, climaxing.

He buried his face in her hair and hung on.

"Are you okay?" Alex's deep voice was right in her ear, so close his breath made her shiver.

Was she okay? Caitlin took stock, wriggling her fingers and toes. Moving anything else was impossible, since he lay sprawled on her and he weighed a ton.

She had to consciously expand her lungs to breathe and could feel her joints creak from the weight.

"Peachy," she gasped.

He felt delicious on top of her though. Her arms could barely encompass his shoulders. Even under those boring work clothes it had been clear that Alex Cruz was a fit man, but she really hadn't suspected all these muscles. Thousands of them, deep, hard as steel, covered with acres of the most luscious golden brown skin she'd ever seen.

"I want to go down on you," his deep voice announced in her ear, and her whole system jolted at the idea. God, could she stand it? Her heart had nearly stopped as it was with the force of her orgasm. He hadn't even had to do much. Nothing, actually. Just...be inside her. That had been enough to push her right over the edge into the strongest orgasm she'd ever had.

"That's nice." She did her best to pull in another chestful of air, pushing against his weight on her. "I'd like that."

She might not *survive* it, but she'd certainly like it.

"In just a minute," he said, words coming out slowly. "I'm on it."

He certainly was. On her, actually. And in her too. Still hard.

His breathing was slowing down, heavy breaths shifting her hair. A lock of it tickled her cheek but she didn't dare brush it away. Didn't dare move.

This was just so wonderful, she wanted to commit it to memory. The feel of his steely muscles under her hands, the thick mat of hair covering his chest tickling her breasts and stomach. The feel of his hot, hard cock inside her, a touch softer than before but still much harder than Marvin had ever managed on his best days.

"Give me a second." His voice was slurred, as if he were drugged.

"Take your time," Caitlin said softly, running her fingers through his thick hair.

He grunted.

His weight somehow settled more heavily against her and he let out a soft groan. A second later, a faint buzz-saw sound echoed in her ear.

He was snoring.

Caitlin grinned at the ceiling, arched her back to get a little oxygen into her lungs and turned her head until her lips met his massive biceps.

Inside of a minute, she was fast asleep too.

Chapter Seven

Caitlin realized that up until now, she'd woken up beside boys. Alex Cruz was *definitely* not a boy.

She tried to stretch but he was still sprawled mostly on top of her, her legs still around him. His golden-toned skin made a fabulously interesting contrast with the white sheets.

Alex looked intimidating and powerful. Even sprawled on a bed, fast asleep, he looked like what he was — a predator.

His subconscious was telling him that there were no danger signals in his immediate surroundings so he slept through the small noises she was making. But Caitlin had no doubt that at the first sign of real trouble, Alex would be instantly awake, alert and dangerous. And reaching for the gun which was kept in its holster, hooked over the bedpost.

Strength and character were carved into the harsh planes of his face. She turned her head and examined the hand splayed next to her. Large, graceful, long-fingered, with thick veins rising on the back. And yes, she'd seen correctly that first morning in his office. He had a barbwire tat on his wrist, obviously a relic of his gangbanger days. Barbwire tats were the mark of the Eightballs, a particularly vicious gang whose members' average life expectancy was nineteen. He'd been lucky to get out in time.

On the adult Alex, Mr. Straight and Narrow, Mr. Law and Order, the tat looked unbelievably sexy.

She shivered, remembering how that hand had touched her last night.

There was a gentle hum in the air, a soft murmuring like…

Rain.

Rain?

She turned her head to look out the window and saw that it was indeed raining outside. The light that filtered in through the open window was silvery and dim. Cool air drifted in through the partially open window. The rain created a gentle, upbeat patter which suited her mood.

She wanted to get up, dance around the room, take a shower, go get some coffee.

And, well, go to the bathroom.

Caitlin wiggled, hoping she could get Alex to roll off her without having to wake him up. He was so amazingly heavy. She pushed gently on his shoulders, trying to roll him enough to slide out from under, but it didn't work. He was dead weight, so deeply asleep he could have been in a coma.

She, on the other hand, was revved. Energy pulsed through her veins and she felt tinglingly alive from her hair to the tips of her toes. Staying in bed one second more was not an option, she had to get up.

He was breathing very heavily. Snoring again, actually, if you wanted to be technical.

"Alex." Caitlin dug her fingers into his shoulder, finding little purchase. The man's muscles had no give at all. Louder now. "*Alex.*"

He gave an inelegant snort and his eyelids flickered. She put her lips close to his ear. "I need to go to the bathroom. You need to move."

It must have penetrated into the deepest recesses of his brain, because he rolled, just a little, just enough for her to slide out from under him. His semisoft penis had still been inside her. Her movements pulled him out of her and she missed him immediately. Her nether muscles had instinctively clenched, trying to keep him inside.

Caitlin stood beside the bed, just a little shocked at what her body was feeling—stiff, sore, whisker-burned, with a

A Fine Specimen

heaviness in her breasts and between her legs. In some insane way, her body was still feeling his. Between her legs, it was as if he were still inside her. She felt stretched and a little sore there, as if he had somehow branded her.

He'd branded her in another way, as well. Caitlin couldn't even begin to imagine any other lover pleasing her, fulfilling her the way Alex had. She'd spent twenty-eight years without having a clue as to what sex was really about. After Alex, she would undoubtedly spend the rest of her life never finding anything like this ever again.

It wasn't so much his technique. Last night there hadn't been any technique at all. It had been more of a slam-bam-thank-you-ma'am kind of thing. It didn't make any difference. He'd been massively overexcited and therefore fast. She forgave him—and how. That someone like Alex, who could have any woman he wanted, could be incredibly excited about *her* was its own turn-on.

Not to mention what *she'd* felt. If he'd been fast, it didn't matter because the entire evening had been foreplay. Just being near him, breathing the same air, touching him, was foreplay. She'd had no idea her body could respond like that to a man. It hadn't ever before and probably never would again.

She shook her head. No sad thoughts. Not today. Alex was like a comet flashing through her life, showering it with heat and light. The comet would burn itself out, because that was its nature. So she had to hug each moment tightly, appreciate it, and be able to let it go at the end, because that was *her* nature.

Gingerly, she made her way to the bathroom, wincing a little.

Alex's en suite bathroom was big, with a huge window looking out over a garden, privacy guaranteed by a row of tall poplar trees fencing in the garden. Caitlin opened the window and took a huge breath. The rain had almost stopped and the air was clean and fresh. It might turn muggy later if the sun came out, but right now it was like air at the dawn of time, fresh, rain-scented, brand new, rich with promise.

Unsurprisingly, Alex's bathroom was decorated with black and white tiles. The fixtures were white porcelain with old-fashioned brass taps. Beyond a good brand of soap, a cache of disposal razors and shaving cream, shampoo, a comb and a brush, toothbrush—one, she was happy to see—and toothpaste, he had no personal care items. No cologne, no aftershave, no creams, nothing. A big open shelf held a stack of folded white towels, and that was it.

She couldn't find a shower cap, so she wrapped a big towel around her head and stepped into the shower. The strong jet of hot water soothed her sore muscles.

She stretched, on top of the world. Turning around under the spray, she couldn't remember when she had felt as great as this. Her experience in mornings after was limited, but this morning after very definitely topped her personal list of favorites.

Once she'd dried off, she contemplated her nakedness.

Her dress was still downstairs. Caitlin thought of it fondly. She'd had to give up breathing to fit into that nipped-in waist but the look on Alex's face when she had emerged from the elevator had been worth it. Like the ad said, it had been priceless. Who needed breathing anyway?

Smiling, she lifted Alex's shirt from the floor and put it on. It hung to her knees. When she rolled up the sleeves, it was as modest as a summer dress. She inhaled deeply. There was a faint scent of soap and something that was unmistakably Alex. No aftershave. Alex didn't need aftershave. He emitted godzillions of utterly male pheromones all on his own. An eau de cologne would have simply masked it. And there was no commercial cologne on earth as riveting as Alex's smell. God, it was enticing.

She closed her eyes and inhaled again. Smells go straight to the limbic system—the dark, primitive part of the brain that operates on the senses and has no use for thoughts. For an instant, thoughts fled her brain entirely as the smell evoked powerful memories of the night before. Alex's smell was unique—slightly woodsy, slightly musky, laced with clean sweat.

For a second, Caitlin stood there, electrified. Her legs wobbled and her thighs clenched. Breath whooshed out of her and she found it hard to breathe, remembering. Her vagina contracted once—a sharp, muscular movement as if it was clenching around Alex's penis—and a soft sound escaped her.

She whipped around to see whether she'd woken him up but Alex was sleeping like the dead, one arm off the mattress, hand curled on the floor, the other spread over the rest of the bed, as if she were still there. His strong back rose and fell regularly, his dark, thick lashes didn't even flutter. He was out like a light.

A predator like Alex only slept like that when he knew there was no danger in the room. And there wasn't. The danger was all in the other direction. To her, not to him.

Caitlin caught a glimpse of herself in the dresser mirror and the expression of yearning on her face was...embarrassing. This man was going to break her heart if she wasn't careful. Sleeping with him had been fantastic. Incredible. Overwhelming.

And, well, a terrible idea.

The mirror showed a pink-faced Caitlin, mouth swollen and red, whisker burns on her cheeks, hair a wild cloud around her head. A walking advertisement for sex.

Needing a distraction, she checked out the bedroom, searching for clues to the endlessly enticing mystery that was Alex Cruz.

Last night she'd been too blasted by lust to look around her, but in the soft morning light the room spoke volumes. Alex's bedroom was like his office and his living room. Clean, neat, with just the essentials to be able to function as a bedroom. Oddly enough, the bedroom had artwork on the walls—a series of black-and-white photographs in simple, narrow black frames.

They were very good—a shell on the beach, an old bicycle against a crumbling wall, a close-up of a branch in bloom, all showing an excellent sense of proportion and balance. Had he taken them himself or had he bought them? Either way, it was a little window into an unexpected artistic streak.

Curiosity about the man who had just become her lover overcame her.

She wrenched the closet door open. It was so different from her own closet it could have been intended for another species. But it was definitely Alex Cruz's closet. A thick, black cashmere trench coat hung neatly from a padded hanger, together with four pairs of neatly pressed black jeans, ten pairs of slacks and ten men's jackets, all black and all identical. In neat stacks on shelves were piles of identical, white long-sleeved shirts, white short-sleeved shirts, a pile of black turtlenecks, white tee shirts and black tee shirts. The closet smelled of starch and clean fabric. Looking down, she saw eight identical pairs of black lace-up shoes and two pairs of Nikes. The one pair of loafers he had were clearly for living dangerously. Like last night.

Stripping the laces from one of the shoes, Caitlin tied her hair back and, humming softly, made her way downstairs to the kitchen. The rain had finally stopped and she could see large, fluffy clouds rolling across the pale blue sky through the kitchen window. Magnificent sky. Magnificent clouds. Magnificent morning. The best morning ever, since the beginning of the world.

A shaft of bright sunlight glanced off one of the poplars, making the raindrops glisten as if the leaves were made of diamonds. She hugged herself in delight at the sight. It was all so wondrous, so perfect. Life was so exquisitely beautiful.

Caitlin was perfectly familiar with the biochemistry of infatuation. The technical term for it was *limerence*—and it was a killer. Right now, norepinephrine was cascading wildly through her system, triggering the breakdown of glycogen and triacylglycerols, providing a massive spurt of energy, making her heart beat faster, her senses more acute, switching off the logic circuits in the brain.

In all the important ways, the biochemistry of infatuation mirrored insanity. She knew that academically, but *feeling* it, for the first time—well, that was something else.

Opening the back door, she stepped out and took a big breath of the clean, pristine air, feeling the oxygen flooding into her system right down to her toes.

This particular back garden could only belong to Alex. If he could have had a black and white garden, he would have. Still, he had the next best thing. The garden was a small, neat expanse of close-cropped grass in a square area. Each corner had a box shrub pruned into a severely square topiary. Not a blade of grass out of place. Not one flower or ornamental plant besides the box shrubs and the poplars backing them. The garden practically cried out for some color and shapes.

For an instant, Caitlin let herself go and imagined creating a small herb garden off to the right, near the kitchen door, a rockery straight ahead and a flower garden on the left. She would plant pansies right about now, the soft purple and fuchsia kind—

Whoa. Talk about hormonal overload and the insanity it brings! Caitlin shook herself and turned back into the house. Who even knew if Alex would want to see her again after last night—and here she was planning his garden? That way led to heartache and it was way too nice a day for that. Besides which, she was hungry and it looked like Alex wasn't going to be doing the honors.

Cooking breakfast was fine with her, she liked cooking. It was the cleaning-up-afterward part she didn't like.

Caitlin checked the fridge, frowned, then checked the shelves.

Preparing breakfast was going to be a major undertaking. Alex didn't believe in food shopping. Finally, after a thorough and disgusted check of his supplies, she managed to put together the makings for French toast. The bread was stale, with suspicious green flecks, the butter was almost rancid and she didn't want to think too hard about how old the eggs might be. But—technically—it was food. And including the major food groups too—grease, carbs and cholesterol.

She cracked the eggs into a clean white bowl and whisked them. The yolks were anemic-looking, but they'd have to do. The coffee machine was in a cupboard, together with a radio. Caitlin twiddled the dial until she found a soft rock station and settled in contentedly to a program featuring the best of the '90s.

Madonna. "Ray of Light". Perfect.

Humming softly, hips moving gently in time with the beat, she put on the coffee and lit a burner for the French toast. She turned to the cupboard again—then gave a start at the large, dark figure standing in the doorway watching her out of dark, unreadable eyes.

The gray morning light gave his dark skin a metallic tone. His tight, hard features looked almost otherworldly, like a member of a future race that had been honed and perfected over several millennia. He looked like the captain of Starfleet Command.

"Oh!" She smiled, heart hammering. "My goodness, you scared me. I had no idea you were up. Breakfast will be ready in just a few minutes, so… Alex?"

He just looked at her unsmilingly, his eyes fiercely locked on hers.

"Got unfinished business," he said finally in a hoarse croak, as if his voice hadn't been used in a long time. "You and me."

God, he looked better than any male had a right to in the morning. He had pulled on pajama bottoms and the soft cotton

A Fine Specimen

clung to his lean hips, the drawstring waistband dipping low on his flat stomach. His chest, covered in crisp black hair, was just magnificent. Good thing he kept that chest covered up during the day with a shirt and jacket. If he lived in a nudist colony, he'd be jumped constantly by the female population.

Caitlin had felt every inch of that chest against her the night before. Her heart thumped at the sight of him and she found awkward bits of her body softening. Her heart, her knees, her sex.

"Alex?" she asked uncertainly when he didn't move. He simply stared at her, face expressionless. "Is something wrong?" He came away from the doorframe and walked silently toward her on large bare feet. Damn him, even his feet were gorgeous, long and lean, high-arched and beautifully shaped. There was something in his walk which reminded her of a panther's pace. A panther stalking prey.

He was aroused. The big, plum-colored tip of his cock was poking up from under the waistband of the soft pants. Oh God.

"Alex?" she ventured again. "Are you angry because I rummaged around for food and— Mmmf!"

Alex hooked his arm around her neck and caught her mouth with his. Her neck fell back over his arm and her bones loosened. His kitchen, his garden, Baylorville, the whole world started spinning around her as he leaned into her, and she had to clutch his bare shoulders for balance.

When his tongue touched hers, she felt the electric shock down to her toes. His large, calloused hand touched her thigh under the shirt and glided upward, smoothing over her bare hip.

"Saw your panties on the bedroom floor," he breathed into her neck, once he released her mouth. "Figured you wouldn't have anything on under this."

"You figured right, Dick Tracy, excellent deductive powers," Caitlin murmured, then bit her lip as his hand traveled leisurely up her side to caress her breast.

"Mmm." He pulled her even closer. "But I had to find out firsthand. Says I have to right in the Detective's Manual. Rule number one for a detective—check your facts."

He reached out to turn off the burner and hooked a kitchen chair with one gorgeous bare foot. He sat down, Caitlin straddling his lap.

She looked at his face. From this vantage point, what she could see was mostly square jaw, black stubble and absurdly long black eyelashes. He shifted his arms until she was nestled up against him, chest to chest, nose to nose.

She could feel the pulses of blood in his penis every time her belly touched it. Each surge was echoed in her womb.

He watched her eyes, watched her reaction to his arousal, hot and hard as steel against her belly. Caitlin couldn't have hid her own reaction to him if she'd tried.

She knew she was flushed, she could feel it down to her breasts. Her nipples were so sensitized that the thick, starched material of the shirt almost hurt them as she brushed against it. At least the material was so thick it hid the fact that her nipples had turned hard as pebbles.

Alex's gaze left her eyes, lingering on her mouth before dropping to her breasts. When his gaze rose again, his eyes were so hot they scorched.

Maybe he had X-ray vision.

"What—" Oh God, the heat inside her was so intense she could barely huff out the words. "What unfinished business do we have?"

"Foreplay," he growled. He pulled her to him for a kiss so hard and so hungry she was shivering when it ended.

"Completely forgot foreplay last night, it went straight out the window." His hand slid up her rib cage, his thumb rasping across her nipple. Goose pimples broke out on her arms. "It was like I was in some kind of a race to see how fast I could get into you. Sorry."

The last word was said against her neck, his teeth and stubble scraping down a tendon. She shivered.

"I forgive you," she whispered.

His mouth moved against the skin of her neck in a smile. "That's good. I am humbly appreciative and hope to make it up to you. However..." His hands went to the front of his shirt. "You stole my shirt. Do you know what happens to stolen goods?"

He slid the buttons from their holes, slowly, one by one, watching carefully as the shirt widened, exposing the swell of her breasts.

Caitlin was mesmerized by the look on his face. Every feature tight. Pupils dilated. Sharp, searing heat. He suddenly looked up at her and every cell in her body flashed heat.

"Do you?"

Do I what? she thought, dazed. He was teasing her. She should be responding but there was no moisture in her mouth. She couldn't even swallow. He'd asked her something. She shook her head slowly, side to side, without looking away from him.

The shirt was completely unbuttoned, caught on her breasts. Alex put his hands on her shoulders, opening the shirt even farther.

"The police have to confiscate stolen goods." His hands slid down her arms, taking the shirt with it. It dropped to the floor. "That's the law."

She was naked on his lap. Her heart was pounding so hard she was sure he could see it pulsing against her skin. He was seeing something, because his eyes were locked on her breasts. He cupped a breast in his hand, his skin dark and tough against her white flesh. The contrast was vivid, arousing.

He bent his dark head and licked her nipple.

Caitlin jolted. Her womb contracted with each movement of his tongue. She was breathing in short pants, embarrassed at how aroused she was at such simple touches. His hand at her breast, his tongue at her nipple. Her heart was knocking against her rib cage so hard she was surprised it didn't make a racket.

Alex lifted his head and kissed her again, hard, one big hand cupping the back of her head, as if she'd escape if he didn't bind her to him.

Silly, silly man. She wasn't going anywhere. His kisses were making her so weak she could barely stay upright. His other hand left her breast to cup her bottom, edging her closer to him, so close the lips of her sex met his huge, material-clad penis. It surged against her, lengthening and thickening.

She sucked in her breath and let it out shakily.

He pulled her even more tightly to him and kissed her again, so hard she sagged against him helplessly. Caitlin's body immediately prepared itself for lovemaking. Her breasts felt heavy and swollen and her lower body softened, like a flower unfurling.

Had he felt that? He felt something, because he jolted and moved fast, in a blur. He lifted her, using only one arm around her back and positioning her over him. With the other hand he pushed the material of the pajama bottoms down, pulled his penis away from his stomach and held it, lowering her over him. His hips pushed up as she sank down on him so that in an instant she was completely impaled, full to bursting with hard, aroused Alex.

It hurt, just a little. Not actually *pain*, no. More like stretched and invaded. And hot. It was like having a burning brand of steel inside her. He was so tall her feet didn't touch the floor so she had no leverage to control the depth of his invasion, the full weight of her body sinking her down on him. She wriggled a little to find a more comfortable position and he groaned.

A Fine Specimen

"Oh God." Alex's forehead fell to her shoulder with a little thunk. "Not again."

She wriggled a little more and felt him, impossibly, swell inside her as she moved on him. "What?" she asked, breathlessly. It was almost impossible to breathe, as if her body couldn't do two things at once—have Alex inside her and pull in air.

"Foreplay." His muffled voice floated up. "Fuck. I forgot again."

It was hard to think of him doing anything that could excite her more than she already was. The slight discomfort was gone and she was so aroused she was shaking with it. Alex's entire body was one huge turn-on. The crisp chest hair that tickled her breasts and stomach and that turned wiry around his groin, rubbing roughly against the delicate flesh of her sex, the steely thighs under her legs, shoulders so broad they exceeded the span of the chair.

And that smell, oh God. Pure Alex. Pure sex.

"It's okay," she said shakily. "Another time."

His head lifted at that and he gave her a half smile, one corner of his beautiful mouth tilting up. "No," he said, his deep voice low. "Now."

Eyes narrowing, watching her face carefully, Alex reached down to where her body joined his. Carefully, delicately, he touched her clitoris. It was like being touched by lightning. She jolted.

"That's it," he murmured, rubbing her lightly. A wash of heat so great she almost burned up with it rose from her groin area, together with a wash of juices. That was it, indeed.

His finger slowly, carefully traced her pussy all around where it was clenched on his penis, opening her up just a little more. The thighs under her turned even harder and his hips rose, just a little, reaching somehow even more deeply inside her.

"Bend back," Alex ordered.

Caitlin was almost beyond understanding English. "What?"

"Over my arm. Bend." Alex's voice was guttural now, hoarse. He had a steely arm holding her, and she tipped her head back.

"Yeah. That's it." It was more a puffing out of breath than words. Bending to her, Alex licked a nipple. Caitlin whimpered. She was breathing in fast, shallow pants that sounded loud in the quiet kitchen. With a low, approving sound coming from his throat, Alex opened his mouth over the tip of her breast and sucked. Hard.

Her vagina clenched around him.

A noise came from his chest that sounded like a purr.

Each movement of his mouth set off a reaction in her inner muscles, which caused his penis to jerk inside her. Like a positive-reinforcement machine.

Caitlin's muscles were completely lax. If she hadn't been held up by his arm, impaled on his penis, she would have fallen to the floor.

Alex switched breasts and the contrast between one nipple in the heat of his mouth, the other tip wet in the cool morning air, made her shiver.

Alex's mouth left her breasts and moved up, slowly, kissing her skin every inch of the way to her neck, where he ran teeth and tongue over a sensitive tendon. She broke out in goose bumps all over. She could feel Alex smiling against the skin of her neck.

"That's it," he whispered against her skin. "Now open more for me."

Caitlin blinked. Open more for him? How could she possibly be more open? A shifting of his hands on her back, an adjusting of her thighs and she found herself leaning forward, plastered against his chest, her thighs opened wider by his legs and Alex, impossibly, even more deeply inside her.

"Oh yeah," he breathed. "Just like that."

A Fine Specimen

His thighs under her hardened even more as he moved inside her. At first gently, a light rotation that brought him into contact with every single erogenous zone inside her, then harder as he started pumping. Short, lazy strokes that soon grew deeper.

Caitlin's head had fallen to his shoulder. They couldn't kiss. His strokes moved her up and down too much for that. And a kiss would be wasted right now anyway. Caitlin loved Alex's kisses. He was amazingly good at kissing. He never made her feel crowded or like she couldn't breathe, like other men's kisses had. No, Alex knew exactly what to do and how to do it, and she loved it.

But right now, all her attention was centered on the heat between her legs.

With difficulty, she lifted her head slightly and opened her eyes. It was mesmerizing, watching where they were joined. The contrast between their coloring was electrifying. With each stroke that pushed him inside her, strands of her pubic hair intertwined with his, pale ash to black. When he pulled out, his penis was darkly earth-toned and glistening, a contrast to her bright pink flesh.

She was so wet, pearls of moisture glistened in her pubic hair and made his penis glisten when he pulled out of her. An intense smell, the unmistakable smell of sex, drifted up. His churning penis made small sucking sounds as he worked her. A blind man could smell and hear what they were doing.

The strokes were becoming harder, deeper, faster. Her chest rubbed against his, the friction almost as exciting as the friction of his cock inside her. Almost, but not quite. The friction of his penis was burning her up from the inside, a whirlwind of heat so intense she couldn't move, could only stay with her head on Alex's shoulder, watching the two of them, a sight so erotic her skin prickled.

Alex was moving so fast and so hard now, both big hands clenched hard around her backside, holding and lifting her for him, moving quickly into the violent rhythms of climax.

Caitlin slowly raised her eyes from where he was pumping in and out of her, up over the strong stomach muscles rippling with his thrusts, up to his face, flushed and hard, predatory, the broad chest beneath her hands bellowing in and out as if he were running a marathon. A lock of thick black hair had fallen over his forehead, tap-tap-tapping in time with his thrusts. His narrowed gaze held hers intently, watching her carefully.

His jaw muscles moved and stomach contracted as he drove into her, over and over again.

It was all too much. Caitlin drew in a deep breath and held it, shaking, on the edge of a precipice and then—yes! She fell right over the edge with a cry, tumbling onto him as her body erupted in tight convulsions, so hard they were almost painful.

He rode her through it, intensifying the pulses of pure sensation, a level of pleasure she'd never felt before, pure animal sex, hard and fast.

Caitlin shook and shuddered, eyes tightly closed because she couldn't take any more sensory input, what was happening inside her was too sharp, too intense. Her loins were drenched, she was sweating all over, even her closed eyes were leaking water.

Her body was starting the long slide to the other side of orgasm when Alex's strong arms tightened around her so hard he cut off her air. He punched his hips up in one hard thrust that raised her high, swelled inside her even more and gave a huge shout, jetting semen inside her so hard she came again, a short, intense little orgasm, like a hiccup or a cough.

Dazed, Caitlin felt Alex settle back in the chair and felt his breaths slow in time with hers. They sat, foreheads on each other's shoulders, plastered together by sweat and semen...and simply breathed.

She opened her eyes slowly, astonished to find the room exactly the way it had been before. The buzzing frantic energy between them had been so strong she wouldn't have been surprised to see that it had swirled in the room, knocking glasses and plates off the counter, tipping chairs.

But nothing had changed except her.

She closed her eyes again, feeling her muscles relax, one by one, her breathing slowly returning to normal, her other senses slowly awakening.

Finally, Alex stirred and raised his head. He turned her face toward him with a finger. Her muscles had turned to water. She didn't even have the energy to open her eyes.

"Look at me," he ordered softly.

Yeah, right. Her eyelids flickered then subsided. Not going to happen.

He shook her a little.

"Caitlin, look at me." Oh God, that was the Alex Cruz Voice of Command, as impossible to resist as the voice of God from a burning bush.

Her eyes popped open.

"Are you okay? Did I hurt you?" He was looking grim now, as if expecting bad news. How sad. She wanted to wipe that expression off his face, right now. What they'd just shared was...terrific. Mind-bending, actually.

She opened her mouth to tell him so and her stomach emitted a loud growl, startling in the silence of the room.

Alex lost the grim expression and laughed. He closed his eyes and bent his head forward until it touched hers again. His mouth curved in a smile. "Much as I want a second round, I've guess we've been ordered to make other plans." He lifted her gently and reluctantly off his lap. "What were you doing before?"

"Cooking," Caitlin said. She stood on shaky legs, looking down at his still-erect penis. Desire burned in her bloodstream and she was about to bend back down to him when her stomach rumbled again, loud and strong and embarrassing as hell. With a sigh, she bent to retrieve his shirt from the floor and gave herself up to satisfying at least one type of hunger.

"Can you cook?" Alex asked curiously. He was so outrageously sexy sitting there bare-chested in a kitchen chair, with a dark, bristly jaw, half-closed eyes, cock still so engorged she could make out the veins. She could barely keep from flinging herself at him.

Now he wasn't the straight-arrow, button-down upholder of law and order. Now he looked rough, tough and dangerous. He looked like someone he should arrest.

He was relaxed, but Caitlin knew he could move quickly when necessary, like a cheetah, springing from immobility to blinding speed in a second.

He hitched up his pajama bottoms, covering that intriguing stalk of hard male flesh with its large, plum-colored head, the source of such amazing delight. She nearly sighed as it disappeared under the drawstring pants.

Caitlin tried to get her mind away from the strong set of his shoulders and his flat stomach with the thick vee of hair arrowing intriguingly into the pajama bottoms...

She shook her head and tried to remind herself not to get too sentimental about Alex Cruz, considering that he often behaved as if he'd studied at the Mordor School of Charm, under the Dark Lord himself.

He'd asked her a question.

"I like good food and can't afford to eat out much, so yeah, I can cook. If I have food to cook with." She planted her hands on her hips and tried to look sternly at Alex. It was hard while he was looking at her through slitted eyes, the dark heat so enticing. "I managed to scrounge some scraps for breakfast, but you need to do some serious shopping."

"We can go on a food run later," Alex said lazily, getting up to put plates on the table. "You can fill my pantry to your heart's delight."

A Fine Specimen

"Sounds like a fun way to spend a Sunday." Caitlin turned the burner back on. She whisked the eggs and milk a bit more and dipped the stale bread in them. The butter started sizzling. "Tell you what, I'll help you stock up and cook you lunch. And then later in the afternoon you can drive me back to the hotel."

"No." Alex's deep voice was flat.

"No?" Caitlin's hands faltered then shook. Damn her fair skin and the fiery blush of humiliation she could feel rising. Her face would be a hot pink right now. She cursed her pale complexion and the faint hope that had risen in her heart.

Oh God. It was starting already.

Though she'd lectured herself all morning not to expect anything from Alex, her traitorous heart had betrayed her. The prospect of spending the rest of the morning and the early afternoon with this new, seductive and playful Alex had been so enticing that she hadn't stopped to think at all. She'd simply opened her mouth and, like an idiot, let her hopes plop out. She could have slapped herself.

Everyone at the station house had emphasized that Alex never took a day off. Ever. Not even Sundays.

He didn't want to spend the day with her. After the shopping, he wanted to head back to work. And maybe, she thought, as an even deeper flush of embarrassment washed through her, maybe he had another date this afternoon or tonight. The fact that no one knew anything about Alex's private life didn't necessarily mean he didn't have one. Alex Cruz was an incredibly attractive man. He probably had women falling all over him.

They'd had a brief affair—well, call it what it was, a one-night stand—and it was over. Caitlin swallowed heavily against the acid bile rising in her stomach, telling herself that it was the thought of eating that moldy French toast, though she knew better. It was her idiotic hopes for more than casual sex that were roiling her insides.

Foolish, foolish Caitlin. She'd known what to expect, no use feeling disappointed. *Well, play it cool, Summers,* she told herself, turning away—and knocking a mug off the counter.

Alex moved with lightning speed to catch it before it shattered on the floor. Her flush deepened. Caitlin didn't even want to think about how she and Alex could have cleaned it up. They were both barefoot.

This was awful, a repeat of last night's pants fiasco.

"Sorry," she whispered, her gaze going out to the backyard so she wouldn't have to look at him.

"Listen to me." Alex placed the mug back on the counter and caught her shoulders. A long, lean finger turned her head to face him. "I'll drive you back to the hotel after lunch all right. But just to get your things. You're not staying in that hotel anymore."

Caitlin frowned. He'd gone from amazingly attractive, lazy, sexy Alex to Stern Cop Alex, who was, unfortunately, just as attractive. "I'm not what?"

Alex's jaws jumped as he clenched his teeth. "Staying in that hotel. Ever again."

"I'm...not?" Caitlin searched his dark eyes.

"No." Alex shook her slightly. "You're going to stay here. With me. At least until you can get yourself set up. I already called the hotel and told them you'd be checking out today. We'll swing by to get your things this afternoon. I don't ever want you in Riverhead again. Is that clear?"

Caitlin blinked. She opened her mouth and nothing came out.

"I...see," she said finally.

"Are we clear?" Alex repeated. She nodded.

The coffee machine began to hiss and sputter and Caitlin turned it off. She didn't know what to say...so she started talking. "Sit down. The French toast is almost done. I couldn't find any syrup or jam, so you can sprinkle some sugar on them instead. There won't be enough milk after the French toast to put in the coffee, so I hope you like it black. I like a touch of cream myself but..." She shrugged. She took a deep breath, bit her lip and served Alex before sitting down across from him.

She stared at her breakfast, which didn't look too appetizing, then lifted her eyes to Alex, who did.

"I'm going to stay here with you," she repeated. "For a while."

Alex nodded and dug in with a fork.

Caitlin blew out a breath in frustration. It was what she wanted, but he hadn't even asked, he'd simply told her.

Clearly, the country of Alex was no democracy—and its diplomatic corps wasn't too functional either.

Alex didn't have too much experience in politely asking people to do things. In the first half of his life, no one would have done anything for him no matter what he asked or how he asked it. His parents had been lost in their own dark, cruel and desperate world of drugs and alcohol, with nothing left over for him.

And in the second half of his life, he just gave orders and they were obeyed. Cop shops were like the military. They sure as hell weren't democracies. So this whole notion of asking someone to do something they might or might not do, depending on their mood, was completely foreign to him.

Maybe he should have asked Caitlin if she'd like to stay with him while she was doing whatever it was she was doing in the station house.

No!

His entire nature balked at the thought. He could ask Caitlin what she'd like for dinner. He could ask her what movie she'd like to see or if she'd like to go for a walk. But her sleeping at the Carlton, in Riverhead, was not an option. It was absolutely out of the question. He'd been crazy to let her stay in the Carlton even one night.

Riverhead was a place where the druggies and the punks came out of the woodwork after dark. During the day it was only the loonies and sad drunks, so he'd felt more or less satisfied that she wasn't out and about at the most dangerous times.

He hadn't had alarm bells ringing in his head, so against his better judgment, he'd let her stay there. But now they'd had sex. She wasn't Ray Avery's anymore, she was *his*. For the time being, anyway. Her safety was now his direct concern and staying in Riverhead didn't figure into the equation at all. Riverhead was for scumbags, not gorgeous young scholars.

She was so beautiful this morning, wearing his shirt, that glorious hair tied back with a shoelace. He'd watched her fussing in his austere kitchen, making a mess, humming softly along with the radio. He'd leaned against the doorframe, drinking in the sight of her and rubbing his chest, where something inside had started aching.

She was like a fairy, a good fairy come down to earth just for him, to make him stale French toast and to make sure he broke his three-year record of going into the office every Sunday. Right then, watching her hips sway under his shirt, the idea of going into the office on a Sunday had struck him as insane. Why had he been living like that? Sundays were for gorgeous fairies with their asses swaying gently to the beat.

"What?" Alex paused for a moment before forking in another bite. She'd said something.

"I said that's very kind of you." When he looked up, startled, she blushed. "To let me stay with you."

Alex snorted and sipped his coffee. He wasn't kind, he was selfish. Having her stay here was purely self-serving. He knew she'd be safe, he wouldn't have to worry about ferrying her to and fro and he'd have her available for sex whenever he wanted. And now that his dormant hormones had woken up and smelled the roses, he wanted. A lot. But hell, if she wanted to ascribe good-guy sentiments to him...hey.

"It will only be for a few more days, anyway," she said earnestly.

"Yeah?" She was so cute when she was serious. Alex put down his cup. "How so? I thought your study was going to last at least a week."

"Oh it will." Caitlin leaned forward and Alex almost did too, looking for a glimpse of cleavage. He stopped himself, ashamed. It was purest instinct. He didn't need to grasp this opportunity though. Her breasts, her luscious, pale, round breasts were his for the asking. All he had to do was reach over and unbutton his shirt, and she'd let him. Oh yeah. She was right here, in his house, and all he had to do was reach out to have her.

"I'll be looking for an apartment next week. The news isn't official yet, the announcement will be on Thursday...but it looks like I'm going to be awarded that Frederiksson Foundation fellowship I told you about! I can rent a nice apartment with the stipend that comes with the fellowship."

What?

"Well, that's...that's good news," Alex said slowly. The old joke—good news and bad news. The good news was, she'd be sticking around Baylorville. The bad news was, she wouldn't be in his house. "How long does a fellowship last?"

"A year, with an option for renewal for two more."

A year of Caitlin. Here in Baylorville. *Okay.* He could work with that. Alex chewed his stale French toast with renewed enthusiasm.

"I'm so excited!" Caitlin beamed. "The focus of my project will be on August Vollmer. The Frederiksson has extensive archives, particularly for the period I'm interested in, which runs from the Peelian reform in England to the founding of the IACP. I'm hoping to gather enough material for a book."

What the hell was she talking about?

"Vollmer?" Alex pursed his lips, thinking furiously. "Isn't that an...unusual choice?"

"Not really." Caitlin frowned. "I mean, if you stop to think about it, a modern professional police force would be unthinkable without his theories of management. Why, you could almost call him the precursor to community policing."

"You're right. Of course." Alex deepened his voice and looked thoughtful. "August Vollmer *would* make a really interesting subject for a book."

Who the fuck is August Vollmer? Alex had some vague memory of a hot summer afternoon in the academy and the most boring professor on the teaching staff mentioning August Vollmer, but for the life of him, he couldn't remember a thing.

At the academy, he'd aced every subject that he considered practical and pertinent to policing, including law. *Especially* law, once he'd made the decision to uphold it instead of break it. He'd had top marks in Surveillance Techniques, Self-Defense and Marksmanship and good marks in everything else except for Police Theory.

August Vollmer had been somewhere inside the boring part, but where? He didn't give a shit right now. Right now, all he wanted was to get her out of the Carlton and settled in his bed. Er, his *house*.

"Okay." He slapped the table with open palms."We'd better get started," he said, rising to put the plates in the sink. "Otherwise we won't get back in time for you to cook me a fabulous lunch."

Caitlin laughed and stuck her tongue out at him. She ran up the stairs and Alex followed, enjoying the view of her bare legs, with tantalizing, glimmering glimpses of bare ass. It was very tempting to think of sliding his hands under his shirt, cupping those firm cheeks while kissing her, but if he did that they'd end up in bed, which as ideas went was a good one. A really good one.

His cock, which had been at half-mast as he watched those pink lips and small pink tongue as she ate — and had swelled as he watched her run up the stairs — twitched in

A Fine Specimen

eagerness at the idea. *Down boy*, he told himself. For now, anyway. He had to get Caitlin checked out and get some food in the house before they could play.

And while he was at it, he was definitely going to have to haul some of his old academy textbooks out of storage and bone up. August Vollmer, eh? He was going to have to work hard to keep up with Caitlin Summers.

* * * * *

"We've got enough food to feed Baylorville for a month when civilization breaks down," Caitlin complained. Alex had restocked with a vengeance, including a bottle of real French champagne. To celebrate her fellowship in style, he'd said.

They had just left the Carlton, where she'd packed up her few possessions and checked out. Alex now headed into a rabbit warren of dark, dank streets. She looked at the bleak surroundings. "And judging by this neighborhood, that day might not be too far off. Where are we, anyway?"

"We're in the bad part of Riverhead. I'm taking a few shortcuts home."

Caitlin had been staring out the side window but when she heard him, she turned, startled. "You mean the Carlton is in the *good* part of Riverhead?"

He looked over at her, just a quick glance out of dark eyes. "Yeah."

Caitlin sat back, blinking. The sky was darkening with storm clouds, more every passing minute, but it wasn't the sun behind the clouds which gave the area such a forsaken air.

Almost all the buildings were boarded up—or worse, with doors and windows ripped off and mounds of rubbish piled up inside. The streets were almost deserted. This whole section of town was abandoned, as if a war had been lost and conquering troops had passed through, wrecking everything in their path.

The few Dumpsters there were had been tipped over and ransacked. Black, charred circles on the cracked sidewalk showed where bonfires had been lit. A number of rusted hulks of cars, most with the tires long-since stolen, were parked haphazardly along the street.

Sullen, too-thin men loitered on door stoops, tipping their heads back and drinking out of bottles wrapped in paper bags. Others were clearly drug addicts.

Some of the houses looked as if they had been bombed. Caitlin supposed that the owners had set fire to them in hopes of collecting insurance money. There wasn't a business open, there wasn't a human being in sight who looked purposeful. Though it wasn't cold, Alex drove with the windows up and the doors locked.

He'd made her put her purse in the footwell and had put her things and most of the groceries away in the trunk.

Alex was in full cop mode, silent, utterly vigilant, eyes flickering constantly to the rearview mirrors.

Caitlin shivered at the stares of some of the men. There was no way for them to know that Alex was a police officer, but the hatred in their eyes as Alex's sleek, expensive car drove through the neighborhood, as out of place as an alien spaceship, was unmistakable. He didn't have to be a cop for them to hate him. Alex belonged to a different world, a world they would never join, and that was enough.

She pulled her new cotton sweater close around her midriff and shuddered. "What an awful place," she said.

"Yeah, it is." Alex's voice was grim. He took a deep breath and let it out slowly. "I grew up here."

Caitlin shot him a startled glance. Alex was looking straight ahead, but she wasn't fooled. She could feel his concentration centered on her, wondering what her reaction would be.

This was fascinating. She'd known that he'd grown up on the wrong side of the tracks. It was part of the legend surrounding Alex. How he had been a punk and Ray had saved him. But somehow, being in the area where Alex had grown up made it clearer just how greatly the odds had been stacked against him and how far he'd come in life.

Caitlin felt her heart swell, but not with pity. Alejandro Cruz didn't need her pity. He didn't need anyone's pity.

Caitlin had worked in the inner city on a sociology project for three summers straight. She knew very well how a bad neighborhood could suck its young into its own negative gravity of hopelessness and despair.

But Alex had been strong enough, smart enough to get out and prevail over his background. He was an alpha male, and alpha males win or die trying. He'd made a success of his life, despite the odds against it. Caitlin felt only admiration for what Alex had done with himself. Admiration...and something more.

She'd been close to falling in love with him and, right there, in a car driving through the 'hood, Alex staring straight ahead, his knuckles white on the wheel, she slid all the way in.

It wasn't just the sex, she thought almost sadly. It would be easier if it were. Falling in love with Alex Cruz was not a smart move, but there it was.

"It's a tough neighborhood," she said gently.

Alex nodded, his face tense.

"But you were tougher."

He swiveled his head and Caitlin smiled at him. Alex stared at her for a second then turned his attention back to the road. He was quiet for another mile, then one corner of his mouth lifted in that half smile she was starting to know so well. "Yeah," he said softly. "I was tougher."

They drove in silence. Alex clearly knew his way around the area. Caitlin had long since lost her sense of direction. The sky was turning purple and sheet lightning flared on the horizon. A big fat raindrop splattered on the windshield, then another.

Alex turned a corner and nosed the car into what looked like an alleyway. Caitlin wondered what he was doing when he turned another corner onto a broad avenue which she recognized. He'd shaved twenty minutes off the drive.

"It wasn't quite this bad around here when I was growing up," Alex said finally.

"No?"

Alex shook his head. "Oh, it was a rotten neighborhood all right. But you could live a life here, of sorts. Over there," he nodded at a burnt-out two-story building, "was a little supermarket, and there," he pointed to a boarded-up storefront, "that was a clothing store."

Caitlin blinked. It was hard to imagine organized life in this place. "So what happened?"

"A lot of things happened, but *mainly* what happened was Angelo Lopez."

She'd heard the name before. "Angelo Lopez?"

"Yeah. A major scumbag. But scumbags are a dime a dozen, we put them away by the ton. This guy's worse. He's a loan shark and runs a protection racket. He's dangerous as hell. He'll bomb your shop in a heartbeat if you don't pay up. He'll send his goons to kneecap you and then he'll go after your wife and kids. Five years after Lopez started operations here, the neighborhood collapsed. Anyone who had the energy or the wits to run a business had left."

"Well, that wasn't very smart of him, was it?" Caitlin frowned. "Sort of like killing the goose that lays the golden egg."

"That's not how these guys think, honey." Caitlin started at the endearment and told herself she was a fool to feel warmth spread through her. "They don't care. Lopez certainly didn't. He probably cleared five million in as many years. He sucked the place dry and then he moved on to greener pastures. He's operating out of Barton now."

Caitlin sucked in a shocked breath. Barton was an old neighborhood that was gentrifying—and it was where her friend Samantha had found a little fixer-upper of a house. "He's got to be stopped before he ruins Barton too!"

Alex glanced at her. "We'll get him," he said softly. "It's just a question of time. We're going to pull in his numbers man, his accountant. You might remember me talking about him. He took the protection money and the prostitution money and the drug money and washed it whiter than white for Lopez. You'd better believe he'll—" Alex stiffened, his words ending abruptly.

"Alex?" Caitlin hung onto her shoulder strap as Alex swerved violently to the side of the road and braked sharply. "Alex, what's the matter?"

The car was still rocking as Alex unbuckled his seat belt and reached into the glove compartment. Caitlin's eyes widened when she saw him draw out a gun. It was a Glock 19, bigger than his service weapon. He held it with complete familiarity. A sharp snick sounded as he switched the safety off. "Lock the door after me, and *don't* move," he said as he slid out of the car.

Caitlin didn't even have time to answer. Alex slammed the car door shut and started sprinting down the street.

There he is!

Alex hadn't been wrong. Scrawny build, narrow face, long nose, scraggly whiskers. Ratso was unmistakable, as ugly as his namesake. Alex had been thinking about Ratso, savoring putting the pressure on him—oh-so gently so the DA couldn't say jack shit about it—and watching him crack wide open to let them reel Lopez in, when *wham*!

There Ratso was, walking down the street as if Alex had conjured him up himself out of his yearning to see the fucker behind bars.

Ratso had turned around at the sound of a car braking abruptly, but when he saw Alex shooting out of the car, he started running down the street.

Alex was off-duty, with a civilian, in his own personal car. Going after Ratso right now was a no-no. A *big* no-no.

But...damn it! He could almost taste Ratso's testimony. He could almost *see* Lopez behind bars.

Ratso had about a hundred yards on him, but Alex was in good shape and Ratso wasn't. Ratso looked over his shoulder at Alex gaining on him and darted into an alleyway.

Alex grinned. Of all the cops in the world, Alex was the only one guaranteed to catch Ratso in the dark, winding alleyways of Riverhead. He knew these streets like a mother knows her child. Ratso could never shake him here.

The adrenaline of the chase coursed through Alex. This was what he needed, this was what he had been born for—the hunt. He drew even with the alley, glancing swiftly backward before plunging into the labyrinth of alleyways—and stopped dead.

Though it was only late morning, the sky was almost completely black. The brewing thunderstorm gave the shabby, derelict buildings a sinister bruised look. Even through the window of the car, Caitlin's pale face and pale hair glowed in the darkened street like a beacon.

Some of the groceries were stacked in the backseat, an open invitation to a fist through the window. Caitlin herself was probably the most delectable thing any of the men in Riverhead had seen in years. She was as juicy a prey to the predators of Riverhead as a lamb tethered to the stake.

Even at this distance, Alex could see her watching him anxiously. Leaving her there alone and unprotected was literally unthinkable. A thousand eyes were watching. The instant he headed into the alleyways, the scum would come swarming out of the woodwork.

Without a second thought, Alex put his Glock in his jacket pocket and headed back.

As he walked toward Caitlin, it occurred to Alex that, for the first time in his adult life, he had put something before law enforcement.

It didn't seem real, but there it was. His decision had been instantaneous, he hadn't even had to argue with himself. All he knew was he couldn't possibly leave Caitlin unprotected.

When Caitlin saw him heading back toward her, she gave him a shaky smile and his heart gave a kick in his chest, just as it had in his kitchen this morning. Alex rubbed his chest absently.

Maybe he should be seeing a cardiologist.

Chapter Eight
❦

At eight o'clock on Monday morning, Alex marched Caitlin up the broad granite steps of the station house and into the high-ceilinged lobby. "Marched" was the right word too. Alex looked like a man on a mission. A soldier with one goal in mind—getting her up the stairs of the station house, no matter what.

They'd argued about it all morning and, not surprisingly, Alex had won. Caitlin wanted to take a bus in and arrive at a different time from Alex, but Alex had refused in a way that made a brick wall look reasonable. When she'd broached the topic, he'd simply said, "No," and that was that. Reasoning and pleading and even anger hadn't budged him an inch.

Entering the building together on a Monday morning was more or less the equivalent of having HEY! WE'VE BECOME LOVERS! tattooed in red ink on their foreheads. Apart from the embarrassment, it was terribly unprofessional to engage in an affair with the subject of a study in the first place, let alone publicizing it. Caitlin had broken a lot of personal rules this weekend and had been hoping to get away with it. After all, who had to know? She'd simply assumed that in public, Alex would behave toward her exactly as he had before, in his usual brusque, bordering-on-rude manner and no one would be the wiser.

She would soon be out of the station house, her study completed, with no more professional barriers to an affair with Alex Cruz. She hardly dared to hope that their…relationship, affair, whatever it was, would last out the week. But if it did, then afterward, she was a free agent.

However, in the meantime, Caitlin deeply, *deeply* wanted to pretend that there was nothing going on between them.

The embarrassment at having an entire cop shop know they were sleeping together was compounded by the fact that, though they'd had copious, fantastic sex all day yesterday — Caitlin was sure she'd used up her sex quota for the next couple of years — Alex hadn't said one word that made her think it was something *more* than sex.

It was true that at times his touch was delicate and affectionate, but he hadn't given any indication whatsoever that this was anything more than hormones gone wild. Caitlin was afraid to ask outright, because she didn't want to know the answer. Something told her Alex was always brutally honest and if she asked him whether they were in a relationship, and he answered no, she'd shrivel up and die.

If they became a couple, people would quickly forget that it all started at work, during a research project, which was pretty much a no-no. Couples become part of the woodwork very soon.

If everyone knew they were having an affair, and if it ended right away, people would never forget that she'd been sleeping with a senior police officer. She was going to become a fellow at the Frederiksson Foundation and, as such, was expected to entertain good relations with the law enforcement community. If this...thing with Alex somehow ended badly, right away, Caitlin was going to be up the proverbial creek without the proverbial paddle, and she'd have started her fellowship, her first big chance, with a big black mark next to her name.

Those were all really strong reasons why she didn't want to walk into the station house at the same time as Alex. All she had to do was walk in a quarter of an hour after him and behave impersonally toward him all day and her reputation would be salvaged.

She'd tried every iteration possible on "let's keep a low profile". *I can catch the bus* and *I can call a taxi* had been repeated so often she would throw up if she said the words one more time. For all the attention Alex had paid, she could have been reciting the Gettysburg Address.

Every single variation of "I don't want to walk into the cop shop with you" had been tried and found failing.

She'd dawdled as long as she could this morning, hoping Alex would finally just go off on his own and she could call a cab. But no—Alex had waited patiently downstairs until she was ready. Then, when he had parked the car, she had stated that she absolutely, desperately needed another cup of coffee and that Alex should just go on ahead. But he had simply steered her into a coffee shop just across the street from the entrance and waited until she gulped down a boiling-hot, unwanted espresso.

There seemed to be nothing she could do to shake him off. He had a tight grip on her elbow, as if he knew she wanted to escape. With a feeling of dread, she walked up the big granite steps side by side with Alex at exactly one minute to eight.

"Hey, boss." A young, sandy-haired police officer greeted Alex and matched his pace with theirs as they walked up the staircase.

"Boyd." Alex nodded, barely sparing him a glance.

"So...anything good happen yesterday?" the young officer asked. "I was off duty."

Caitlin knew that in cop talk, "good" meant a juicy murder or at least an armed robbery. Cops lived for the excitement.

"I don't know." Alex's voice was clipped and his face remote. "I didn't come in yesterday."

"Yeah, riiiight," Boyd answered with a laugh. "That'll be the day. You've come in every Sunday since the Jurassic era."

Alex turned his head slightly and Boyd blinked at Alex's look. Suddenly he seemed to register Caitlin's presence, Alex's hand on her arm and her flaming face, all at once. Caitlin watched in an agony of embarrassment as the young officer looked from her to Alex then back again, finally putting the whole thing together.

"Wow." He shook his head and raised his eyebrows. "Sorry, boss. Bad case of foot-in-mouth disease." He bit his lip to keep from smiling and coughed into his fist. "Ah...I guess I...gotta go get a...a report. Right *now*. Bye." He loped up the rest of the staircase then turned for a moment at the top to stare at them, smiling. He stuck his hands in his pockets and walked away, whistling.

Knowing how news traveled in offices, Caitlin was certain that in half an hour, the entire station would know she was having an affair with the Loot. There would probably be a pool on how long it lasted.

Alex didn't seem at all perturbed. Caitlin tried once more to gently pull her arm away from Alex's grip but it didn't work. She tried a little less gently.

"Stop tugging," Alex said irritably, "or you'll hurt yourself."

"Well, then let me go," Caitlin hissed, a big smile pasted on her face for the benefit of the officers passing them on the stairs and staring. She tugged again.

Alex gripped her elbow harder. "No."

Caitlin understood what he was doing. He'd been halfhearted about having the station house cooperate before—and now he was making it plain that she was under his protection and that everyone would cooperate fully.

It was a nice thought but he could have done it more subtly.

There were at the top of the stairs, walking down the corridor. The grapevine had been at work faster than expected and heads were popping up out of cubicles like prairie dogs at a whistle. Alex seemed not to notice.

"What do you want to do this morning?" he asked her as they walked into the squad room.

"Um..." It was hard for Caitlin to think straight with all those curious glances directed her way. She desperately needed someone familiar, friendly.

Curly brown hair, a round lined face... "Kathy!" Caitlin called out, pleased. "Do you have a few minutes to spare?"

"Sure." Kathy Martello smiled and beckoned. "Come on over to my desk."

Alex released his death grip on her elbow. Caitlin scurried over to where Kathy was sitting filling in a form on her computer. An open box of donuts sat next to the monitor, a little trail of sugar and crumbs leading to the keyboard.

Caitlin dumped her book bag onto Kathy's desk and started hauling out her questionnaires. Alex watched her for a moment then turned to walk away.

"Uh...Lieutenant?" Kathy called after him.

Alex turned back. "Yeah?"

Kathy shifted her weight in the chair and loosened her shoulders, the way wrestlers do before going a round. "Look, Lieutenant, I was busy all weekend and I just couldn't get around to that report on the Barton shooting. But I'll have it on your desk by early afternoon, promise." Kathy visibly braced herself.

Alex raised his eyebrows and one corner of his mouth lifted. "Okay, Sergeant. Just make sure I have it by three."

Kathy's mouth opened then closed with a snap. "Yes sir," she said, stunned. "I...I'll be sure to do that."

Caitlin and Kathy watched Alex's departure. Kathy let out her breath in a little huff of surprise and turned to Caitlin.

"What just happened? He didn't chew me out, not even a little! Usually, you're late with a report and he reams you a new one. Hey, wait." Kathy frowned suspiciously, eyes narrowed. "Was that the Loot just now or do they have a pod in the basement with Alex's name on it? Because that wasn't like him *at all*. Believe me, when he says he wants a report, he wants it yesterday, so that just *can't* have been him saying I have until three o'clock to hand it in. And not only that..." She looked at Caitlin, puzzled. "What was Alex doing with his *mouth*?"

Caitlin sighed. "As someone who has spent the past ten years studying human behavior, Kathy, I think I can safely say that the lieutenant was smiling."

"Smiling?" Kathy looked from Caitlin to Alex's back as he disappeared into his office and then back at Caitlin. She blinked. "*The Loot*?"

"My word as an expert."

Kathy mulled that one over. "Listen, hon." She put her hand on Caitlin's arm and leaned in close. Caitlin could smell bad coffee and the donut she'd just eaten. "Whatever it is you're doing to him — don't stop."

* * * * *

Midmorning, while Alex was trying to catch up with paperwork on the computer, Ben Cade stuck his head in Alex's office. Ben leaned his shoulder against the doorjamb.

"Hey, guess what?"

Alex abandoned his mouse and stretched his arms above his head. He hated writing assessment reports and they seemed to multiply like rabbits. Maybe he should have Caitlin study how many man hours were lost to this bullshit paper chase. Then he could go to the brass and have it cut down in the name of efficient use of resources.

"Dunno, but I'm sure you'll tell me in the next ten seconds."

Ben sauntered into the room and settled comfortably in the chair in front of Alex's desk "Okay, man. You're really going to like this one. Take a guess who was sighted this weekend?"

Oh God, riddle time. Still, it beat writing up the monthly account of ammunition use, which was next. "Elvis. Back from the dead."

"Nope." Ben looked sad as he shook his head. "But Jesus, wouldn't *that* be fabulous? Guess again."

"Okay." Alex tilted his head to one side. "Judge Crater."

"Noooo." Ben was enjoying himself. "Try again."

"Jimmy Hoffa."

Ben grinned and shook his head. "Nah, he's sleeping with the fishes. Come on, you can do better than that."

"I give up." Alex shrugged. "Who?"

"Ratso Colby." Ben looked smug and tilted his chair back. "He didn't skip town after all. Guess where he was seen?"

"Riverhead."

"Well, *hell.*" The front legs of Ben's chair hit the floor with a thud. "Why don't you just tell us you're psychic so we can save ourselves the trouble?" he asked in disgust. "How'd you guess? Riverhead is the last place Ratso shoulda been caught in. Guy knows he only escaped by an act of God and thanks to his skinny ass. He shoulda skipped town days ago. How'd ya know he's still around?"

"I saw him myself," Alex said, regretting it even as he said it. "Yesterday morning."

"Oh yeah?" Ben sat up in interest. "You *saw* him?"

"Mmm-hmm." Alex kept his face expressionless.

"I swung by yesterday and you weren't here. Threw me for a loop. Since when are you not here on a Sunday? Wondered where you were. So now I know! No wonder you weren't here, you were making the collar. Good work!" Ben grinned. "So when are we gonna put the fucker in the box? Or is he there already?"

Alex hesitated a moment. This wasn't going to be easy and it wasn't going to be fun. He let out his breath on a huff. "He's... Ratso's not in custody."

A Fine Specimen

"Yes he is." Ben frowned. "You said so yourself. You said you saw him. Yesterday. That's what you said, just now."

"Saw him. I didn't say I caught him."

"Well," Ben began, confused. "If you saw him, why didn't you collar him? That runt can't outrun you."

Alex mumbled something and stood up. Ben was like a terrier when he had something between his teeth. He never let go. It was a good trait for a cop to have, except for right now. "Don't you have some recruits to see to, Ben?"

"No," Ben said. "Recruit day is tomorrow and you know it. Sit down, Alex. You need to tell me how come you let Ratso Colby slip through your fingers. An hour with the guy and it's done — we can issue a warrant for Lopez. You've been gunning for Lopez for two years now. So what's the deal? Why the fuck did you let Colby go?"

Alex leaned back in his chair, trying not to grit his teeth. "I...wasn't alone on Sunday."

"You were on *patrol*?" Ben asked, confused. "Why?"

"I wasn't on patrol. I was...with someone." Alex scowled at Ben, willing him into giving it up. But Ben's genetic makeup included pit bull DNA. He had never given up on anything in the fifteen years Alex had known him.

"I still don't get it," Ben complained, drawing bushy, gray-red eyebrows together. "We've been after Ratso for, like, forever. You chewed my ass out for letting him slip through a window just a coupla days ago! Then you spot him and you let him go just because you were with...someone..."

Ben's voice dropped away. Alex could actually *see* him thinking. It was like watching ball bearings roll around in an empty space. Ben's eyes widened and a broad, wicked grin spread slowly across his face. "Wait a minute. Could that someone you were with by any chance be," he held his hand a little over five feet above the ground, "'bout yay high, big blue ones, blonde hair, very pretty?"

153

"That's none of your business," Alex said, jaws clenched. "What I do on an off-duty Sunday is none of your concern."

"Nope. Sure isn't." Ben's blue eyes danced with devilry. "But that don't mean it's not interesting just the same." He slapped his knee in delight. "Hot *damn*! I was wondering when you'd take the fall. Had to happen sometime. Even to big, bad Alex Cruz! I want to be invited to the wedding. No, wait—I want to be best man! Fuck, after all the crap I've put up with over the years I deserve to be best man. And I want at least one home-cooked meal a month. I want that in writing. Been eating junk food since the last wife left."

Alex shuddered, panic rising in his throat. "Whoa, now, wait just a minute here. Not that it's any business of yours, but it's not like that. It's *nothing* like that. It's just...we're just...seeing each other. Not that it's any business of yours," he repeated, feeling like a broken record.

"Sure," Ben said equably as he stood up. "I hear you. I'm outta here. Gotta go get measured for the tux."

* * * * *

Meanwhile, Caitlin and Kathy were bonding over truly disgusting station house coffee.

"God, this stuff is terrible," Caitlin grimaced. It was like drinking essence of burnt rubber and gym socks. "Do they brew it like that on purpose?"

"Well, that's one theory." Kathy blew on her cup and eyed Caitlin with amusement. "The female officers used to think it was a male conspiracy. To see whether we could stand the coffee or not. We drank gallons of it in the beginning just to show that we were man enough to stomach it and ended up with ulcers. But it wasn't a test of our manhood, it was just that the pot is never washed out." She shrugged. "And we're not the maids so it *still* doesn't get washed out, and that's why it tastes like week-old crap."

A Fine Specimen

Caitlin was pleased to note that the female officers hadn't been pressed into dishwashing service. Or had refused to be. "Did you encounter any gender prejudice when you started as a police officer?" she asked curiously. "Did you have any problems because you were a woman?"

Kathy thought about it. "Not really. All my problems were related to the nature of the job. Being a cop is a hard job for anyone and getting through the academy isn't easy. The physical requirements are really tough. However, the instructors treated the women exactly the same as they treated the men — like shit."

Caitlin studied Kathy carefully. Kathy looked like every other good cop Caitlin had ever met. She looked smart and tough and competent. As if nothing could ever disturb her or throw her, as if she were in complete control of herself and the world. Caitlin envied Kathy her air of control. She couldn't even control her own hair.

By the time the day ended, Caitlin would be a mess. Her hair would be curling wildly around her face, her brand-new outfit would look rumpled and ten years old, her new shoes would be scuffed and any makeup she might have put on that morning would have long since worn off. She would have ink stains only on her hands if she was lucky, on her new shirt if she was unlucky.

By the end of the day, Caitlin knew, Kathy would still look spic-and-span, leather shoes and leather gun belt polished, shoulders straight, not a hair out of place.

"Command presence" it was called in the Police Academy, and it was taught on day one. Officers were taught to control situations with their presence and behavior, and not with force.

The human response to aggression wasn't quite as ritualized as that of, say, highland gorillas. Caitlin doubted whether a show of teeth, loud grunts and slapping the ground would frighten off a delinquent, but many potentially dangerous situations were defused by a police officer's calm voice and air of command.

Though command presence was taught as a conscious technique, Caitlin was certain that most police officers were born with it and it was simply refined during training and on the job. Certainly Alex had been born with it. She was sure he had made an impressive criminal too.

"Did you always want to become a police officer?" Caitlin asked. It was a question she'd asked many of the officers. Most of them said yes.

"Not really." Kathy drained the last of her coffee and made a face as she put her cup down. "God, if that doesn't put hair on our chests, nothing will. No, I wanted to become a nurse. I had actually enrolled in nursing school when an old high school friend of mine invited me out on patrol with her. That night, there were two stabbings, a jewelry store robbery and a murder." Kathy shook her head fondly. "Jesus, who could resist after a night like that? It was the most exciting thing I could think of to do with my life. The next day I applied for the academy. Hey!" Kathy angled her head to see what Caitlin was writing. "Is there going to be a quiz?"

Caitlin laughed and shook her head. "No, and if there were, you'd ace it."

Kathy, like most police officers, was a dominant personality. Strong, confident, needing the rush of challenge and excitement.

At times like this, Caitlin marveled at how the world was put together. She herself was happiest squirreled away in the library reading about dead people. Her favorite challenge was how to organize her footnotes. She'd make a lousy cop.

They spent another hour on a special psychological test Caitlin had devised then Kathy left to go on patrol.

Caitlin went into an empty room and spread her material out. She couldn't wait to start collating her results. And once she was a fellow at the Frederiksson Foundation, she could

A Fine Specimen

send her questionnaire out under the auspices of the Foundation to other police stations throughout the country. There could be a paper and—who knows?—maybe even a book to be gotten out of it. The thought pleased her so much she barely noticed the time passing.

"Your pen is leaking." The deep, familiar voice startled her out of her reverie.

Caitlin looked down and, sure enough, there was a blue splotch on the questionnaire folder. The middle finger of her right hand was ink-stained and there was a faint stain on the front of her brand-new and expensive blouse. She sighed and turned around.

"See?" she said accusingly. "That's my point exactly."

"Yeah?" Alex asked mildly. "What point?"

"*You* wouldn't get ink all over yourself, would you?"

"Well...no."

"They probably taught you how to make inanimate objects obey you at the academy," Caitlin grumbled.

Alex's mouth lifted in a half smile. "No, but they did teach us neatness, which is something your fancy education seems to have neglected. Come on, Caitlin. Put your things away and I'll take you out to lunch."

"It's lunchtime already?" Caitlin asked, startled. She looked at her watch. It was 12:38. Suddenly, she realized she was ravenous.

Several of her textbooks were perched precariously close to the edge of the table and her papers were scattered all over the surface. She couldn't leave this mess behind. Smiling up at Alex, she reached across the table for her books. "Okay. Where are we going?"

"There's a good deli with table service around the corner," Alex said. "Gather your things up and," he neatly sidestepped, avoiding by inches the pile of heavy hardbacks that fell to the floor, "watch those books."

"Oh Alex." Caitlin's eyes widened as she stooped to pick the books up. "I'm so very—"

"Sorry," Alex finished for her. "Uh-huh. I know you're sorry, honey. It's okay. I've learned to be careful and watch my step around you. You're a real dangerous lady."

She sucked in an outraged breath. They were in a building full of armed alpha males and females, trained for violence, and *she* was dangerous? "I am *not* dangerous. You take that back!"

Laughing, he evaded her punch and took her elbow in that special grip of his. The grip that seemed to convey he wanted to prevent her from floating away or running off.

It would be nice if he didn't use that grip in the station house, but complaining was pointless. Alex did what he wanted, when he wanted, how he wanted.

Chapter Nine

※

Caitlin described her new questionnaire to Alex as they walked to the deli. He half-listened, enjoying her ideas, enjoying the sound of her voice even more. It would be a good questionnaire, he knew that much about Caitlin. No doubt it would be the best questionnaire in California, in the country, the best questionnaire in the history of the world.

It's just that it was hard to concentrate on double-blind samplings and the DSM-IV on a day like this. The air was warm and clear, bright with buttery sunlight, and it reminded Alex that he'd been holed up in a windowless room all morning.

Jesus, since when did he mind spending the day in his office? Since when did he go out to lunch as opposed to ordering in and eating at his desk? Since when did he notice the frigging *weather*?

He found himself smiling as he walked into Sam's Deli. The food was so great here. Why didn't he eat here more often? Why did he chow down stale sandwiches at his desk?

The only bad thing about Sam's was that it was a hangout for the dreary drones working at the three banks, two insurance corporations, four internet service providers and three financial services companies in the area — and they were all freaking out about the economy, ruining the vibe of the place. Alex hated business people, but he supposed they were necessary. For something, anyway. Otherwise, why would there be so goddamn many of them?

He steered Caitlin to the line where customers waited for the small bistro tables to be freed. He loved taking her by the elbow. She had the softest skin he'd ever felt. Though she definitely had good muscle tone, her biceps weren't hard and stringy like some slender women. It took an effort to remove his hand.

"I need to ask you a favor, Alex," Caitlin said.

"Sure," he said, craning his neck to see over the heads of two insurance agents in front of them. They were talking about the tanking derivatives market, premiums and the prime rate. Market share and the Nasdaq. Recession and 401(k)s. The subprime market and CDOs. Washington bailouts and the FDIC.

Alex shuddered, glad for the hundred thousandth time that he was a cop, and that his only worry was putting the bad guys away. Market upswings, market downswings, recessions and bubbles, he didn't give a fuck. His salary got deposited into his bank on the first of every month and that was the one and only time he ever thought about money. He owned his own home, he earned more than enough to cover all his needs and one day he'd be getting a good pension. What more could he want?

Money was boring, the hugest yawn he could imagine. Bagging bad guys—now *that* got his rocks off. The thrill of the chase, the intellectual challenge of putting a case together that would hold up in court, the camaraderie of the officers in the cop shop—even when they drove him crazy—it was all he had ever wanted.

And now he was getting laid on a regular basis by a fabulous woman. Life just didn't get any better.

Two couples were getting up from their tables as Alex checked out the blackboard on the wall. The miso soba sounded good. He smiled down at Caitlin, thinking about soup and sex. "What was this favor you wanted?"

"I want to go on patrol," Caitlin said. "It would really help me with my study. Ron Torrance said it was okay with him, but to check with you first."

A Fine Specimen

"Absolutely not." All thoughts of food and sex fled right out of Alex's head. "Out of the question. You're not going on a ride-along."

Caitlin was taken aback at Alex's vehemence then a hurt look came into her eyes. Alex glanced away. He didn't want to see it, though she could send hurt looks his way from now until kingdom come and it wouldn't change his mind. *No way* was Caitlin going out on a ride-along, and that was that.

"Alex...listen. Ron said—"

"Sorry," Alex interrupted, though he was anything but apologetic. "It's against station-house policy. Ah, I think our turn is coming up. Come on, let's get ourselves something to eat." The two tables had been cleared. Alex was glad to see that they were far apart from the guys in front. He didn't want to sit next to any suits and have to listen to them gab about how much money they were losing in the lousy economic environment.

He placed a hand to the small of Caitlin's back and felt her jerk away from his touch. She was offended. Well, there was nothing he could do about it. She wasn't going on a ride-along. He knew only too well how a placid, routine patrol could turn violent in seconds.

Caitlin hurried ahead of him, back stiff. She was angry at him and he didn't know how to make amends, other than to give in. Which was out of the question. There wasn't any doubt in his mind at all about that. Better Caitlin in a snit than Caitlin caught in a crossfire.

She sat down before he could pull her chair out and waited patiently while he took his seat across from her.

"It is *not* against station-house rules." Caitlin leaned forward, her expression impersonal and serious. Alex understood that she was trying hard to be objective and not to presume upon their personal relationship. "I distinctly remember Peter Cannell doing a series on the Baylorville PD for the *Chronicle* and he went on patrol with the officers. Often. He wrote some very effective stories about it."

It was true, dammit. Peter Cannell had become a familiar and welcome figure around the station house and his sympathetic articles had even won him a few minor awards. He still stopped by occasionally to renew the friendships he'd made at the station. Alex always welcomed a chance to buy him a beer and swap war stories.

But Peter Cannell was a tough, wily Irishman, totally unfazed by the violence and degradation he'd observed throughout his investigation. He wasn't Caitlin.

"Policy's changed," Alex said curtly. "Someone got hurt and sued the PD."

Caitlin pulled in a deep, calming breath. "You can be protective of me, Alex," she began quietly, "but you *can't* treat me like a fool. I know perfectly well that I would have to sign a waiver before riding along. Everyone does. So no one has sued your department. And of course I would never sue your department if something bad happened."

If something bad happened. Alex's heart jumped in his chest at the idea. At the idea of Caitlin hurt, injured or—God!—dead.

"All right," Alex said angrily. "I made that up about the lawsuit but someone *did* get injured a few months back. A friend of Kathy Martello's, as a matter of fact. Ask Kathy about it if you don't believe me. Her friend wanted to ride with her and the patrol car responded to an armed robbery call. There was a shootout. Kathy's friend took a bullet."

It had been a ricochet, the bullet having spent most of its force before creasing the woman's arm. Basically it had been a flesh wound, requiring just a few stitches, but Alex wasn't about to tell Caitlin that. He wanted her to think of the risks, he wanted her scared and, above all, he wanted her away from any possible danger.

A Fine Specimen

There was another kind of danger now, in Caitlin's face. She wasn't pouting. He'd somehow known she wouldn't pout. For all her girlish looks, he knew Caitlin well enough to know that she was at heart a mature woman who was serious about her profession. No, it wasn't a pout—it was something more serious than that. She looked...disappointed.

In him.

"Alex." Her voice and expression were cool. "I won't insult you by threatening to pull rank on you and calling Ray Avery. I will, however, remind you that this is pure discrimination. Either your department has a ride-along policy or it doesn't. As far as I know, it does. And that means that everyone—everyone except me, it seems—has a chance to ride in a patrol car. I find that unfair and discriminatory."

"Can I take your orders? My name's Sergio and I'm your server today." A tall man with dark hair pulled back in a ponytail slid two menus written on a sheet of butcher paper in front of them. "Today's specials are up on the blackboard."

Alex turned gratefully at the distraction. What happened to his lighthearted lunch with a woman he was massively attracted to? He felt aggrieved. *I don't get enough shit back in the office?* he thought. This whole situation was going south, fast.

Caitlin was studying the menu as if it were the key to passing an exam. She didn't look up once at him. Alex's jaw muscles bunched as he slid the sheet of butcher paper away. He looked up at their server. "I'll have whatever she's having."

"Don't be silly, Alex," Caitlin said coolly. "Order what you want."

"No. No, I'm fine with whatever you're having." She was trying to make him feel like a chauvinist pig, a control freak. He wasn't. He'd give her control over every aspect of his life, if she wanted. She could choose his diet, his wardrobe, his furnishings. She could choose every film they saw for the rest of time. Just not this. He didn't want her hurt in any way. He didn't want her even near a place where she could potentially be hurt. He didn't want her near a place where someone could *think* about hurting her.

"They have burritos. You like burritos." Still not looking at him. Damn it! Her face was as smooth and expressionless as a doll's.

"No, I'll have what you're having," he repeated stubbornly.

"All right." Calm, collected, Caitlin tilted her face up to the server. "We'll be having the cream of broccoli soup. And the steamed broccoli salad with blue cheese dressing." She smiled faintly.

Alex hated broccoli. And Caitlin knew it.

"And to drink?" Sergio asked, pen hovering over his pad.

"Two glasses of celery juice, please," Caitlin said with relish. She was enjoying this, getting her revenge. Alex barely suppressed his shudder. Celery juice. Gah. Whoever heard of drinking celery juice?

Caitlin didn't say a word until the food arrived. Alex didn't open his mouth, either. That way he couldn't stick his foot in it.

For the first time, Alex realized how much he counted on Caitlin smiling every time she saw him. How much he liked it when she hung on his every word. How important it was that there be softness in her gaze when she looked at him.

No smile, no softness now. Her face was closed to him. For the first time, she was cool and reserved. It was as if a chasm had opened up between them.

The food arrived and Alex was reminded once again why he hated broccoli. It was so goddamn sour and...and *green*. He managed to choke down half the soup before he pushed the bowl away and attacked the salad, trying surreptitiously to eat the dressing lettuce and leave the other vegetables.

Caitlin was steadily making her way through lunch in silence. Alex had a bitter taste in his mouth and it had nothing to do with broccoli. He took a big swig of the celery juice and nearly gagged. How on earth could anyone be expected to drink something green that wasn't dyed beer on St. Patrick's Day?

"Something wrong?" Caitlin asked sweetly.

Alex bit his lip. And then—maybe it was all those vitamins in the fucking glop he'd chugged—inspiration struck.

He heaved a huge sigh, as if in defeat. "Okay, honey, you win."

"It's not a contest, Alex." Caitlin's voice was low. She patted her mouth with the napkin. "I understand your reasons for not wanting me to ride in a patrol car. I don't agree with them, but I understand them. You are, of course, free to do as you see fit. And, of course, I am free to try to do whatever is necessary to complete my study."

"Like I said, you win." Alex held up his hand. "Okay, okay, it isn't a contest. It isn't a test of wills." *Like hell it isn't.* "So listen, how about this? Pederson and Martinez are going out on a special mission this afternoon. How about if you tagged along with them?"

It was worth it to see that smooth, impersonal expression disappear and her face light up. "Oh Alex. That sounds wonderful!"

Caitlin got up in a rush and threw her arms around him—tipping the rest of the green crap in the glass onto his pants. *Better on my pants than down my gullet,* Alex thought philosophically.

"Sorry, Alex," Caitlin said automatically, mopping up the mess with the little napkins she tore out of the holder. Her smile could have lit the deli. "Let's get going. I can't wait to go out on the special mission. I knew you weren't as pigheaded as everyone says you are. I just *knew* it!" She was hopping with excitement.

"Yeah, yeah," Alex said wryly, taking the napkins out of her hands. She was making the mess on his pants worse. "Thanks. I think. Just don't let word get around. My reputation as a badass comes in handy and I don't want to spoil it." He took her elbow. "But you owe me, Caitlin. I want a really special dinner since you made me eat this crap."

* * * * *

That evening, they had grilled chicken breasts, steamed green beans with sesame seeds, garlic bread and lemon mousse for dessert. It was delicious and Alex ate every bite.

"You thought you were so smart," Caitlin said, watching Alex as he loaded the dishes into the dishwasher. She lowered her voice in a very bad imitation of his bass growl. "'Pederson and Martinez are going out on a special mission'. Special mission, my foot. A special mission to give a talk at a middle school. When Pederson and Martinez told me where they were going, I could have strangled you with my bare hands! But then I started listening to what they were saying to the kids and it was really interesting, you know? And the question and answer session was fascinating. What the kids said fits right in with Huntington's theories."

"That right?" Alex didn't have a clue who Huntington was, but if this Huntington kept Caitlin happy, he was Alex's newest favorite author.

Happy and replete, Alex wiped the counters and watched the sky over his garden turn flamingo pink. He switched the dishwasher on and turned around to look with pleasure at Caitlin sitting at his kitchen table.

The kitchen was filled with the glowing light of sunset and Caitlin seemed to glow in the light as well. In the mornings, she managed to beat her hair into a semblance of submission, but by evening she gave up the attempt and let it curl wildly around her head like rays around the sun. She'd changed into a tee shirt and shorts and was barefoot. She looked about twelve as she rambled on about theories of community policing. As always, she made a lot of sense— when what she was saying could penetrate through Alex's fog of lust.

Jesus, if he could just keep his head out of his pants and listen to her more, it would be like getting himself another master's.

It was hard keeping his hands off her. The sex they'd had in the past couple of days should have slowed him down some, but he stayed in a constant state of semi-arousal around her. He was aware of her, always, as if his skin had become this sort of receiving station for whatever it was she emitted.

He and Caitlin had slipped into an easy domestic routine. Caitlin set the table and cooked, and he cleared the table, loaded the dishwasher and cleaned up.

If there was going to be any order in his kitchen at all, he was the one who was going to have to create it. Caitlin was a messy cook, though a fabulous one. Cleaning up after her was a small price to pay for the delicious meal he'd just eaten.

She was talking earnestly, something about community relations as understood by Horace Westin who said something about community policing, which was different from what whoosis in England postulated. Alex listened with half an ear, too delighted at the picture she made to take in much of what she was saying.

God, she floated his boat. During the day, he managed to keep his mind off his cock by immersing himself in the details of the hunt for Lopez and he knew she worked hard to stay out of his way. He was glad. She tried to stay out of his way as a professional courtesy, but he avoided *her* because just watching her breathe was enough to give him a hard-on. Like he didn't have enough problems at work. But at home, well...

Like right now. She wasn't wearing a bra. The red tee shirt she wore was ancient, faded to a dull pink and baggy. It had been washed so many times it was also very soft and outlined her gorgeous breasts lovingly. He could even see the tiny mole on her right breast through the soft material. Her breasts were perfect. He just loved them. Loved touching them, nuzzling against them. Soft yet firm, slightly large for her narrow rib cage and all hers.

He resolved never, ever to go to bed with a woman with plastic sacs of silicone under her skin. Ever again.

Actually, it was getting harder and harder to imagine any other woman pleasing him as much as Caitlin. Well, he didn't have to imagine it. She was right here, and welcomed his every touch.

"Don't you think?" she asked, when she came to the end of her point, whatever it was. She looked up anxiously at him out of enormous blue eyes.

"Absolutely," Alex said firmly. "Couldn't agree more."

"I'm so glad you feel that way," she said with relief. "Not everyone does, you know. Why, Willard Bates argued that— What are you doing?"

Alex cupped her elbow and urged her to her feet. "There's a fantastic sunset. Let's go watch it." He took the bottle of unfinished white wine, grabbed two clean stemmed glasses from the cupboard and opened the door into his garden. He breathed in deeply. The air was fragrant with evening dew and pine from the big pine tree in his neighbor's yard.

"Come here." Alex sat down on the top step and patted the place next to him.

"This is nice," Caitlin said as she sank gracefully down next to him.

"Mmm, very." Alex poured them both a glass of wine and set the empty bottle down. His garden faced west and the sky was spectacular. Light cirrus clouds floated lazily across his neighbor's treetops, their underbellies painted a bright pink slowly fading into purple. A deep sense of peace seeped into his soul.

When was the last time he'd watched the sun set over his garden? He'd bought the damn place because it had a garden and he never used it. As a kid growing up in a rented, broken-down, filthy hovel of an apartment, he'd dreamed of a house, a proper one with a garden and maybe even a dog. And here he'd done it, paid his house off even, and though there was no question of having a dog, he couldn't even remember the last time he'd been in his garden.

He'd been pulling double shifts for so long—what they called eight-to-eights down at the cop shop—he'd come to think of a twelve- or fourteen-hour day as normal. And yet they'd been warned against overdoing it at the academy, and even Ray had chewed his ass out over and over again.

"You're going to burn out, boy," Ray had growled, his bushy gray eyebrows drawn together in a frown. "You'll crash and burn and for what? The bad guys will always be there. They're forever. Working yourself into the ground won't change anything."

Ray was right, Alex suddenly realized. He'd started coming home later and later simply because there was nothing for him to come home *to* and it was easier to stay at work than face the emptiness here. But the last hours of his day weren't productive and he always came home beat. Today, he'd worked efficiently all day, quit at five and he felt great.

And here he was, watching a spectacular sunset with a spectacular woman. He sipped his wine. Things were definitely looking up.

"You know what?" Caitlin asked.

Alex made a "hmmm?" sound in his throat, too lazy to even form words. This was such a perfect moment. The last rays of the sun had turned her skin a delicious pearly pink, like the inside of a seashell. He turned his face to her and pulled in a deep breath. He could smell her soap and shampoo, mixed in with the Chardonnay and pine. If sunset had a smell, this would be it. Caitlin and wine and his neighbor's big pine tree. Especially Caitlin.

It was so perfect. The dramatic, darkening sky edging toward night. The soft sounds of evening. A dog's bark carrying faintly from far away. A cicada revving up, ready to start the nightly concert. The dark, exotic smell of coming night. There was magic in the air.

Alex wasn't a fanciful man, would have scoffed if anyone had said that he was susceptible to romance, but there was definitely something in the air. It was as if the world had taken a huge breath, ready to make a leap into something new, something almost frightening in its intensity.

He was a practical man, not given to fancies—and he hardly recognized himself. But what the evening offered him was too enticing to resist. Alex opened his heart and took it in.

Caitlin waved her hand at the garden. "I think you should plant an herb garden. Herbs are pretty, low upkeep and you can use them for cooking." She slanted him a teasing glance. "Not that you do much cooking."

No, she took care of that, he thought with satisfaction. She wanted an herb garden? Hell, he'd give her an herb garden. Long as she did all the work. It would be fun to watch that cute little ass bending down over the plants. "Okay. What do you want planted?"

"Mm. Well, rosemary, sweet basil, parsley and sage, for starters."

He hummed "Parsley, Sage, Rosemary and Thyme", off-key. "And thyme. Don't forget thyme."

"And cilantro and chervil, and dill and mint."

"Gotcha." What the hell was chervil? No matter. Alex gave in to temptation and brought his mouth to her neck. Each time he touched her, the softness of her skin surprised him all over again. She felt like silk against his mouth. He planted a necklace of soft kisses along her collarbone and when she tilted her head slightly, he took it for the invitation it was. His mouth rose along her neck, feeling her heartbeat speeding up under his lips. He put his glass down behind her, taking hers away as well, and ran his newly freed hand under her tee shirt to cup her breast.

He was right. No bra. Oh God. Just a soft, round breast. He was going to hide her bras so she never wore one at home.

Her breath sped up further as he slowly, gently circled her nipple in exactly the same rhythm as his tongue circling her ear.

He could feel her heart beating fast now against his hand, her lungs expanding as she started panting.

Jesus, he was hard as a rock.

"We need to take this inside," he whispered in her ear. "If we do what I want to do out here, I'll have to arrest us."

"Okay," she whispered, turning to put her arms around his neck.

"Come with me," Alex said, his voice thick. His mouth closed over hers, the kiss deep and hard. He rose, his hand under her elbow, taking her up with him. Two short steps and they were against the kitchen door, Caitlin's hands on his back, under his tee, fingers curled into his skin.

They stumbled inside. Alex closed the kitchen door with his foot and walked her, lips still locked together, into the living room. He hurriedly stripped off his tee shirt, letting it fall to the floor as he scrambled to pull her tee off too.

His hands covered her breasts, firm and smooth. "Don't ever wear a bra again," he murmured against her mouth.

"Never," she whispered. "Ever again, I promise."

"Burn them. Give them to charity," he said between nibbles of her mouth.

"Okay."

Her shorts, his pants...somehow he got through the barriers between his flesh and hers. Their mouths never parted. It was impossible to leave her mouth, so soft and welcoming.

But he had to leave her mouth because he wanted to kiss something else.

It was amazing to him how little foreplay they indulged in. It was like he was always in this race, eager to just get inside her and start moving. And yet he knew better. He'd been fucking since he was twelve, when he'd nailed Maddie Harrison standing against her back door. And he'd been developing his technique since his early twenties. He knew what women liked. God knows they stated it clearly enough. Some of his lovers gave directions like backseat drivers. *To the left, now the right, a little lower, there you go...*

Alex was a cop. He was a listener and an observer. If you'd asked him, he'd have said he knew exactly what women wanted, how they wanted it and where.

So why did he always behave like a rabid wolverine with Caitlin, of all women? Caitlin, who still had that aura of innocence about her, who was actually smaller than most women? All his self-control just melted around her. In the sack, his basic technique was to jump her bones and stay inside her as long as he could, like a horny eighteen-year-old. Gah.

It was a very, very lucky thing that Caitlin desired him. No matter how little foreplay there was, she was always ready, always welcoming, tight little cunt warm and wet, just for him.

Oh yeah.

He batted down the heated images in his head before they got out of control. Before *he* got out of control. He needed to take it slow this time, if only to prove to himself that he could.

She sat on his couch, naked, soft, looking up at him with a smile on her face. Her eyes traveled down his body and blinked when they got to his cock. Yeah, well, he knew what she was seeing, he didn't have to look down. He was hard as a club.

Her breathing sped up as she looked at him and damned if he didn't swell a little, just from her eyes on him.

A Fine Specimen

Oh Jesus, no — his spine was tingling and his balls start to rise. This wasn't good. He was going to blow his wad the instant he got inside her. He'd done that too many times.

Alex recited a few sections of the Traffic Code in his head and dropped to his knees, taking his dick out of sight range.

"Oh." Caroline's startled gaze met his. She was surprised he wasn't jumping her bones. This wasn't good. He'd trained her to think that his erection meant instant fuck. Well, how was she supposed to know otherwise? It had been his MO up until now.

That had to stop.

He put his hands on her knees and gently pressed her legs apart. Ah. She opened up like a little flower, pink, puffy girl flesh, already shiny and slick and he hadn't even touched her there yet.

The color of her little cunt was delightful — a deep rose matching the color of her nipples and mouth. Everywhere else she was as pale as moonlight but here, oh yeah. Here she was the color of passion.

Unable to resist, Alex bent and put his mouth on her, feeling her jolt with surprise. He drew in a deep breath, nearly dizzy with delight. Caitlin always smelled good but *here*, her scent was wild, concentrated. When they had sex, their smell had a sweet undertone — and it was all her.

He tasted her, an experimental lick, holding her down easily as she nearly came up off the couch. God he loved how incredibly responsive she was. So prim and proper and scholarly outside the bedroom — or in this case the living room — but wild in his arms. She tasted wonderful, like sunshine and honey. He didn't usually like going down all that much — it was awkward and uncomfortable — but right now he was as excited as she was.

He kissed her cunt exactly as he'd kiss her mouth, tongue deep inside her, swirling and licking like she was the world's most delightful lollipop. He was enjoying it so much he relaxed into it, completely forgetting about himself and his hard-on. He just dove into her, listening to the small moans she was making, feeling her thighs tremble.

He licked and sucked to his heart's content, stealing glances up at her face now and again. She was bright pink, the blush extending down to her beautiful breasts. He sucked gently at her clitoris and felt her tremble sharply, her hands suddenly in his hair, pulling, panting wildly. He sucked just a little harder and she gasped, her cunt contracting sharply. In a second she'd be coming...

Alex quickly pushed her onto her back, opened her with his fingers and pushed his dick inside at the *exact* second she started coming in sharp little contractions, groaning in his ear.

The plan had been to stay still until the climax ended then start moving, but the plan was blown out of the water by the feel of those tiny muscles milking him, her arms and legs holding him tightly, long neck thrown back...

Without moving a muscle, just by being inside her, he went off like a rocket, pushing hard against the arm of the couch with his toes so he could get inside her as far as he could possibly go, feeling every inch of her climax against the super-sensitized skin of his cock. His climax was so hard it was entirely possible he spurted every ounce of liquid in his body into her, because when it was over he collapsed on her, utterly spineless.

They lay there until the light had drained from the sky, the only illumination in the room coming from the streetlight outside. Caitlin's wriggling shook him out of his near coma.

"Alex." Her voice was breathless. She pushed at his shoulders without budging him an inch. "Get up."

Get up? Why? Things were absolutely perfect exactly as they were. He loved lying on her soft, slender body, lips against the skin of her throat. It was his favorite position in all the world.

A Fine Specimen

"Mm." He was playing possum, but he genuinely didn't want to get up. She wriggled some more and his dick started growing again inside her. She wanted more? Oh yeah. Just give him a minute here...

"Alex." Her voice was sharper now. "Get up, please. I need to shower. I need to...to go to the bathroom."

Ah Christ.

He placed both palms flat on the couch seat and lifted himself up. She scooted out from under him and he mourned the cool air that hit his dick. It had been way more comfortable, snug and warm inside her.

She disappeared into the downstairs bathroom and he didn't stir for a long, long time, thinking nothing, just feeling.

He looked at the heap of their clothes, his on top of hers. She was going to come out naked from the shower. His dick hardened happily at the thought.

Waiting for her, he looked around his living room. Caitlin's presence in his house had changed it almost beyond recognition.

She had cut some branches from the shrubs in his backyard and put them in vases. The effect was odd but dramatic. Her laptop had taken up residence on his desk. Her books were scattered over the coffee table and her papers were piled on every available surface—the seat of a chair, on top of the entertainment center, under the phone.

Yesterday's cotton sweater was still hanging over a dining room chair and one of her slippers peeped out from under the couch. God only knew where its mate might be. Knowing Caitlin, it could be anywhere from the bathroom to the bedroom, or even in a corner of the kitchen.

He hardly recognized the place as his own. His house usually looked as if no one lived there. Now the house looked messy—but lived in. The house looked like a home.

Caitlin was, hands down, the most low-maintenance woman he'd ever met. She didn't require constant attention or flattery or enormous amounts of money. He hadn't once heard a version of "how do I look in this?" The eternal question that was such a freaking minefield.

Alex'd had a couple of affairs that had spilled over into temporary living-together arrangements and he still shuddered at the memories. He'd felt hunted in his own home, required to constantly dance to the women's moods and thoughts and whims. Making an effort and always coming up short.

Caitlin was the opposite. Give her a table, a chair, her laptop and a book and she immediately sank into a study coma. Went a million miles away. If anything, Alex sometimes found himself making noises or even once harrumphing, simply to get her attention. He felt like a high-schooler doing handstands to impress the pretty new girl in school.

She came out of the shower, smelling of his soap and Caitlin.

"Tomorrow night," Alex said, picking up her tee shirt, slipping it over her upraised arms, "let's see if we can make it to the bedroom."

"Sounds enticing." Caitlin lifted the heavy mass of her hair and let it spill outside the shirt. "But I'll be busy tomorrow night. Or rather, tomorrow afternoon. I don't know how long I'll be, so maybe it would be better not to plan on dinner."

His hands stilled but he kept his voice casual. "You'll be busy?"

"Yeah." Caitlin's voice was muffled as she bent down to find her shorts and flats. "I have an appointment with a real estate agent at three. I'll start house-hunting tomorrow. I'm going to have to hurry because I'll be starting my new position next week and I'd like to have found a place to stay and be settled in." Caitlin shifted some papers on the coffee table, a wry smile on her face. "The sooner I get out of here, the sooner you can go back to having a neat house. I'm pretty hopeless at keeping things in order."

"I'll come with you." Alex stood to pull on his jeans.

"You'll what?" Startled, she let the papers drop again.

Alex patiently picked them up. "I'll come with you. I know this town inside out. I can help you find something suitable."

"That's nice of you, Alex," Caitlin said, looking up at him uncertainly. "But really, there's no need for you to go out of your way. You'll be busy. You have this pesky thing known as a job."

"I can take some personal time off. No problem. I'll help you look for a new apartment," he said.

Over my dead body, he thought.

Chapter Ten

ಬ

"Well, you're no help," Caitlin grumbled three days later as she and Alex walked into Alex's house.

She'd received official notification of the fellowship from the Frederiksson Foundation and was due to start the following Monday. The good news was that the Foundation was going to pay her an extra ten thousand as a housing allowance — and the bad news was that she didn't have a house to rent yet. After three exhausting days of house-hunting, she was no nearer to her goal that she'd been at the beginning.

It was after eight and she was tired and dispirited. She dumped her purse and a bag of groceries on the kitchen counter.

"How can you say that?" Alex asked reasonably. He ferried in the rest of the groceries from the car and started putting them away. "I saved you from making some huge mistakes. Remember that split level in the boondocks? I swear you could hear the coyotes howling. And what about that apartment over on Southside? You practically needed a passport to get there."

"Well, okay," Caitlin conceded. "A few of the properties were a little out of the way, that's true. But come on, Alex, Baylorville isn't L.A. Everything's reasonably close to everything else. And anyway, all the apartments were close to bus stops and I intend to buy myself a car soon anyway. What about that last apartment? That was smack in the center of town."

"That last apartment we saw had termites, I'm sure of it. I could hear them crunching. Speaking of crunching, what's for dinner?" Alex asked. When she glared at him, he shrugged and started setting the table.

Caitlin planted her hands on her hips. "Alex, the building was made of brick and steel! How could it have termites?"

"Insidious little creatures," Alex agreed. He folded the napkins and brushed his hands. "Probably mutants. Hey, didn't we have some beer around here somewhere?"

"I put a six-pack in the fridge behind the lettuce. Stop changing the subject, Alex. Do you realize that we've run through three real estate agents in three days? I start at the Frederiksson Foundation on *Monday*. I'm never going to find an apartment at this rate."

"We'll find something, don't worry," Alex soothed. He brushed her cheek with his lips and pushed her glasses back up to the bridge of her nose.

She rolled her eyes. "Not like this. Not if you keep nitpicking. Nothing the agents show us is good enough. The apartment's either too hot or too cold or too expensive or too big or too small."

Alex clucked and shook his head. He reached into the fridge, grunting with satisfaction when he found the six-pack. He cracked one open and took several slugs from the can. "I can't help it if there are so many lousy properties on the market."

"Look, Alex, all I need is a small apartment. I don't need the Taj Mahal. What was the matter with that cute little place on Greenwood?"

"It faced north, honey." Alex took another swallow and shrugged. "Can't have that."

"Alex," Caitlin took a deep breath, "I'm not a *tree*. Moss will not grow on my north side. It was comfortable and convenient and cheap."

"You'll have sky-high heating bills this winter."

Caitlin held her breath for a count of three then let it out slowly. "We're in Southern California. How much heat can I consume?"

"What about el Niño?" Alex frowned, considering. "Or la Niña. Or El Niñito. Whatever. Hey, do we have any peanuts?" he asked, grabbing a second beer and carrying the cans into the living room.

"Here." Caitlin pulled out a drawer next to the sink. She picked up a packet of salted peanuts and tossed it at Alex from the living room door. He caught the bag one-handedly, ripped it open with his teeth and dumped the peanuts into a bowl which he set on the coffee table. "For your information," Caitlin began, "el Niño—"

But Alex was gone. As always when he got home, he ran upstairs and changed into sweats. A few minutes later, he padded back downstairs barefoot and cleared some of Caitlin's papers off the couch to sit down. She walked around the couch so she could see him.

"For your information," she continued, "el Niño was years ago and la Niña's over and el Niñito doesn't exist. And what was so wrong with that apartment off Carson?"

Alex thumbed the remote. "Ah...did you see the color of those walls? Puke brown. Come on, Caitlin, you would have had nightmares with those walls."

"Walls?" Caitlin frowned. The apartment had perfectly normal off-white walls. "There wasn't anything wrong with the color. The color was—" But Alex wasn't listening. He had settled with a heavy sigh into the sofa and the sounds of baseball commentary drifted from the TV.

"What's for dinner?" he asked over the announcer's voice.

Caitlin looked at Alex watching the game, rolled her eyes and gave up. "How about those steaks we bought? And maybe a salad."

"Sounds great." Alex cracked open another beer. "Well done, please. I hate blood."

A Fine Specimen

Caitlin turned on the kitchen radio and started preparing dinner. She marinated the steaks, washed the salad and made the vinaigrette dressing, her heart heavy.

He hadn't once asked her to change her mind. He hadn't asked her to stay. If he hadn't asked by now he wasn't going to. That was simply a fact.

And it made finding a new place even more imperative. She was starting her new position on Monday.

She didn't have great expectations. Her old place in Grant Falls had been a cheap one-roomer, masquerading as a studio apartment. Every single property she'd seen in Baylorville was better than what she had been living in.

She hated not knowing where she was going to live. It was going to be hard enough starting a new position, meeting all her new colleagues at the Foundation. Trying to strike the right note as the new kid on the block who didn't want to make waves but who *did* want to contribute. Hit the ground running. She needed a stable home base. She wanted to have that part of her life settled before facing a new job and a new life.

She was so rattled, not knowing from one day to the next what she was doing.

Of course, Alex was sabotaging her attempts at finding a place to stay, which would have been fun to watch if the subtext were "don't go away, stay with me". But it wasn't. He hadn't once offered to simply extend their live-in arrangement. He never gave any clue at all that her future plans had anything to do with him.

Every time he passed up an opportunity to tell her he'd like her to stay, her heart cracked a little. What was the point of getting straight A's since she was five, of getting a PhD, of being really book-smart if she was going to be so dumb about her private life? She'd been telling herself from day one that Alex was going to break her heart and then telling herself right back that she was just along for the sex. Have an affair with a man whose hotness quotient was off the charts, just for the experience, then leave. She'd lectured herself a thousand times not to get emotionally involved, but here she was.

Ha, ha.

The eternal tug of war between head and heart. She was just like so many others in academic life. Book-smart and life-stupid.

She absolutely loved living with Alex. Not just for the sex, though that was...yeah. Whew.

It was hard for her to admit how lonely she'd felt before, but now it was impossible to fool herself. Being with Alex was incredible, the best thing that had ever happened to her. It was as if she'd been color-blind up until now, and the world had suddenly exploded with color.

What a fool she was. In a fit of optimism, she'd even bought packets of herb seeds to plant then, at the last minute, had a return to sanity, quietly flushing the seeds down the toilet before Alex could see them. He'd vaguely mentioned buying some herbs but he hadn't. If she planted them herself it was a big fat statement dug right into his garden that she wanted to stick around.

Everything was like that, bending over backward not to make a statement, doing her best to leave a small footprint. She made sure she used as little room as possible in his closet, kept her few cosmetics in a small bag on the floor of the bathroom, made sure she didn't buy any new books because she'd already added too many to his overflowing shelves.

But you can't try not to cast a shadow forever. She was making herself sick trying not to impose on him, searching his face endlessly for some clue as to what he felt for her, trying to read his body language. Oh, the sexual body language was easy enough to read. No problems there. He wanted her. That was plain to see. But sex alone wasn't enough.

It was so *hard* playing it cool. She found herself wanting to talk about her plans with him, what working at the

A Fine Specimen

Frederiksson would be like, sounding him out on the Baylorville power structure so she'd be better positioned not to step into holes like a newbie. But of course, planning her future with his advice presupposed he even cared what her future *was*, which wasn't a given.

And worse...she'd reach out to smooth back a lock of hair that had fallen across his forehead, but then clench her nails into her palms to stop herself. Sex was fine and when they were in bed, she could touch all she wanted. The more the better. Out of bed, there seemed to be some moratorium on shows of affection.

It was madness and a recipe for deep unhappiness. She deserved better.

It was absolutely impossible to know what Alex wanted.

He wanted nothing at all, apparently, because he never talked about it. All his discussions were relentlessly based in the present. He hadn't shown any signs of tiring of her presence in his house, but he never talked about the future in any way. It was as if the future tense had been banished from his vocabulary.

He certainly hadn't asked her to leave. But then again, he hadn't asked her to stay, either.

Caitlin grabbed one of Alex's razor-sharp knives. Using it to cut the lettuce was probably overkill but she had no choice. Alex didn't have plain old salad knives—all he had were pricey samurai blades.

She thought of the dull, cheap department store knives with the faded plastic handles back in her apartment in Grant Falls. Alex wouldn't have stood for dull knives. Like Alex himself, all his equipment was in superb shape.

She should get out of his house before she dropped one of his expensive knives on the floor or cracked one of his imported terracotta pots or tipped over one of his fancy designer floor lamps. She should get out before she ruined something important to him.

Should I stay or should I go now? The song got it exactly right.

The thought of just staying on was so incredibly tempting. Alex wouldn't say no. But Caitlin needed some stability, her things around her, as she faced her first big, important job. Just staying, without Alex inviting her, meant she could be out on her ear in a heartbeat.

And yet, living with him was just so wonderful.

It was easier than she would have expected. Though she'd had two affairs with fellow students, she'd never actually lived with a man before. She hadn't really known what to expect.

A week ago, the thought of sharing quarters with Alex Cruz would have terrified her. She had found him so intimidating, so overwhelming. She could never tell what he was thinking or feeling. He was this huge, sinfully attractive puzzle, which she was certain she couldn't ever possibly solve.

To her surprise though, he never browbeat her. Incredible as it seemed, he dialed down a lot of that I'm-King-of-the-Mountain macho authoritarianism when they got home. The small temporary household they'd created had turned into a participatory democracy instead of a dictatorship.

Alex wasn't aggressive with her, he asked her opinion on things and—miracle of miracles—he picked up after himself. He even picked up after *her*, being much neater than she was. And surprisingly enough for a neat freak, he never complained about her messiness and lack of organization.

The passion that flared up between them still surprised her. She had never thought of herself as a passionate woman, but when Alex touched her, kissed her or even looked at her in a certain way, she melted instantly. They were so big and scary, these feelings she had for Alex. But Alex wasn't a forever kind of guy. She had to remember that, pound it into her stubborn, oh-so-foolish head.

He wasn't looking for a life mate or even a short-term partner. She didn't need for him to tell her that, it was evident in the way he lived. She had never seen anyone as completely self-sufficient as Alex Cruz. He didn't need anyone, for anything at all.

Ben Cade told her that it had been years since he and Alex had gone out carousing. No one called in the evenings. It would have been sad if it weren't for the fact that it was clearly Alex's choice. He could have any kind of company he wanted, whenever he wanted it.

He didn't appear to be a womanizer, which was a relief. But according to station-house scuttlebutt, there hadn't been a woman in his life for a long time, which was odd in a man as attractive as Alex.

It looked like he'd more or less written off having a stable relationship in his life.

In a way, Caitlin could understand him. Just like he never spoke about the future, he rarely mentioned the past. But from her interviews with the cops, she'd pieced together a tragic picture of a neglected, even abused youngster who'd adopted toughness as a shell until it became his defining characteristic. Breaking through that shell was impossible. She was breaking her own heart instead.

She had no idea what Alex's feelings were about their affair. Maybe he didn't have feelings. Maybe he didn't even realize they were *having* an affair. Maybe he hadn't thought about it at all. Maybe he was just enjoying their time together, assuming it would be over when she moved out. Maybe she was presuming too much, staying on. Maybe she should have looked for another hotel right away instead of accepting his invitation, maybe...

A noise behind her made her whirl around.

"Whoa," Alex said, pushing her hand away from the region of his groin. "Take it easy and point that knife somewhere else. I like my private parts right where they are."

Caitlin was always off balance when she was jerked out of her thoughts. And she was always off balance around Alex anyway. He was too close for her to be able to collect her thoughts. "Alex?"

"Right here."

Alex reached past her to turn the radio off. There was a sudden silence in the kitchen and Caitlin realized that he'd turned the TV in the living room off too.

Alex always smelled so good, Caitlin realized as he moved even closer to her. Even at the end of the day, when everyone else smelled of the emotions they'd experienced, Alex still smelled good, as if he could control that too.

Caitlin had read somewhere that males in a fight could smell each other's fear. Alex wouldn't ever smell of fear, he'd smell of himself. And win.

He put his arm around her and looked into her eyes. His gaze was fierce and penetrating. Caitlin couldn't even begin to imagine what he was thinking, except that whatever it was, it was intense. His dark eyes were slightly narrowed and his mouth was drawn into a tight line.

"Alex?" she asked again. "Anything wrong?"

"No," he said and put his mouth on hers.

Caitlin breathed in shakily, her nose next to his cheek. Alex's kisses were always different, taking her completely by surprise each time.

Sometimes he was so passionate she felt seared to her bone marrow. This one was sweet, hot, deep. Sweet enough to drown in, hot enough to ignite her, deep enough so she could never find her way out again.

Alex's mouth moved on hers and Caitlin felt a wave of desire move in her bloodstream.

Alex tasted of beer and himself as he took the kiss ever deeper. He was holding her head in both hands, his fingers burrowed in her hair. He was connected to her only by the kiss, by his mouth on hers, his hands in her hair, and she wanted to be closer to him than that. She arched up against him, drowning in his kiss, moving ever closer, feeling her muscles go lax...

And heard a soft *boing*.

They broke apart and stared at Alex's heavy, needle-sharp knife quivering in the hardwood floor a hair away from his bare foot. A touch to the right and it would have skewered it.

He looked up and smiled into her eyes, a hot, secret smile just for her. He shook his head slowly. "You're a dangerous woman, Caitlin Summers," he said.

Chapter Eleven

ಬಿ

Alex was sweating. Danger on the horizon.

He was trying to keep his cool, but it was hard. It was Saturday and he and Caitlin were looking at their fifth apartment of the day. All the other apartments they'd viewed had been reasonably attractive, reasonably well maintained and reasonably priced.

Shit, the last one had been in a nice neighborhood, in a pretty apartment complex with a pool, spa and gym and wasn't expensive. The real problem was that it was all the way across town from his house. At least an hour's drive away.

It had taken him a sweaty half hour to talk Caitlin out of it. He'd had to become increasingly inventive in finding excuses to reject everything they saw and he could tell that the real estate agent was getting annoyed.

The agent was a tall, tough-looking lady with big hair an improbable shade of red. Her name was Karen Lowden and she and Caitlin had hit it off immediately. By the second house, they were calling each other by their first names and now, by the fifth, you'd think they were lifelong buddies.

At first Karen had addressed both of them, thinking they were looking for an apartment to share. Alex had felt a pang in his chest when Caitlin had made it clear that she would be living alone. After Alex found one problem after another with the apartments they viewed, Karen totally ignored him and spoke only to Caitlin.

Why the fuck was Caitlin so hell-bent on finding herself an apartment? They were doing just fine the way they were. Weren't they? He didn't have any complaints and he hadn't heard any from her.

A Fine Specimen

Why did she want to move out? Was she waiting for him to say something? It wasn't as if he hadn't thought of it, because he had. He had a feeling that if he asked Caitlin to stay, she would.

Or maybe she wouldn't. Who knew? What did he know about these things? Nothing.

He didn't want to find out. And anyway, asking her to stay would somehow formalize the arrangement, which he wasn't sure he wanted to do. He wanted the situation to remain exactly as it was, for as long as possible, because it was just *fine* the way it was.

They could both walk out of the arrangement at any moment though he knew that right now, he'd rather have root canal work on every single tooth in his head than to see Caitlin walk out of his home. She seemed perfectly happy too. They were doing just fine. Why the fuck fix it if it wasn't broken?

Alex wasn't dumb. He knew there was a time limit on their time together. Caitlin was, by any measure or definition, a "good girl". If she lived with a man for any stretch of time, she would start thinking marriage. And she would have every right to.

She had so much to offer. She was kindhearted, gentle and mind-blowingly beautiful without a shred of vanity. She was very smart — probably smarter than he was — and she kept him on his toes. She had a wry sense of humor which was enchanting. She cooked like a dream. She had a fascinating mind and he loved to hear her take on things. Even her messiness was charming.

Alex knew — because everyone made a point of telling him, over and over again — that he'd been easier to get along with at work lately, something everyone attributed to Caitlin's influence on him. And they were right. He was feeling more relaxed than he had in years.

Caitlin Summers would make someone a delightful wife someday.

But not him.

Alex had never thought much about marriage. The few times marriage had flashed across his mind, his reaction was— *no fucking way*. He couldn't see himself as anyone's husband. What could he possibly know about happily ever after? About making a marriage work?

Alex had always made a point of never asking about people's backgrounds, because he wasn't prepared to reciprocate. But Caitlin had volunteered the fact that, though her father had died at a young age, her parents had had a happy marriage. Alex couldn't even begin to imagine a happy marriage. The whole concept was foreign to him.

Happy for a *lifetime* with someone? What the fuck was that about? It was a minor miracle that he'd managed to be happy for a full week with Caitlin. How on earth could anyone manage a fucking lifetime?

His parents' marriage had been made in hell and he'd spent his entire childhood and adolescence watching up close and personal how badly two people could damage each other and everyone around them. No happy families in Riverhead.

His own relationships never lasted more than a month or two at the most, he'd seen to that. The instant the woman got that faraway, I-want-a-ring-and-a-fancy-wedding look in her eye, he cut loose.

It didn't happen often, thank God, because he usually chose his women carefully. They expected nothing but a good—though short—time from him and that was exactly what they got. No more, no less.

Caitlin had somehow blindsided him, sneaking up on him while he wasn't paying attention, and now it was too late. She was under his skin and the thought of losing her gave him a cold feeling in his gut.

Too bad, because right now it looked like she was going to walk.

A Fine Specimen

She was ooh-ing and ah-ing over what the agent called the "crown molding". So what was so fucking great about a little stucco work around the upper walls?

Caitlin had smiled with delight at the Jacuzzi in the pale-rose-and-cream bathroom.

The agent was ecstatic. A trickle of sweat ran down his back and his chest felt too tight.

The apartment was in the center of town, had slightly more room than the average apartment in that price range and was right next to a bus stop. It was in a new building and the previous owner had stated her willingness to leave the brand-new blue-and-white kitchen appliances and a collection of thriving houseplants.

It was perfect.

Alex hated it.

"Say," he said in a conversational tone. "Wasn't a murder committed here a little over a year ago? I'm sure I read this address in the report. It was right in this building. In this apartment, if I'm not mistaken." He gave an exaggerated shudder. "It's enough to give you the willies."

"Alex, please..." Caitlin murmured.

"No, officer—" Karen Lowden began, her strong jaw muscles working.

Alex turned to the red-haired woman and bared his teeth in what could be called a smile. Just.

"That would be 'Lieutenant'," he said, narrowing his eyes.

"*Lieutenant.*" Karen drew a deep breath and lowered her voice. "Lieutenant, there has never, *ever*," her voice was rising again, "been a murder here. I can guarantee it!"

She turned to Caitlin, clearly the reasonable one of the two.

"You can rest assured on that account, Caitlin. This building was constructed in 2005 and the only tenant this apartment has ever had was Helen Montgomery. Mrs. Montgomery was a high school teacher who moved away when she retired to live with her daughter. She moved to Billings, Montana," Karen added, as if that were further proof of the irreproachable pedigree of the previous owner.

"Nice place, Billings," Alex said as he ambled toward the bedroom. Might as well torture himself with the thought of Caitlin sleeping there instead of in *his* bedroom, where she belonged. "Low crime rate. Not like Baylorville. 'Specially in this area of town."

The real estate agent shot Caitlin a can't-you-do-something-about-him look and hurried after Alex in an effort at damage control. She probably felt her commission retreating every time he opened his mouth. Damn straight.

Karen shouldered past Alex and made for the wall closets.

"You see, Caitlin," she determinedly pulled open the louvered doors of the walk-in closet, "there's plenty of storage space. That's really important if you want a neat and uncluttered living area."

The agent ignored Alex's loud snort.

"You see how large the closets are? That's such a plus nowadays when many apartments skimp on that sort of thing."

Alex peered in. "Perfect place for an intruder to hide," he said pleasantly. "Lots of head room."

"If you *please*, Lieutenant." Karen Lowden's voice was a touch above absolute zero. "Now, Caitlin, as I was saying—"

"I'll take it," Caitlin blurted.

"Good!" Karen Lowden said.

"You'll *what?*" Alex asked at the same time.

"When would it be available?" Caitlin asked.

"Look, Caitlin, maybe you want to think it over—"

Karen pretended he wasn't speaking. "Right away. When would you like to move in?"

"Now wait a min—" He tried to keep a calm voice.

"Tomorrow." Caitlin said. "If Sunday will work. I'm starting a new job on Monday and I want to be settled in."

"Tomorrow it is." Karen opened a purse large enough to be an apartment itself and hauled out some papers and a Montblanc pen. "Just sign this lease and the apartment's yours!"

Alex tried to block Caitlin with his body but she was nimble and quick. A minute later the lease was signed.

He didn't have any moves left, short of picking her up and throwing her over his shoulder.

Check and mate.

Alex gave up. "I'll help you move," he said on a sigh.

Chapter Twelve

※

"Are you sure you don't want to think this over for a while?" Alex asked for the tenth time over lunch at a pleasant diner around the corner from her brand-new apartment. "What's the rush?"

Caitlin insisted on paying, saying she wanted to celebrate. It was the first time he'd allowed her to pay for a meal. It was supposed to be a celebration, but it felt more like a wake.

"You wouldn't want to do anything rash. That real estate agent looked like a shark."

"Alex." Caitlin sighed, her head bowed. She looked up again, searching his eyes for...what? Whatever it was she was looking for, it wasn't there. The only thing in his eyes was impatience, because he wasn't getting his way. "I made the right decision on the apartment and Karen isn't a shark. She seemed like a perfectly nice lady. It's a lovely place and right on the bus line for the Foundation. It's in good shape, it's large and it's affordable. I was very lucky."

God, signing the lease contract had been so *hard*. She'd had to stiffen her muscles to hide her shaking hands and had held tears at bay by sheer willpower.

But she was doing the only thing she possibly could. She needed a home base, she needed her books and her things, he wasn't asking her to stay...ergo, she had to find an apartment. No other way around it. If there was one thing twenty-three consecutive years of school had taught her, it was logic.

Logic really didn't have too much to do with her feelings though. Perfectly aware that she was doing the right thing — the *only* thing — it had still been like cauterizing a wound. Painful and necessary.

Who knew what Alex was thinking? He was scarfing down his lasagna, face remote and closed. Not talking.

Well, it was his show all the way. If he wanted her to stay, he had to say so, loud and clear.

Though part of her wanted to weep, another part of her understood.

Alex was a loner and, though it felt as if her heart were being ripped from her chest, she had to respect that. He obviously didn't want her to go—but he just as obviously wasn't willing to ask her to stay.

Which left her where she had somehow always known she'd end up with Alex.

Nowhere.

She pushed her food around on her plate, plastering a serene expression on her face. After a lifetime's silence, Alex cleared his throat and Caitlin looked up.

He forked up the last bite and pushed his plate away. "That was good."

Food. Okay, they were going to talk about the food. She could do that. "Yeah. Mine's delicious." It *was*—a creamy, warm goat cheese salad. Fabulous, except that every bite stuck in her throat.

"Uh-huh." His mouth lifted in a half smile. "If you're a goat. Or a rabbit. Fantastic." He made of habit of ribbing her good-naturedly about her light eating habits, mostly salads and whole grains. "How'd you know about this place? I didn't know about it and I've lived here all my life."

"Karen told me."

His face closed up. Well, that was a conversation stopper. Dropping the K-bomb.

Silence. Complete and utter silence.

Get used to it. Once she moved into her new apartment, there was the possibility that they might see each other a few times. A lunch or two. Dinner, maybe. Maybe even go to bed together, and she'd get dressed and go back home, not knowing when she'd see him again. That was number one hundred forty-six in her Scenarios for Heartbreak.

A clean break was best, the smart thing to do. The only thing to do. So why did it hurt so much?

She finished her salad and sat back, hands in her lap, waiting to see what his next move would be—if there *was* a next move. Maybe this was It. One last meal, clearing out her stuff and she'd never see him again.

She breathed in and out, past the pain of the thought.

Alex cleared his throat. "Caitlin, I, ah, I wanted to ask you if, ah…" He stopped.

She blinked. That was totally unlike Alex's normal speech patterns. He spoke crisply, well and always to the point. She'd never heard him stammer, not once.

Caitlin's heart started pounding. She leaned forward. "Yes, Alex?"

He pulled apart a slice of bread and started rolling the bread into little balls. "I was wondering if you would…"

"Mmm?" she murmured, heart beating triple time. "If I would…what?"

Oh God, maybe he was hurting as much as she was! Maybe the finality of signing the lease woke him up. Maybe the thought of her leaving was worse than the thought of trying to live together on a long-term basis.

Maybe—

She gave herself a little shake. *Listen to what he has to say.*

Alex looked her full in the face then and she saw him struggling with something. He swallowed. "This is hard."

Oh yeah, it would be, wouldn't it? Maybe he'd never asked a woman to live with him. Of course it was hard. She'd make it as easy for him as possible.

"Just ask, Alex," she said softly, hope flaring.

A Fine Specimen

"Okay. Okay." He blew out a breath, sucked another one in. "I...ah...would you..." His jaw muscles were working overtime and he swallowed hard. He looked away for a moment, shook his head sharply then looked back at her. "Would you...would you go shopping with me? I told you before, I really hate shopping. Maybe it won't be so bad with you around. I need some clothes and I'd like your input." He narrowed his eyes at her, as if just now noticing her sitting across the table from him. "Do you have the time? I don't want to interfere with your schedule or anything."

She coughed to loosen her throat. "Yes, I have the time," she answered. "It won't take me long to pack."

Going clothes shopping. Caitlin's heart sank down to her toes. He wanted her to go shopping with him. Actually, she was possibly the worst person on the planet to go clothes shopping with. She didn't know any of the shops in town except the one boutique where she'd bought her few new items—including the do-me dress, and she didn't think spandex or Lurex would suit him.

He knew she didn't have an eye for clothes. He just wanted to spend more time with her. Without, of course, actually coming right out and saying so. The coward.

"Sure, Alex." A clenching of teeth, upturned mouth and a smile was forced out. "And maybe we can go crazy and buy some colors. Dark gray or even," she blinked back tears, "even navy blue."

* * * * *

Dawn was about half an hour away. Caitlin lay on her side, eyes wide open, and watched the day begin outside the window. A faint pale blue glow was lighting up the sky, enough for her to start distinguishing the night sky from the poplars bordering his backyard.

She'd been watching the utter blackness of the window all night, barely blinking, hardly breathing. She hadn't slept at all.

She hadn't even been able to close her eyes. Her body had lost even the notion of sleep. She'd lain awake, staring out the black window, listening to Alex's even breathing. He was utterly still, not moving a muscle. If she hadn't heard him breathing, she would have thought he was dead.

Not having slept at all wasn't a good thing. She had a really busy day ahead of her and she was moving out of Alex's house at the end of it. Getting through today would require every ounce of self-control she had. The last thing she needed was to be groggy from lack of sleep.

If she'd been in her own apartment, she would have gotten up for a glass of milk or to make herself a cup of herbal tea in the hope of falling back asleep. But she hadn't wanted to wake Alex up, so she simply lay on her side all night, staring dry-eyed out the window.

For the first time since she'd moved in, she and Alex had gone to bed without making love. Or, rather, having sex. The term "making love" was a misnomer. A scholar should try to call things by their correct names.

They'd come home, Caitlin had packed her few belongings, buried her nose in her questionnaires—though she'd die before she'd let Alex know she hadn't absorbed one single word—and they'd gone to bed early. Alex had quietly said good night and rolled over. She'd listened to his breathing grow heavy, wishing she could simply follow him into Sandland. Instead she'd watched the sky reach its deepest black, stay dark for a bazillion minutes and was now watching it lighten again.

Sometime during the night, Alex had rolled back over. He was lying on his side, facing her back. She could feel his intense body heat all along her back, head to toe. Any other night, she would have rolled toward him, instinctively reached out to him, touched him. Not now. Even though only inches separated them, those inches were like an endless, unbridgeable gulf.

A Fine Specimen

She no longer had the right to touch him whenever she felt like it. This hadn't been spoken aloud, but then these things weren't communicated in words. She'd had affairs and they'd ended. She knew perfectly well when you lost the right to touch your partner at will.

The thought was painful but real. Alex wasn't hers anymore, in any way. All that intimacy and fun and sensuality — gone, as if it hadn't existed.

God, the whole night had been so painful, a study in suffering. Breaking up with someone had never been this painful before. Sometimes — as with Marvin the Unready — breaking up had actually been a huge relief. But not now. Now she felt as if her heart had been ripped out of her chest, leaving a dull black void.

As a little girl, she'd hated going to the dentist, wishing she could just press a button and fast-forward life to after the dentist appointment. The grown Caitlin wished the same right now, fiercely. Staying here, listening to Alex breathe, separated by only a few inches that might as well have been a continent, was so painful it hurt her chest. How she wished there were a Life Remote Control that could let her fast-forward past this morning. Be on the other side of it without having to go through it.

Getting up, having a silent breakfast, the silent ride into town, trying to smile as she said goodbye...

God, she just hoped she could do all that and keep her dignity.

The sky lightened to pewter, leaves on the trees started to appear. A lark sang somewhere nearby. The sky was cloudless. It was going to be a glorious morning. A really good morning to start the rest of her life. Usually that kind of inner happy talk was enough to lift her mood, but not right now. The rest of her life stretched before her like a bleak, empty, lonely plain.

Caitlin stared out the window. Was it too soon to get up? She couldn't just wander around the house like some lost soul.

She was quick in the morning. Even stretching things out, she'd be washed and dressed and waiting downstairs hours before Alex awoke. The only thing she could do was sit on the couch and wait for him, which on the Fun Scale was about zero.

Maybe she could—

Her thoughts short-circuited when she felt a big hand land on her hip, at the point of her hipbone, warm and heavy.

She stopped breathing.

Slowly, the hand smoothed over her hipbone, long fingers covering her belly. Her stomach muscles clenched, a reaction she couldn't stop to save her life. How embarrassing. At his lightest touch, her body instantly responded, no matter what her head was telling her. She could tell herself to stay still, keep calm, but it was as if a riot had broken out inside her.

The big hand caressed her stomach muscles, moving in a slow circle, round and round. She held her breath, held herself still. As if his hand were some woodland creature and moving would scare it off.

It had been a warm night and the sheet only half covered her. Looking down, she could see his hand on her belly, his beautiful golden skin a shocking contrast to the paleness of her own.

Every sense in her body was concentrated there, where his hand touched her. Warmth swirled, following the movement of his hand. She had to breathe but found it hard. His hand moved lower, rubbing softly, and she bit her lip to keep a moan back.

There was utter silence in the room. She'd noticed that all night. There had been no traffic, no wind, not even dogs barking. And even now, with the morning beginning, they were cocooned in silence.

She was breathing shallowly, finding it hard to suck in enough oxygen, desperate to keep from panting. Alex's hand cupped her, widening her thighs. A hard, hairy thigh slipped

A Fine Specimen

between hers, holding her legs open. A long finger slid along the outside of her sex and she stifled another moan. She was already slippery with arousal. He could feel it. She didn't want him to hear her panting and moaning from his light touch.

Alex knew he turned her on. How *much* he turned her on was something she wanted to keep as her own secret, particularly now, at the end of the affair. Over the past few days, Caitlin's body had turned into a sex-response machine that only switched on at Alex's touch.

Her eyelids fluttered as his fingers began a slow exploration of her labia, lingering over her clitoris. For such a hard man, Alex's touch was so very soft. Perfect. The exact right amount of pressure moving gently over her most sensitive flesh, not sawing at her as most men did, thinking the harder they rubbed, the more excited she'd get.

They were wrong.

This excited her, so much she had to work not to arch her back, move her hips in the rhythm of his finger. Around and around the finger swirled, slowly, delicately, his touch electric. Caitlin bit her bottom lip to keep from crying out.

Her breath left her chest in a long whoosh when a finger dipped inside her, in and out, imitating his cock at the beginning of their lovemaking. Just the memory made her vagina clench and a rush of wetness drench her sex.

He felt it. His finger paused for a second then another finger penetrated her, delved deeply. He spread his fingers, opening her up.

A second later she felt his cock, right there at the opening, the huge head hard and hot. He moved his penis up and down along her labia, nearly causing a heart attack when he rubbed the head over her clitoris. It was as if she'd been jolted by an electric prod.

She held herself as still as she could. Though the sky was lightening up by the minute, it was as if they were strangers, making love in the dark. He touched her only in two places, his big hand—now back on her hip—and his cock, barely inside the entrance to her vagina.

He didn't move, staying perfectly still. She burned and fisted her hands in the sheets. She knew precisely what they looked like together. Though she was staring at the wall and the window, she could imagine perfectly the image they presented, as if there were a camera in the ceiling.

His head was above hers on the pillow, long, muscled legs continuing way past her feet. The long, thick shaft of his sex between them, connecting them. Tall, small, dark, pale, broad, slender—a study in contrasts.

Then all thoughts flew from her head as his hand on her hip tightened, holding her still as he thrust slowly into her, stopping when he could go no farther, rough pubic hairs thick and scratchy against her bottom.

She stopped breathing, every sense concentrated between her legs, feeling every inch of the hot, hard column of flesh inside her. He'd slid smoothly in without any difficulty, testimony to how often they'd made love and to how much he excited her.

Even men much smaller had sometimes hurt her, just a little upon first entering, but not Alex. He was huge, but she was always ready for him, as if she'd been designed for him. All he had to do was touch her and she opened to him, completely and totally, like now.

Her head knew that they were...estranged, for want of a better word. It knew perfectly well that she was leaving his house today and that it was very possible they'd never see each other again, but something had intercepted this message from her brain to her body. Her body didn't get the memo. It was open for him, always and—probably—forever.

She closed her eyes at the thought just as he started moving, deep, powerful thrusts that touched all the hot, secret places inside her that had never been touched before. That seemingly only Alex could touch.

A Fine Specimen

The feeling was electric, so arousing it was almost painful.

Alex's hand slid down from her hip to her thigh, pulling her leg higher and even farther back so that, impossibly, he could plunge even more deeply inside her.

The room wasn't silent anymore. The bed creaked rhythmically, the headboard banging against the wall, Alex's breathing harsh, almost grunting in time with the heavy thrusts. The sounds filled the room.

Quickly, so quickly, she felt that slippery, hot slide. He was already bringing her to orgasm, an unstoppable tide, a wave poised to crash over her. She hung right there on the brink, shaking.

He thrusts grew heavier, irregular, and he swelled inside her, growing impossibly larger. He was close too, so close.

She held her breath, her vagina fluttering, heat prickling in her veins. He was pounding into her now, faster, harder...

Caitlin opened her eyes and stretched her neck to finally look at him. She loved the look on Alex's face as he was nearing orgasm. His face flushed under that golden-olive skin, making him almost glow, the sweat of exertion and excitement dotting his forehead. His mouth became red, suffused with blood, sensual as hell. His eyes narrowed into black slits, staring intently, hypnotically into hers, as if he could walk around inside her head while she came.

Maybe he could.

Alex was a powerful man in every way and, particularly in the last moments of lovemaking, she felt all that male power concentrated on her, like a sexy and powerful laser beam. The world narrowed to the two of them, so close they could feel each other's heartbeats.

It was her greatest joy, making love to Alex, and her heart soared as she glanced over her shoulder to see him—and froze.

He always had his eyes on her, *always*, as they made love, never looking away. She'd never had a moment's doubt that he was with her every step of the way.

But now his eyes were closed, his head and torso reared back, as far away from her as he could get and yet still be connected to her by his cock.

He wasn't touching her anywhere at all, except for the hand holding her still and the penis in her. He wasn't flushed, he was pale, his mouth set in a thin, hard slash, deep brackets lining his mouth. He didn't look overwhelmed with pleasure as he usually did, he looked cold and remote. Utterly separate from her, except that he was making love to her.

No. No, he wasn't making love to her. They weren't even having sex. *Use the correct term*, old Mrs. Robinson, her high school English teacher, used to say.

Okay.

They were fucking.

Alex was fucking a woman. He'd woken up with his usual morning erection and had found a warm female body with the right plumbing. She could be anyone. He wasn't with Caitlin Summers, he was fucking Anonymous Woman. He didn't even want to touch her more than was necessary. He was holding himself as far away from her as he could and still fuck her.

The thought pierced her heart just as her body—her oh-so-treacherous body—betrayed her. One more heavy thrust of Alex's hips, a flash of intense heat and she erupted, muscles contracting around him as he continued thrusting heavily. She stifled a moan with her hand, suddenly ashamed of reacting so strongly to what was just an anonymous fuck. Her body went haywire, as it always did with Alex.

His thrusts were growing shorter, harder, faster, the bed slamming rhythmically into the wall as a counterpoint to her drumming heart. The hand on her thigh grew sweaty and he had to tighten his grip. Later she'd have bruises but she didn't care because her whole body was caught up in an orgasm so intense she thought she'd faint.

She trembled and shook, her vagina clenching hard around Alex's shaft, so incredibly drenched that he was making wet sounds as he pounded in and out of her. Heat bloomed between her legs, bright and electric, the sharp, hot pleasure overpowering.

It broke her heart.

While her body was convulsing, sweat broke out all over, her entire body wet, as if everything inside her had to come out. Tears sprang out of her eyes, wetting her cheeks.

Alex followed a second later. A thrust so heavy it almost shoved her off the bed and, buried deep inside her, he swelled and started coming inside her, grunting heavily. She heard the beginning of a shout, instantly stifled. He wasn't allowing himself anything but the sheer sex act. Putting his penis in an available vagina and getting his rocks off.

That's all it was. Thinking it was anything else was insane.

Her body didn't really care. It had its orgasm without her, a white-hot rush of incredible pleasure so strong she shook with it.

She was still convulsing when he pulled out of her. Feeling his cock slide out of her was shocking. Like a plug being pulled. The white heat disappeared instantly and the orgasm stopped, as suddenly as if she'd been doused with ice water. Usually, making love with Alex was like this huge high that gently dissipated. At times, even half an hour after coming, she was still holding him, smiling, as her body rocked to earth.

This was instant chill.

He let go of her leg and the bed shifted as he turned away from her.

While they'd been making love—no, *fucking*—the sun had come up completely, bathing the room in a warm, buttery light that didn't warm her at all. She felt frozen, chilled from the inside. Her wet groin was cold in the morning air.

The room was silent, still, as if empty. You'd never know two lovers had just joined.

The smell of their sex was unusually sharp in the air. She'd loved that smell, but now it made her nauseous. Her stomach clenched sharply as bile rose in her throat. Saliva filled her mouth and she swallowed it down. Though her stomach was empty, it was bathroom time, fast, because something was coming up.

Caitlin rolled out of bed, knees nearly buckling. Her stomach clenched again and she knew if she didn't make it to the bathroom right now she'd humiliate herself in front of Alex.

She stumbled across the room on legs that felt too weak to walk, banging her hip against the dresser, pushing uselessly, desperately at the bathroom door until she remembered that it opened outward.

She finally wrenched it open. Turning, she saw him on the bed. He was lying on his back, one arm across his eyes so he wouldn't have to look at her. On his thigh, his semi-erect penis glistened with her juices and his semen. He lay utterly motionless, as if dead. Only the slight rise and fall of his broad chest showed that he was breathing. Sex with her normally left him breathless, chest moving like a bellows to pull in air as he kissed her neck and breasts in a post-coital cuddle.

His body was closed to her. They could have been a prostitute and her john in a hotel room, for all his reaction.

Her stomach clenched once again and she barely had time to pull the door closed, turn on the faucets full blast to hide any sounds and bend over the toilet. A jet of green bile splashed against the white porcelain, then another.

Her knees shook and she had to stiffen them not to fall in a heap over the toilet bowl. Though her stomach kept convulsing, there was nothing else to bring up.

Finally, Caitlin rested, head bowed, one hand holding on to the wall, until she felt steady enough to move away.

A Fine Specimen

The reflection in the mirror over the basin made her wince. Snow had more color than her skin, and the sleepless night showed in the purple bruises under her eyes. She looked like the survivor of a bad accident.

Well, that was okay because in a very real sense, she was.

Switching on the hot water in the shower, Caitlin stepped under the fancy modern showerhead, lifting her face into the steamy stream, letting her tears meld into the water.

Chapter Thirteen

"Well, fuck a duck," Ben said, eyes wide, jaw dropping. "Woudja take a look at *that*?"

One of the female officers gave a loud wolf whistle as Alex walked through the squad room on Sunday afternoon. Fuck this. He didn't have time for this shit. He threw her a dirty look but she only grinned, just one more sign that he'd been way too lax lately. Another officer took up the whistle and the other officers stood up, cheering and clapping.

A grinning Ben got up from his desk to follow Alex into his office. Alex turned at the threshold and looked out at his officers, unleashing his Death Glare, waiting until the commotion died down. "Settle down out here. I mean it. Back to work or I swear to God I'll have you all reassigned to Stolen Vehicles."

If they thought he was going soft because, well, he'd been in a good mood these past few days—okay yeah, he'd admit it, he'd done a lot of smiling lately—then they were in a shitload of trouble, because Hard-ass was back. Big time.

His officers were nothing if not smart. A dozen heads suddenly bent over forms and keyboards. Alex waited a minute then nodded grimly. He'd been getting this goddamn reputation as a wimpy good guy. Candyass was gone, history. Starting now.

Alex walked into his office and sat down behind his desk. Ben stood in front of him, a wide, sloppy grin on his face. Alex stared at him through narrowed eyes. "That goes for you too, Ben. Don't you have some work to do? Or are you dying to explore the finer points of chop shops?"

A Fine Specimen

"Hey, what's going on?" Kathy stuck her head through Alex's door and her eyes widened. "Yowzer."

She walked in, holding a sheaf of papers. After staring at him for a moment across his desk, she walked around to look Alex up and down and shook her head. She hitched a hip on a corner of his desk. "Does Armani know about this?"

"Not you too," Alex said, transferring his fierce, forbidding gaze to Kathy. He liked her, she was a good cop, but right now he hated her.

Her eyebrows lifted, face bland. "I can't believe this. Blue blazer, gray slacks, dark gray shoes. Alex's wearing *colors*. What happened?" She turned to Ben. "I don't think a living soul has ever seen him in anything but black and white. It's like a cult with him." She frowned. "Do you think he's an imposter? Some alien Alex Cruz lookalike?"

Ben fondled his own brightly colored tie and straightened his lime-green jacket. "Nah. He's just finally developed a fashion sense, probably from hanging out with me."

"My fashion sense is just fine, thank you very much," Alex said with a frown. "As a matter of fact, my fashion sense is so keen I think you should turn down the batteries in that tie of yours."

"Aw, you're just jealous," Ben replied, shaking his head sorrowfully. "It's 'cause *you'd* like to have my tie on."

"On what?" Alex asked acidly. "Fire?"

"Ah, ah, ah." Ben wagged his finger at Alex, still grinning widely. "Flattery will get you nowhere."

"Cut it out, you two," Kathy said. She leaned closer and put a hand on Alex's shoulder. "Alex," she said earnestly, looking him in the eyes. "I want you to know that I think this is great. Just great. I think it's the best thing that ever happened to you. And I'm really, really happy for you."

Alex didn't know what the fuck she was talking about, and anyway, whatever she was talking about, it was over. He tried to hide the spurt of panic that jolted him at the thought.

She had walked. Caitlin had turned her back on a perfectly nice situation, completely of her own accord. They'd been having a really good time and then pow! It was over and she'd signed the lease on a new apartment without even asking him for advice.

Well, she was a big girl. She wanted to walk, she'd walk. What the fuck did he care? And if the thought of going back to his empty house tonight gave him a slippery, sliding spurt of panic, well what the hell. He'd get over it. It's not like they were married or anything.

"Thanks for sharing, Kathy," Alex growled. "Now go away." Kathy squeezed his shoulder, looked meaningfully at him then turned and walked out.

Ben was watching him carefully, smile gone. Alex slanted him a glance. "What?"

"You fucked it up," Ben said quietly. He rarely turned serious but when he did, his entire face changed. "God dammit, Alex, you had the best thing in the world going for you and you fucked it up!"

Alex's jaws clenched—hard. "I don't know what the fuck you're talking about, and anyway, it wasn't me, it was *her*." He hated how childish that sounded.

Ben didn't move, just stared, grim-faced and somber. "You dumb asshole," he said slowly and shook his head. "You might as well shoot yourself in the head right now because—"

One swift knock and young Roscoe, their newest recruit, stuck his head in the door. Usually Alex steered clear of excitable rookies, but this was a welcome distraction. He knew Ben and he knew he was about to ream him a new one. "What?"

Roscoe's cheeks were red with excitement. "Lieutenant, Sergeant! Great news! Sorensen and DeWitt have apprehended Ratso Colby! He's on his way. They're bringing him in now!"

* * * * *

A Fine Specimen

Staring at the backs of two cops as big as sides of beef, Ratso Colby sat sweating in the backseat of a black and white. *Shit*! Ratso thought as the police car took a tight turn. He *hated* cops, hated everything about them. Cops had sent him to jail years back and he'd nearly died there. He still had the scars. Now they were trying to send him back. No fucking way. Ratso was *not* going back to County. Whatever it took to stay out, he'd do it.

Except he knew what it would take—staying out meant he had to rat on Lopez and go into Witness Protection. Lopez made him shit-scared. Ratso knew what Lopez would be willing to do to find out where he was hiding. Lopez wouldn't rest until he got him. Word on the street was, Lopez took traitors out to an abandoned warehouse he owned and watched as it took days for the poor fucks to die. Ratso's heart trip-hammered at the thought. They were still finding pieces of the last guy who'd turned on Lopez.

But on the other hand, to be back in a prison system that was home to an entire branch of the Aryan Nation... A fresh torrent of sweat broke out. One of the cops sniffed suspiciously then looked back at him with a sneer.

The badges had caught him. It was his fault. He'd been making some bad decisions lately, starting with the decision to work for Lopez. He shouldn't have accepted Lopez's offer but shit, Lopez was offering almost three-hundred large. He thought he'd be able to keep it a secret but one of Lopez's men had dropped a dime on him. With the cops on his tail, he'd had to run.

He should have just hopped on a bus to Mexico and taken a flight out to Rio from there. A man he'd met in stir could have gotten him a new passport that would definitely have been good enough to get out of the country and fly from a foreign city. First to Aruba, where he had money he'd salted away over the years, then from there to Rio, where no one could ever force him back. But spending the rest of his life in a foreign country required more money than he had, so he'd waited until he could cash in the extra couple hundred thou he was owed here and there, not to mention cashing in on his stocks. Even in the bear market, he'd been making money.

He'd been on his way to meet his broker when the cops nabbed him.

He should have skipped town two weeks ago.

He was so fucked. Massively fucked. Ratso hadn't had much education, but he had always been good at odds and numbers. And right now, the odds were against him and his number was up.

Christ, another day and he'd have been home free, with a new passport, new identity, sipping caipirinhas on Copacabana.

No more dirty work. No more collecting blood money for Angelo Lopez, no more scurrying along with thick-necked goons to terrorize a shopkeeper or entering protection money into a Palm Pilot to stash away in Switzerland for Lopez.

Another day! All it would have taken was one more *day*. Now there was no way he could convince Lopez he hadn't talked. Ratso was sure Angelo would get him one way or another. And if he didn't talk, the cops would put him in stir.

Talk about your lose-lose situation.

Ratso's brain worked feverishly as the black and white pulled up in front of the station house. He had to get away. He had to. He *had* to.

Because otherwise, whether in prison or in Lopez's warehouse, his life was over.

* * * * *

"We're really sorry to see you go," Kathy said. "We're all going to miss you."

Caitlin nodded as she put her papers away, looking around the squad room where she'd spent so many intense hours.

A Fine Specimen

She had to clear her throat to get it to work. It felt tight, hot, incapable of uttering a sound. She studiously avoided looking at Alex's closed door but it was next to impossible, there every time she turned around. He was behind it and staying there. If there was even a tiny hope left in her that there might still be something between them after this morning, there was her answer.

It was definitely over, whatever "it" had been, and Alex was going to ignore her until she left. But professional and personal pride wouldn't allow her to let Kathy see how upset she was. She turned, pasting a big smile on her face. "I'll miss you guys too."

"Give me a call when you get settled into your new job," Kathy said, picking up a few stray papers which had fallen to the floor and handing them to Caitlin. "We'll get together for some coffee that doesn't belong in Dr. Kevorkian's IV line."

Well, that was something. Life would go on. She knew that, intellectually. She'd go to work at the Frederiksson, maybe write a book, decorate her new apartment. Have dinner with Kathy occasionally. Maybe Kathy would keep her up to date on what was going on with Alex—

Whoa. Caitlin nipped that thought in the bud. It was too pathetic. There had to be a clean break. She couldn't pine forever. "Yeah, that would be nice."

"Count me in," another officer, Sally Devoe, chimed in. Sally had been a fun interview. She'd been delighted when Caitlin had told her that in the wild, lionesses did all the hunting in the pride. Sally now gave her male colleagues a mock roar every time she walked by.

Caitlin had interviewed her extensively and found her to be smart and funny, just like Kathy. That was two possible new friends.

"Me too." Tom Roscoe, a new recruit from the academy, picked up a book Caitlin had left on a chair. "You can't make it a chicks-only gathering," he said, grinning as he handed her the book. "That would be discrimination."

"Here." Kathy walked over to the soda pop dispenser and put in some change. When nothing came out, she kicked it in the side and two cans of Diet Coke popped out. She walked back smiling and thrust a can into Caitlin's hands. "There you are, it just needed a little percussive maintenance. So, Caitlin, before you go, I propose a toast."

She raised her can high and her voice took on the solemn tones of a toastmaster. "To Caitlin Summers, the woman who did the impossible—she singlehandedly turned Lieutenant Alex Cruz into a human being." She opened her can with a flourish.

"I second the motion." Sally put change in the machine, kicked it viciously and brought back a can. "Alex actually smiled the other day. I've been here ten years and I can't recall him ever smiling. And damned if he didn't! *Twice*, if I'm not mistaken." Her brow furrowed. "*Trés* weird."

"And a few days ago I caught him *humming*," Tom added. "'Memory'." He shook his head. "Can you imagine? In the academy, the older officers used to joke about him being immortal. To kill him you'd have to put a wooden stake through his heart."

"And we owe it all to you," Kathy said, slapping Caitlin on the back. Caitlin staggered and coughed. Officers were drifting over, sensing the opportunity to rag one of their own. Kathy raised her can again and looked around at her colleagues. "Another toast. To Belle! Who tamed the Beast!"

"We talking about Alex?" someone asked.

"Who else?" someone else called out.

"No, really," Caitlin said, looking around at the grinning faces. This was too horrible. No way could she announce that their relationship—or whatever it was—was over. Not here, not now. Later, maybe, she'd confide in Kathy. Much later, when she could talk about it. In the meantime, though the dog didn't deserve it, she felt Alex needed a little defending. "I didn't do anything. And come on now. Alex couldn't have been all *that* bad-tempered."

There was a polite silence.

Caitlin remembered what Alex had been like on that first day.

Okay. She'd done the adult thing and now she'd shut up.

"So," Kathy said, slinging a friendly arm around Caitlin's shoulders, "we can now rest easy in the Baylorville PD and come to work with a smile on our lips. We really owe you a lot."

"Who owes who a lot?" The desk sergeant walked by and Kathy put a can of pop in his hands. "We do," she said and pointed her own can at Caitlin. "Her. We owe Caitlin. For taming Alex."

* * * * *

With every step he took, Ratso's terror grew until he was shaking and trembling. He was sweating so badly the booking officer had to throw away the first set of prints in disgust and take another set.

Coming into the station house, Ratso had seen Eugenio Carlucci, aka Ginny the Gun, one of Lopez's men. One of Lopez's *nastier* men. Ginny was known for blowing out kneecaps if you looked at him sideways.

Ginny had recognized him. Those black eyes as flat and cruel as a shark's had narrowed, focused in on Ratso. Lopez would spring Ginny in a couple of hours then Lopez would know he was with the cops. A minute later, Lopez would already be making his plans to get rid of him. Lopez was a fast mover. He would figure something out. Undoubtedly he had someone on his payroll in the BPD. Unless Ratso could get away — *now* — he was a walking dead man.

Dripping with sweat, Ratso looked around, conscious of each second passing. The officer who had taken his prints had disappeared and, for the moment, no one seemed to be paying him any attention even though the squad room was packed. Ratso flexed his hands. Whatever he was going to do, he couldn't do it in handcuffs.

"Hey!" he called out when the officer reappeared without his prints.

The officer looked over at him, frowning. "Yeah?"

"Fucking hurts." Ratso held out his handcuffed hands. "Come on, gimme a break."

The officer looked him over, then pulled out a key and unlocked the cuffs. Ratso rubbed his sore wrists. He still didn't know what he was going to do but at least he wasn't in handcuffs anymore.

"Okay," the officer said, attaching the handcuffs to his belt. "You just sit still until the lieutenant comes out. He's been waiting to talk to you for a long time."

The lieutenant. Christ.

Ratso looked around desperately. There had to be something he could do. *Think!*

He had the use of his hands and his legs. And his head, which had never failed him before. He knew his looks fooled a lot of people, but he was smart. The only really dumb thing he'd ever done in his life was to keep Angelo Lopez's accounts. He hadn't drawn a carefree breath since.

Ratso took in everything while making sure he wasn't making eye contact with the cop across the desk. The cop wasn't paying him any attention anyway. It looked like there was a little party going on two desks down, between him and freedom. The uniforms were clustered around a pretty blonde girl. The girl clearly wasn't a cop. She was too young, for one thing, and looked way too innocent. So if she wasn't a cop, who was she?

Whoever she was, the cops cared about her, that was for sure. They were laughing and smiling and pumping her hand.

A Fine Specimen

A vague idea started taking shape in Ratso's mind. But he'd need someone new to the cop shop, someone clueless...

Shifting in his seat as if he were uncomfortable, Ratso moved his chair around so he could study the uniforms. Maybe a female cop. A woman might be weaker...

He looked at the two female cops and changed his mind.

He switched his attention to the youngest-looking cop. Roscoe, someone called him. Barely old enough to grow a beard, rosy-cheeked, he was laughing raucously at something someone had said, oblivious to his surroundings. Clueless.

Perfect.

The party was breaking up and the young blonde girl started gathering her things. She turned full-face toward Ratso and he blinked at how pretty she was. Never mind, he told himself. Didn't make any difference what she looked like. Pretty girls bought it every day. Besides, who knew? She might even live.

Ratso was plotting trajectories and moves when the door to Lieutenant Cruz's office started opening. Panic skittered up his spine. Once Alex Cruz was in the room, Ratso knew he wouldn't be able to get away with anything. It was now or never.

"Feel sick," he mumbled.

The cop who had taken his prints looked up at him with a frown. Ratso knew he was pasty white and he could feel the sweat rolling down the sides of his face. It was terror, not nausea, but the cop wouldn't know that.

"Gotta go to the bathroom." His voice came out thin and shaky. "Gotta barf."

The cop looked him up and down and made a big song and dance about getting up. "Okay," he said, giving Ratso a shove toward the corridor. "Let's go."

"Thanks." Ratso kept his voice low and his eyes to the ground, the very picture of submission. Lieutenant Cruz's door was wide open now. Ratso knew he had only seconds to make his move.

He shuffled forward down the aisle between the desks, toward the corridor, keeping his head tucked low, eyes darting constantly, aware of the pig behind him with every fiber of his being.

They were approaching the little cop party.

With a swift look over his shoulder, he saw Cruz still in his office, talking to a big guy with graying red hair. In a minute he'd be in the squad room.

Now!

Lightning-fast, Ratso's right hand snaked out and snatched Roscoe's Glock from its holster while wrapping his left arm around the pretty blonde girl's neck. He dug the barrel of the gun into her right temple.

"Nobody move!" he shouted. "Or she gets one right through the head!"

At first Alex couldn't make any sense of what was happening. All he could see was a thick wall of blue backs. All of his officers were shouting *"Freeze!"* over and over, their voices raised over the sound of a hysterical man screaming. His officers had their weapons out.

He pulled his own gun from his shoulder holster. Some dumb fuck was actually trying to shoot his way out of the cop shop. Alex smiled slowly.

No way. Not while he was here.

Alex inched forward, sideways so as to present as small a target as possible, gun held in both hands and pointed at the ceiling.

"Put your guns down! Down! Or I'll shoot! I swear I'll shoot!" a man was screaming. "You'll be cleaning her up with a spoon!"

A Fine Specimen

The officers dropped their arms and guns clattered to the floor. Several moved to the side—and Alex got a clear view of what was happening.

His blood froze in his veins. The nausea of panic came at him with a sickening rush.

Somehow Ratso had acquired a gun and he was holding it to Caitlin's head. And he was choking her. Even from ten feet away, Alex could hear Caitlin wheezing, trying to bring air into her agonized lungs.

Ratso was dragging her, almost a dead weight, toward the door. Caitlin clutched his arm, trying to pull it away from her throat.

Caitlin saw Alex and her eyes widened in recognition. She gazed entreatingly at him, eyes huge in a pale, shocked face, fingers scratching at the wiry arm locked around her throat, cutting off the windpipe.

Ratso was beyond feeling scratches. Sweat was pouring down his face as he moved backward, dragging Caitlin. He screamed at the officers over and over again. "Don't move! Don't nobody move or I'll shoot. I swear I'll shoot! Blow her brains out all over the wall!"

Alex finally broke out of his paralysis. As a rookie cop, he'd faced down a three-hundred-pound biker high on angel dust. Three hundred pounds of violent craziness, wielding a knife. The biker had ended up facedown on the ground, cuffed. Alex hadn't broken a sweat.

He thought his childhood had inured him to fear. When you've faced death and degradation in your own family, what could scare you?

He feared nobody and nothing. He'd thought.

Right now he was so terrified he couldn't breathe. Watching Ratso screw the muzzle into Caitlin's temple made him shake with terror. The gun's safety was off. Ratso was sweating so hard it looked like he'd just come out of a shower. His hands were slippery with sweat. Alex's heart gave a huge thump of terror when he saw Ratso tighten his grip on the weapon, finger in the trigger guard.

The gun had a four-pound pull, about the strength it would take to pull the tab on a can of beer. Nothing. A slip of his finger and the bullet would travel at twelve-hundred feet per second straight through Caitlin's head, exiting in a spatter of bone and brain and blood so intense it would send up a pink mist, and Caitlin would be gone, forever.

Ratso wanted her alive as a hostage, but he was scared and he wasn't an operator. He'd always been a petty criminal at best. Right now the chances were very good that he'd shoot Caitlin by mistake. He'd never make it downstairs dragging her with him. He was growing more agitated and sweaty by the second.

The instant he shot Caitlin, he'd be taken down by at least twelve shots. Suicide by cop.

And Caitlin would be wiped off the face of the earth, as if she'd never existed. She'd crumple to the ground like a broken doll, bloody and torn. All that loveliness and light, the beauty and the good humor, the affection and softness...all of that gone, snuffed out like a candle.

Alex had seen a lot as a cop. He knew exactly what the bullet would do, exactly what Caitlin's lifeless body would look like.

Like heartbreak.

While Ratso and the officers screamed at each other, a blinding truth exploded in Alex's chest, complete and whole. He didn't have to think it through, it just was, a central fact of his life, as much a part of him as his hands and feet. As incontrovertible as the fact that he breathed and moved. That the sun rose in the east and set in the west.

He loved Caitlin Summers.

He loved her with all his heart. He had been only half a man, only half alive before she had come into his life. She had given him happiness and hope and the promise of love. If

A Fine Specimen

Ratso put a bullet through Caitlin's brain, he would be putting a bullet through Alex's heart at the same time.

All that bullshit about not wanting a committed relationship was just that—bullshit. He'd spent the most miserable night of his life last night, in bed with Caitlin but not touching her. The anonymous, emotionless sex this morning—the kind of sex he'd had all his life—had nearly ripped his heart out. He had touched her as little as possible because the temptation to simply grab her, hold her tight, never let go, ask her to stay with him forever, had been so strong he'd had to grit his teeth to resist it. He'd been so terrified. Terrified of watching her go, terrified of asking her to stay.

More bullshit. That wasn't terrifying. *This* was terrifying, watching a man crazed with fear hold a gun to Caitlin's head. Every cell in his body was locked down in dread and horror, making his fear of commitment of a few hours ago seem ridiculous.

The pistol slipped in Ratso's sweaty grip and he tightened his fingers. At the same time he tightened his arm around Caitlin's neck. She struggled for air, lips already blue.

"Easy, Ratso," Alex murmured, moving unobtrusively forward. "You're choking her. She won't do you any good dead."

"Back off, Cruz!" Ratso shifted his grip and dug the rim of the barrel harder into Caitlin's temple. "All of you back off! I want a car with a full tank of gas waiting for me downstairs. If I so much as sniff another car trailing me, I'll shoot her in the head and dump her by the roadside. Is that clear?" He dug harder with the gun and Caitlin's mouth opened in agony. Her eyes were starting a slow roll to the back of her head. Ratso's chokehold would kill her before they made it downstairs. "Is that clear?" He trembled and sweated. "*Huh?*" he screamed. "*Is that clear?*"

Alex didn't dare look away from him to see what his men were doing. He stared into Ratso's eyes, gauging. The instant he thought Ratso was going to shoot or that Caitlin was suffocating, he'd take the shot. A small hope was better than none.

"You won't get far, Ratso." Alex knew his voice was calm and his face expressionless. Only *he* knew his heart was pounding. Only he knew how sick he was with fear. "And now we'll have to add assault and kidnapping to the charges."

"I won't be around!" Ratso gave off a hysterical, high-pitched giggle. "You won't get me and Lopez won't get me. I'll disappear off the face of the earth. I should have done it days ago!"

"Ratso, listen to me." Alex took a chance and stepped forward casually. "You can't—"

"Get back!" Ratso screamed, scrambling backward, pulling Caitlin with him. She was paper-white, feet scrabbling for purchase on the linoleum floor.

Then time slowed down and events unfurled in a deadly, slow-motion dance. Alex knew there were people shouting but he heard nothing, saw nothing.

The only thing he saw was Caitlin's foot catching on a chair leg, her slow fall, Ratso's grimace as he felt her weight sag in his arms, Caitlin's leg caught between his, Ratso's slow-motion fall to the floor…

A gunshot sounded and time sped up again.

Alex felt the blood drain from his body and wondered dimly how he could still be standing when his heart had stopped.

The officers moved in a disciplined rush, weapons whisked from the floor and ready. They surrounded the area where Ratso and Caitlin had gone down. Alex couldn't see anything except their backs and for a moment he was glad. For one more second, he would allow himself the thought of Caitlin alive. Alive, and not bloody and still on the squad-room floor. One more second and—

The officers parted and, like a miracle, he saw Caitlin rise, torn, bloody, unspeakably beautiful.

With a cry she ran toward him and he caught her, crushing her fiercely to him, his heart pounding so hard he thought it would pound its way out of his chest.

"Alex!" Caitlin was crying, her arms wound tightly around his neck. She was trembling and sobbing. He didn't even feel the tears coursing down his own cheeks until he noticed that he was wetting her hair. His weapon clattered to the floor and he didn't know if his legs could bear their combined weight.

"Hey, boss." Kathy put a gentle hand on his shoulder. Her eyes were full of compassion. "Why don't the two of you go into your office for a while?" She threw a contemptuous glance behind her. "Let us clean up the garbage."

Alex nodded blindly, picked Caitlin up in his arms and carried her into his office. He slammed the door shut with his foot and walked over to his chair. He sank down with Caitlin still in his arms. He didn't know if he'd be capable of letting her go. Not yet. Not for maybe another hundred years.

He caught her face between his hands. She was dead white, her cheeks still wet with tears. A trickle of blood ran down her right cheek from a shallow scratch.

She had never looked more beautiful.

He kissed her, wildly, crushing her to him as if to absorb her very essence into his skin. His hands speared her hair, ran over her shoulders, dug into her back. He kissed her endlessly, tasting her, reveling in the fact that she was alive, alive and with him.

Forever.

Alex lifted his head, cupping hers between his hands. "You're not going anywhere, do you hear me?" he said fiercely. "You're going to stay with me!" Caitlin nodded, eyes locked with his. "You're going to call up that red-headed harpy and tell her you changed your mind about the apartment and you want to break the lease. If necessary we'll pay a penalty. You're going to tear up that lease and stay with me. Because I love you." He gave her a little shake. "Is that clear?"

Caitlin barely had time to whisper, "Yes, Alex," and then his mouth descended on hers again.

Alex's chest swelled with an emotion that was so big and so new it took him a moment to recognize it as happiness. He lifted his mouth from Caitlin's and laughed.

"What?" She smiled up at him, eyes gleaming, lips rosy and slightly swollen. A little color had come back into her face. Her smudged glasses had slid to the end of her nose. "What's so funny?"

Alex carefully took her glasses off and placed them down on his desk. His eyes circled her beloved face and he knew that the second half of his life, the better half, had begun.

He sighed theatrically. "I've just realized that I'm going to have to rent two tuxes for our wedding. One for me to get married in and one for you to spill the cake on."

Epilogue
Grant Falls
☙

Captain Ray Avery put down the phone with an enormous grin on his face.

He looked at the beautiful woman sharing his bed. She blinked and opened her eyes, the pale blue of a summer sky. Her glorious golden hair, streaked with silver, flowed over her shoulders. "Who was that, darling?" she asked sleepily.

He put his arms around her and nuzzled her neck. He would never tire of holding her in his arms. He blessed the day he'd met Linda Summers, a fellow professor at St. Mary's. She was the love he'd been looking for all his life. He pulled away and smiled at her. She was in her fifties and she was the most beautiful woman in the world. In his eyes, she grew more beautiful every day.

Ray envied Alex the years he was going to spend with her daughter, Caitlin. He wished he'd had them with Linda.

From the moment he'd met Linda's daughter, he'd known she would be perfect for the man he loved like a son. And now it looked as if he'd been proven right.

"That was Alex," he said and winked.

The sleepiness disappeared. Linda's smile broadened. "And?"

"And...our plan worked." Ray brought her hand to his lips. "What would you say, me darlin', to a double wedding?"

The End

Also by Lisa Marie Rice

Christmas Angel
Midnight Angel
Midnight Man
Midnight Run
Port of Paradise
Woman on the Run

About the Author

🕉

Lisa Marie Rice is eternally thirty years old and will never age. She is tall and willowy and beautiful. Men drop at her feet like ripe pears. She has won every major book prize in the world. She is a black belt with advanced degrees in archaeology, nuclear physics, and Tibetan literature. She is a concert pianist. Did I mention the Nobel?

Of course, Lisa Marie Rice is a virtual woman and exists only at the keyboard when writing erotic romance. She disappears when the monitor winks off.

Lisa welcomes comments from readers. You can find her website and email address on her author bio page at www.ellorascave.com.

Tell Us What You Think

We appreciate hearing reader opinions about our books. You can email us at Comments@EllorasCave.com.

Why an electronic book?

We live in the Information Age—an exciting time in the history of human civilization, in which technology rules supreme and continues to progress in leaps and bounds every minute of every day. For a multitude of reasons, more and more avid literary fans are opting to purchase e-books instead of paper books. The question from those not yet initiated into the world of electronic reading is simply: *Why?*

1. *Price.* An electronic title at Ellora's Cave Publishing and Cerridwen Press runs anywhere from 40% to 75% less than the cover price of the exact same title in paperback format. Why? Basic mathematics and cost. It is less expensive to publish an e-book (no paper and printing, no warehousing and shipping) than it is to publish a paperback, so the savings are passed along to the consumer.

2. *Space.* Running out of room in your house for your books? That is one worry you will never have with electronic books. For a low one-time cost, you can purchase a handheld device specifically designed for e-reading. Many e-readers have large, convenient screens for viewing. Better yet, hundreds of titles can be stored within your new library—on a single microchip. There are a variety of e-readers from different manufacturers. You can also read e-books on your PC or laptop computer. (Please note that Ellora's Cave does not endorse any specific brands.

You can check our websites at www.ellorascave.com or www.cerridwenpress.com for information we make available to new consumers.)

3. ***Mobility.*** Because your new e-library consists of only a microchip within a small, easily transportable e-reader, your entire cache of books can be taken with you wherever you go.

4. ***Personal Viewing Preferences.*** Are the words you are currently reading too small? Too large? Too... ANNOYING? Paperback books cannot be modified according to personal preferences, but e-books can.

5. ***Instant Gratification.*** Is it the middle of the night and all the bookstores near you are closed? Are you tired of waiting days, sometimes weeks, for bookstores to ship the novels you bought? Ellora's Cave Publishing sells instantaneous downloads twenty-four hours a day, seven days a week, every day of the year. Our webstore is never closed. Our e-book delivery system is 100% automated, meaning your order is filled as soon as you pay for it.

Those are a few of the top reasons why electronic books are replacing paperbacks for many avid readers.

As always, Ellora's Cave and Cerridwen Press welcome your questions and comments. We invite you to email us at Comments@ellorascave.com or write to us directly at Ellora's Cave Publishing Inc., 1056 Home Avenue, Akron, OH 44310-3502.

COMING TO A BOOKSTORE NEAR YOU!

ELLORA'S CAVE

Bestselling Authors Tour

UPDATES AVAILABLE AT
WWW.ELLORASCAVE.COM

Cerridwen, the Celtic Goddess of wisdom, was the muse who brought inspiration to storytellers and those in the creative arts. Cerridwen Press encompasses the best and most innovative stories in all genres of today's fiction. Visit our site and discover the newest titles by talented authors who still get inspired - much like the ancient storytellers did, once upon a time.

Cerridwen Press
www.cerridwenpress.com

Discover for yourself why readers can't get enough of the multiple award-winning publisher
Ellora's Cave.
Whether you prefer e-books or paperbacks,
be sure to visit EC on the web at
www.ellorascave.com
for an erotic reading experience that will leave you breathless.

CPSIA information can be obtained at www.ICGtesting.com
231677LV00003B/53/P